"Eighty acres is a lot of land," Wade said. "Why should I finance you when a bank won't?"

Ellie sat there a moment, and Wade could see her marshaling forces. "Because you aren't a bank," she said, gesturing with her hand. "You have more sense than a bank. You can see me as an able-bodied human being—not a woman—and can believe I'll pay you."

She was convincing; he'd have to give her that. And sharp, too. He leaned back and looked at her, then chuckled. "Mrs. McGrew, I'd be a fool if I said I didn't look at you and see a woman." He allowed what he meant to show on his face and in his voice. "And I'm no fool, believe me," he promised.

But he must be, he thought, because he still hadn't told her no. And he continued to look into her sky-blue eyes....

Dear Reader,

Sophisticated but sensitive, savvy yet unabashedly sentimental—that's today's woman, today's romance reader—you! And Silhouette Special Editions are written expressly to reward your quest for substantial, emotionally involving love stories.

So take a leisurely stroll under the cover's lavender arch into a garden of romantic delights. Pick and choose among titles if you must—we hope you'll soon equate all six Special Editions each month with consistently gratifying romantic reading.

Watch for sparkling new stories from your Silhouette favorites—Nora Roberts, Tracy Sinclair, Ginna Gray, Lindsay McKenna, Curtiss Ann Matlock, among others—along with some exciting newcomers to Silhouette, such as Karen Keast and Patricia Coughlin. Be on the lookout, too, for the new Silhouette Classics, a distinctive collection of bestselling Special Editions and Silhouette Intimate Moments now brought back to the stands—two each month—by popular demand.

On behalf of all the authors and editors of Special Editions,
Warmest wishes,

Leslie Kazanjian
Senior Editor

CURTISS ANN MATLOCK
Last Chance Cafe

Silhouette Special Edition

Published by Silhouette Books New York

America's Publisher of Contemporary Romance

Special thanks to the gentle giant, singer Don
Williams, whose music enriches my work, my
marriage, my life.
And to KEBC radio in Oklahoma City for playing
the music to stir a country woman's soul.

SILHOUETTE BOOKS
300 East 42nd St., New York, N.Y. 10017

ISBN: 0-373-09426-4

First Silhouette Books printing December 1987

America's Publisher of Contemporary Romance

Printed in the U.S.A.

Silhouette Special Edition

A Time and a Season #275
A Time to Keep #384
Last Chance Cafe #426

Silhouette Romance

Crosswinds #422
For Each Tomorrow #482

CURTISS ANN MATLOCK

loves to travel and has lived in eight different states, from Alaska to Florida. Sixteen years ago she married her high school sweetheart and inspiration, James. The Matlocks are now settled in Oklahoma, where Curtiss is concentrating on being a homemaker and a writer. Other time is taken up with gardening, canning, crocheting and, of course, reading. She says, "I was probably born with a book in hand."

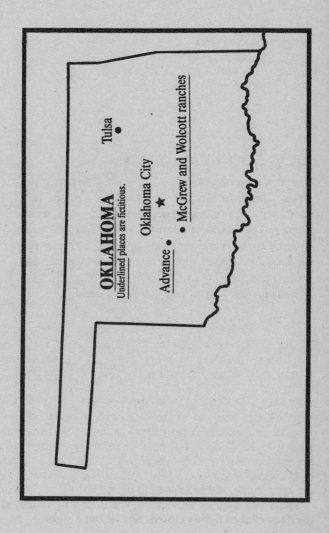

OKLAHOMA
Underlined places are fictitious.

Tulsa

Oklahoma City

★

Advance •

• McGrew and Wolcott ranches

Chapter One

The telephone rang. Though the sound came muffled through the closed door—she'd turned off the extension in her own room—Ellie McGrew jumped. Then she laughed at herself.

She lay very still, listening as it rang again. Then one of the girls must have answered because there were no more rings. The rapid padding of approaching footsteps sounded on the carpet. She closed her eyes as the bedroom door creaked.

She heard breathing, then warm breath tickled her cheek. It took every scrap of willpower not to laugh aloud as she imagined her eldest daughter bending close. She didn't know what told her it was Sara—scent, maybe, or perhaps an inborn instinct every mother has for her child. She just knew. Restraining the impish urge to open her eyes wide and stick out her tongue, she pretended to be asleep.

There was a quick movement, the breathing faded, and the door clicked lightly closed. She let out a sigh.

She scolded herself for being childish, hiding, as it were, but she just could not bear to talk to her mother this morning. This one morning in five years.

Then she experienced a moment of panic as she imagined her mother saying: "Good heavens, Ellie's not up yet? I'll come right over."

Please, God, she thought. *Don't let Mama come over.*

She listened to the sounds of stirring life and longed for a cup of coffee. The chirping of crickets and birds came dully through the closed windows. And Mr. Favor's car backing out of the drive next door.

The low hum of the television sounded beyond her bedroom door, and Poppy's reedy voice began singing a familiar commercial jingle. Immediately another voice in a very loud whisper hushed her. The faucet handle in the bathroom on the opposite side of her bedroom wall squeaked, and water gurgled softly through the pipes. Most probably Sara showering and washing her hair. She'd reached the age when girls nearly washed the hair from their head—oily hair being the cardinal sin.

Today. The word came to Ellie's mind in big bold letters. Today was special.

For one thing, today was her birthday. And she faced the day in a way that only other women who'd turned thirty-four could understand.

She was a widow with three children, and today she was thirty-four.

Heavens—the thought was a bit depressing. It seemed just yesterday she'd so longed to turn twenty-one and had continually had to produce proof of her age.

Well, she certainly hadn't longed to be thirty-four. Yet, it somehow seemed to give her license to do things. To say: *Here I am. I'm me. I can take the world by the tail now.*

Yes, that, and to point out all the things in life that were passing her by, she thought with a soft sigh. She stared at the ceiling.

Today was the day she'd set as the deadline. She had to do something today—or not at all.

She lay quietly a few more minutes, debating, considering. As she had for weeks now. And as she had the previous night, which was why she, Ellie McGrew, still lay in bed at eight o'clock in the morning—a pure sin to her mother— when normally she rose before seven. She didn't get up early because of any great need or principle, but simply because she liked mornings best.

"Today," she said softly. "Today you are thirty-four years old, Ellie. You're going to do something about it."

Flinging back the covers, she slipped from the bed and headed for the small adjoining bathroom. She stood beneath the cool shower spray, allowing the water to pelt her shoulders, and ran a hand down thighs that were sleek and firm. Three children and thirty-four years and she looked pretty good, she thought with pride. And right now she gave thanks for those thighs as only a woman over thirty can do.

She stepped from the shower, her mind whirling with plans. She'd have to tell the children she was going off for the day. And no pussyfooting around about it, making up lies. She was going off, and she wasn't going to tell them where she was going. That was it. She wasn't ready to tell anyone, even her girls, what she was about.

She wrapped her wet hair in a towel, slipped on a robe and peered into the mirror. Was she crazy? She had to be, just a smidgen.

Today she planned to buy a house and eighty acres. All on her own.

Did she really? Ellie asked herself for the hundredth time. There was still time to change her mind.

She was nervous, terribly nervous.

She stopped for a moment and chewed lightly on a fingernail. What she was thinking wasn't a spur-of-the-moment idea. She'd considered and deliberated on it for two months now. And she'd found the exact place for her and the girls. It was a good idea. *Wasn't it?*

It always happened like this. One moment she'd be positive and enthused, the next moment her resolve blew in the wind, this way and that, like brown leaves across the lawn.

With an impatient shake of her head, she opened the bathroom door. One step and she almost bumped right into all three of her daughters.

They stood in a line before her, like soldiers on parade, Sara, the oldest and tallest, at one end. Sara, supple and tall for her age, had only to tilt her head up a fraction to match Ellie blue eye for blue eye. Smiling and with a graceful movement, she held out a card. Ellie's gaze flew to Rae, her middle child, her tomboy, with two braids and one front tooth still only halfway in. Rae held a plate with a sweet roll from which a flickering candle protruded. And then there was Poppy, much tinier than the other two girls had been at her age, with cheeks like two ripe peaches and a perpetual smile. She held a cup of coffee in a saucer. The coffee sloshed dangerously back and forth.

"Happy Birthday," the girls chimed in unison.

"Oh...oh, my!" Ellie looked at them a moment, at their widening grins and the love lighting their faces. Suddenly it was hard for her to breathe and her vision blurred. "I'm the luckiest mom in the world," she said, the words pressing past a lump in her throat. Lord, she was thankful for these girls, loved them with every part of her. She just couldn't let them down.

Quickly Ellie took the coffee from Poppy, who'd begun delicate hopping from one foot to the other.

"Make a wish, Mama," Rae urged, "before the candle melts wax all over the roll."

"Yeah, yeah." Poppy hopped over to the bed.

"Sit here, Mama." Sara smoothed the covers to make a place.

Sparing a moment to smile at her girls, Ellie then closed her eyes and elaborately made a wish. Partly to please her children, yes, but it *was* elaborate for her in that moment. With all her heart and soul she wished that the fantastic plans she'd been dreaming up for the past months would come true, for them all.

With the girls gathered around her on the bed, Ellie balanced the coffee cup and saucer on her leg and shared what amounted to three bites each of the sweet roll.

"What'd you wish for, Mama?" Poppy asked.

"Won't come true if she tells, silly." Rae gave her braids a superior fling over her shoulders.

"Something wonderful for all of us," Ellie told her youngest, giving her a kiss atop her pale, curly bangs.

"Grandma called." Sara regarded her quietly, as if she sensed Ellie had deliberately avoided the phone call.

"You spoke to her?" Ellie said.

"Yes." Sara raised an eyebrow. "It was Rae in the shower," she said flatly, telling Ellie that she knew Ellie had been pretending all along. "She woke up with fleas because she slept with Maynard again last night."

"I did not!" Rae protested and turned to Ellie. "He doesn't have fleas. I was just itchy. A person can get itchy. I don't think you got all the soap out of the sheets. Grandma says that can make a person itchy."

Ellie chose to ignore the argument. "What did Grandma say?" she asked, keeping a smile from her lips at Sara's expression.

"She wanted to know if you were sick, since you weren't there to answer. I told her you were in the shower."

A look of understanding passed between Ellie and her oldest daughter. They both knew Grandma would not want to hear that Ellie was still in bed. Sara was intuitive, mature beyond her years and so very much like Ellie herself.

Ellie gave each one of her girls a thoughtful look. She touched one of Rae's long blond braids, then pulled Poppy up close in the crook of her arm.

"I'm going off today, girls. All day."

"Where?" Came the immediate response of three voices.

"I'm not going to tell you that now. I will when I come back. But this is between you three and me. I'm going to see about something for us all." She gave them a serious warning look. "Don't say a word to Grandma. Just say I went shopping with a friend."

They looked sufficiently curious and awed. Rae was about to press the matter, but after a glance at Sara, she closed her mouth. Poppy persisted.

"If it's a secret, do you gots to do something bad, Mama?" Poppy said.

"Have to," Ellie automatically corrected, laughing and hugging her littlest. "No, darling. But it's sort of like a wish. I don't want to talk about it too much, for fear it won't come true."

Sara lingered while Ellie scrutinized the clothes in her closet, wondering what she should wear.

"Grandma asked me to keep an eye on you," Sara said. "She's worried about you."

"She is?" Ellie pulled tan pleated slacks from a hanger, then paused and cast a quick but studious look at her daughter.

"Yes." Sara flopped to the bed and pulled a pillow across her stomach.

Ellie turned back for a blouse. Her hand hesitated between one with tailored styling and a more feminine one. She chose the tailored one, thinking it would give her confidence.

"You are different—these last months, I mean," Sara said as Ellie began dressing. "You're happier, I think." She paused. "Do you have a lover?"

Ellie gasped and turned to find Sara's gaze, curious and steady, upon her. "What in heaven's name made you think such a thing?"

"Because you are definitely different. Like you're holding a secret or something."

Ellie gave a shaky laugh. "Now tell me when I would have time to find a lover? I'm with you girls all the time. I can't remember a night out alone from the house in five years. If I'm not here, I'm over at Grandma's." She pondered Sara's expression. Sara wanted an explanation. Ellie came and sat beside her.

"No, there's no lover," she said, taking Sara's hand in hers. "I'm not sure I'm the type to have a lover and keep it from my girls. But yes, I am happier. And I am changing."

"Grandma says you're getting a smart mouth."

Ellie, thinking of her mother, allowed a half-grin. "Grandma . . . well, she's just Grandma."

"I know." Sara continued to stare at her. "What's going on with you, Mom?"

"I think…" Ellie paused for the right words. "I think I'm growing up." She smiled and touched Sara's blond hair, which stretched sleek and satiny from her face and hung in a long, thick ponytail over her shoulder. "It's nothing to be frightened of, Sara. I'm fine. It's just that I'm changing, and it means other things will change too. For the better."

"You missed Daddy for such a long time."

"Yes, I did. I always will. But I'm not the same now—at least I don't want to be." She touched Sara's cheek again. "You trust me about today, okay?"

Sara nodded solemnly, then raised an eyebrow. "Something's up, isn't it? Has been for weeks."

"Yes," was all Ellie would say. She couldn't talk about it. The dreams, the intentions and hopes and plans, were too dear to her heart. And when said aloud, they sounded so preposterous and silly. Imagine Ellie McGrew moving out and doing something on her own. She lived in a safe house in the the suburbs, in the comfortable protection and care of her family. Why would she want to change that?

She couldn't say exactly. Perhaps because she found the protection and care too close to dominance. And because she had a need to *do* something, not simply to be. Surrounded by all this comfort and protection, she had been slowly dying. Something stagnant gradually did that, died. A person had to move and change to really be alive. And for the first time in over five years—well, maybe a bit less, since the evening she'd given birth to Poppy—Ellie felt alive.

The girls walked the three blocks to Grandma's, and Ellie drove for forty minutes along the interstate leading west from the city. Turning from the interstate, she drove for another thirty minutes along several blacktop county roads that led through one state park and two small towns. Three miles outside Advance, the second town, she pulled into a narrow, weed-edged gravel drive and came to a stop beside an empty house.

Opening the car door, she slipped slowly from the cool air-conditioned Cutlass out into the hot July sunshine, a gusty Oklahoma wind tugging at her hair. She looked at the house. It was made of fieldstone, colors of the earth: rust and orange and brown. The wood trim and the front and side porches had been painted white; the paint peeled and cracked. The neglected yard of tall grass would take hours of patience to mow. And the picket fence echoing the era of early James Stewart movies sagged in more than a couple of places, reflecting more gray than white.

But in her mind's eye Ellie saw a smooth lawn, a bright white fence; she saw how the stately elm would shade the front porch in the morning. She imagined a swing hanging at the end of the side porch, one in which she could sit in the early morning and late at night. She thought of picking fruit from the two peach trees that scratched the weathered side of the nearby barn.

She turned her gaze to scan the surrounding land. Eighty acres, the For Sale sign out front said. She pictured a vegetable garden, perhaps more fruit trees, and cattle. Their own, all their own.

Her heart picked up tempo. She'd investigated the nearby town of Advance: small, one main street, one bank, one grocery, one cafe—the kind of town where people knew and cared about each other. The school housed all grades, one through twelve. A rambling brick affair, it was more modern than Ellie would have imagined and had a good reputation.

The house with peeling paint, the remote land with only one other house in sight, the town without a single stoplight—it was beautiful to Ellie. It was what she wanted. She knew that in this moment, positively; no matter how much she'd argued with herself on the drive out here that she couldn't possibly go through with her plans. She wanted it and the secure, stable life it represented. For her girls. For herself.

With purposeful strides she walked back to her car. Though she'd already copied the name and number from the sign in front, she looked at the sign again as if to make sure it hadn't changed:

80 ACRES + HOUSE
W. WOLCOTT 376-4008

A hot summer breeze gusted in the car window as Ellie sat and looked at the sign, guessing at the cost for the farm. Her heart dipped. In her search for a place, she'd gone so far as to inquire about a bank loan. But she had no collateral and she was a woman, she'd been told kindly but firmly. She'd visited three banks, and while the melody was different, the tune was the the same: no loan for a widow with no visible means of support—or anyone to support her, she thought grimly.

Couldn't they see that she wanted the land for a job? How stupid. She needed the land to make money. And she had herself. She was her own best asset. She was healthy, with a fine mind. The rules were all so incredibly stupid and unfair. If she'd been a man, if she'd had a man, would that guarantee she'd pay her obligations? She thought not.

Then she pushed the complaints aside. They did more harm than good. This was the world in which she lived, and she'd have to accept it and find a way to get what she wanted. And what she wanted was this farm.

But as she drove back toward the small town and a telephone, the doubts and arguments started once more to revolve in her head. Anxiety clutched her heart.

What was she thinking of? Did she really want to do this?

She spied a telephone attached to a small, surprisingly modern convenience store and gas station. The next instant she slammed on brakes as, there in front of her, only inches from her hood, the rear end of a pickup truck suddenly appeared. Her own fault, she scolded herself, struggling to catch her breath. Caught up in her concerns, she'd not been watching, hadn't seen the truck backing from its parking place.

With a thudding heart, she waited for the truck to drive on before pulling her car in beside the store. She got out and stepped over to the coin telephone. She stopped.

Oh, God, is this the right thing? Will it be the best thing for my girls? For me? Am I being foolish? I don't have much money. I have even less experience. In fact, all I do seem to have is one great big longing, a longing so big it leaves a hollow right through me.

She took a deep breath, let it out slowly and tried to listen to the quiet, answering voice inside herself. Then she picked up the telephone receiver, deposited her money and pressed the numbers with a shaking finger. When a woman's voice answered, Ellie asked for W. Wolcott. She had all her courage gathered into a hard knot in her stomach.

But the woman's voice told her Mr. Wolcott was not at home and that he could most probably be found in town at the Wolcott Machine Shop.

The high expectation drained out of Ellie like a deflating balloon. "Thank you," she said faintly and replaced the receiver.

Okay, so find the Wolcott Machine Shop. In a strange town, with strange people.

How long had it been since she'd talked to anyone other than her family and close friends, with the exception of store clerks? For five years she'd led a very sheltered existence. On second thought, between her parents and her husband Galen, her entire life had been sheltered. They'd always looked after her, cared for her, made the decisions for her.

Now it was up to her.

Instead of asking directions, she got in her car and drove the length of the main street, thankfully coming upon the Wolcott Machine Shop at the far edge of town. She was quite pleased at not having had to ask anyone. She pulled up in front and sat there a minute, rehearsing what she would say to Mr. W. Wolcott.

The heat hit her the minute she slipped from the Cutlass. She blinked in the bright sunlight, even with her eyes shielded by sunglasses. She felt the lumps of sun-warmed gravel through her thin-soled flats.

One of two wide garage doors of the large steel building stood open. Her heart beat wildly. She was exceedingly aware of everything being so new, so strange. Quit being silly, she told herself, trying to relax the muscles of her back. No one is going to bite you. People ask questions every day. And Mr. Wolcott wants to sell his farm.

It was dim and cooler inside the building. Ellie removed her sunglasses and blinked. Two men wearing goggles operated a welder in the back of the building. Giant fans blew from the corners near the ceiling, and large tools, equipment and metal things that she couldn't begin to name were everywhere.

"Can I help you, ma'am?"

Ellie started as a man spoke. He stood in the doorway of an adjoining office. He was short and wiry, fortyish, with unruly gray hair damp from perspiration. He wore darkly stained coveralls. He regarded her with an undisguised look of curiosity.

"I'm looking for Mr. Wolcott," Ellie said, wondering if this was the man, giving a smile she knew was nervous.

The man shook his head. "Sorry. Wade ain't here now."

Ellie blinked. This wasn't what she'd expected. "Oh." She'd missed him again, she thought, her spirits sinking. "Thank you..." She turned and walked back to her car, half aware the man stared after her.

She paused with her hand on the door handle. She'd found Mr. Wolcott's machine shop. She'd talked to two strangers, even if it had been less than ten words each. She should've just asked again where to locate him. And she'd just better march back in there and do it now. Again gathering her courage as if from the very fibers of her body, she turned and walked back into the dim building.

She went to the doorway of the small office, crowded with gray metal file cabinets, a gray metal desk, papers and books everywhere and a Coke emblem clock with a cracked face on the wall. The small man sat in a gray metal swivel chair in front of the desk. He looked up.

"What time do you expect Mr. Wolcott back?" Ellie asked.

The man took a breath. "Hard to say," he drawled. "Sometimes he comes in first thing and stays all day. Sometimes he comes in and only stays five minutes—don't see him again till the next day."

Ellie looked at the man. "Can you tell me where to find him?"

The man looked at her and then at the clock. "Well, now, it's a little early, but I'd guess maybe over at the cafe. Across the street there." He nodded his head toward the large window on his right. "He most generally has lunch there. He could be there now."

"Thank you." Ellie turned, then stopped. "Can you tell me what he looks like?"

"Well, of course I can." The man gave a half-grin. "He's a tall feller, and he'll be wearing a bright red ball cap with Wolcott Machine Shop on the front. Just got a bunch of new ones in last week. Saw him wearing one early this morning. This was one of his five-minute days."

Ellie thanked him and walked back out into the bright sunlight. She stood at the edge of the gravel parking lot and looked, squinting, across the street at the cafe the man had indicated. Last Chance Cafe was printed in red, gold-edged lettering, western style, across the plate-glass window. Red gingham curtains showed through the glass.

Perfect name, she thought as she started across the wide street. She hoped this was the last time she had to go looking for Mr. W. Wolcott. And last chance was exactly how she viewed her entire endeavor to buy a farm. This was her last chance to follow her own dreams, her own star, her own life.

Moving between two parked pickups, she stepped up on the sidewalk. Her heart had begun its nervous pounding again; perspiration ran between her breasts. At that moment, right before her, a tall man wearing a red ball cap stepped from the door of the Last Chance Cafe. And the name Wolcott Machine Shop was printed on the front of the cap!

The man's eyes met Ellie's. "Oh," she said, clutching her purse tightly. "The man at your shop said I could find you here." She stuck out her hand. "I'm Ellie McGrew and I'd like to talk to you about your farm for sale."

The man's eyebrows came together. "Well, hello," he said, shaking Ellie's hand. "You're wanting to talk to me? About my farm for sale?" He let go her hand.

"Yes, I am." Ellie wondered why he looked at her so strangely. She felt him take in her face, then his gaze traveled to her blouse and on downward before it came back up.

"Ma'am, I don't have a farm for sale."

Ellie took in a breath. "But I saw a sign." Something struck her. "You're not Mr. W. Wolcott?"

The man smiled. "No, ma'am. But if it's Wade Wolcott you're wanting—" he inclined his head toward the cafe "—he's inside."

Ellie felt the heat stealing up her neck to her face as her heart plummeted. "I'm sorry," she said. "They told me to look over here for him. I just thought . . . with your hat . . ."

"That's quite all right," the man said, touching the brim of his cap politely. He reached over and opened the door to the cafe. "It was nice meeting you."

There was a grin in his eyes and a definitely complimentary look on his face.

"Thank you," she managed softly, confused and embarrassed as she stepped through the cafe doorway. Once more touching the brim of his hat, the man smiled, then started down the sidewalk.

Ellie stood in the doorway and looked into the cafe. To the far right was a long lunch counter with stools, most of them taken. Two women moved back and forth behind the counter, not quite hurrying, serving their customers. Tables and chairs filled the cafe and red-seated booths lined the walls. It was neat and clean and friendly feeling—and filled mostly with men, several of whom eyed Ellie curiously.

And at that moment she noticed there had to be at least eight bright red ball caps. Three of them, she saw immediately, with the name Wolcott Machine Shop emblazoned across the front.

Chapter Two

Ellie scanned the room again. She felt laughter, an odd kind, welling up within her. Here she stood in a strange cafe, in a strange town, seeking a man whom she didn't know and hadn't the slightest idea what he looked like. She, Ellie McGrew. Her mother would be flabbergasted.

There were maybe only seven women in the crowded cafe, two of whom gave Ellie a thorough going over. She definitely felt the square peg in a round hole, and her mind cast around, seeking a direction to take.

Her first thoughts were hilariously irrational: she could go around to every man wearing a red hat with the name Wolcott on the front and ask his name. Or she could stand up on the counter and call for Mr. W. Wolcott.

Obviously, either plan was beyond her.

She could just turn around and walk out, she thought then.

To keep from doing so, Ellie moved. Heart thumping, she approached the end of the lunch counter closest to herself and farthest from other people. After an agonizing mo-

ment she managed to get the attention of one of the waitresses.

In answer to Ellie's question, the waitress pointed to a
man sitting in the third booth along the rear wall. His back
was toward them. He had brown hair; he wore no red hat.

Ellie made quite certain this was Mr. W. Wolcott. "Only
Wolcott around here," the waitress told her with a generous smile.

Ellie thanked her, grateful for the woman's open friend-
liness as well as the information. Then she sucked in her
breath and headed toward Mr. W. Wolcott's table. Her nervousness wasn't helped by the fact that Mr. Wolcott sat in
the company of a very pretty young woman. Ellie hoped she
wouldn't be too terrible an interruption to them.

Seeing Gayla's eyes widen with curiosity as she stared past
his shoulder, Wade turned his head a bit. His vision came to
rest on beige slacks. A woman's slacks. Covering shapely
hips. Quickly his gaze moved upward over a curvy feminine frame to rest on the face looking down at him. His immediate impression was that if he were to say "Boo," this
woman would turn and run.

"Mr. Wolcott?" she said and gave a small, nervous smile.

Her eyes were blue, very blue, with long dark lashes,
Wade noticed. She wasn't exceptionally pretty, was actually sort of plain. Her clothes, the beige tailored slacks and
matching, obviously silk, blouse spoke of class. She was a
lady. And there was something else about her, Wade noted
with the practiced eye of a man who enjoys looking at
women. A womanliness. A sensual womanliness, hinted at
in the way she moved, the way she looked at a person.

"Yes?" he answered, his gaze continuing to assess her.
Maybe she wasn't so plain after all.

"Mr. W. Wolcott?"

"I'm Wade Wolcott. What can I do for you?" Wade
found this a nice, unexpected happening.

"I'd like to talk to you about the house and eighty acres
I saw for sale outside of town with your name and number
on it." She spoke in a breathless fashion, as if that were a lot

for her to say. She glanced hesitantly at Gayla and then back to Wade. "Is it yours?"

"Yes, it's mine." He saw relief fill her blue eyes.

She looked at him a minute. "May I talk to you about it?" Darting another quick and uncertain look at Gayla, she added, "If you have time."

Gayla smiled, her eyes resting on his for a brief moment. They held a flirting promise, a sexual air as much a part of the young woman as her skin. "I have to be getting back to work anyway," she said. She touched his hand before slipping from the booth. She had a body that wouldn't quit and a way of moving it so everyone was sure to notice. With a smile at the woman, she stepped around her.

"Send over my usual," Wade called after Gayla as she plucked an apron from a hook on the wall. She lifted a hand as a sign she'd heard and gave an extra sweep with her bottom while pulling on the apron.

Wade managed to hold his chuckle in; he was used to Gayla and her ways. But he saw an expression of veiled wonder on the face of the woman who stood beside his table. Then, as if realizing she was staring, she jerked her head back and looked at him. She stood there a second before slipping into the seat Gayla had vacated.

Skittish as a wild mare taken from the mountains, she clutched her small purse until her knuckles were white. Deliberately, though discreetly, Wade took note of the set of wedding rings she wore. He also noticed how the filmy material of her blouse fell over the fullness of her breasts.

Wade considered Gayla a girl and this one across from him now a woman. Taller than average, she had a woman's figure—sturdy, full-breasted and rounded, yet tucked wonderfully in all the right places. Her face was rather square, with pale, smooth skin. She wore little or no makeup. Her hair was dark blond, the color of overripe wheat, and streaked liberally by the sun—and also with a bit of silver. Although wispy curls brushed her temples, the rest of her hair was clipped neatly at the back of her neck. She moved in her seat, and Wade caught the scent of fine perfume.

He extended his hand across the table. "I'm Wade Wolcott.... And you are?"

"Eleanor McGrew," she said, pink tinging her cheeks.

Her grip was firm, but the skin of her hand was soft against his, telling him she didn't do much rough work. Wade held on to her hand and looked into her wide blue eyes. She wasn't plain at all, he realized. A sliver of warmth touched his blood; he felt the pleasure of looking at a very attractive woman.

Her color grew higher, and she pulled her hand away and averted those blue eyes. She glanced to his hat on the table, then back up at him.

"You're interested in buying the place?" He began for her. He wasn't sure she was going to say anything.

"Yes." She paused. "The house and eighty acres?" She raised an eyebrow.

Wade nodded. "You've seen it?"

"I've driven by and looked a couple of times."

Another waitress, Melanie, appeared beside the table and placed a steaming bowl of chili and a frosty glass of cola in front of Wade.

"Thank you, honey," Wade told her, returning her smile.

Looking at Ellie, Melanie whipped an order pad from her pocket. "Would you like to order?"

"Just some iced tea, please," Ellie said. Her voice sounded forced, and her fingers almost played a tune against each other.

Ellie knew she couldn't possibly eat a thing. How had she gotten herself into this situation? It was uncomfortable beyond words to be in this strange cafe talking to a man she'd never met before. A man who looked at her...well...so attentively. It didn't help her nerves at all. She felt distressingly warm and jittery inside.

She wanted to walk away, wished she'd never come into the place, wished she were at home with the familiar—sorting laundry, tending roses, listening to gossip.

Drying and dying.

The thought came sharp and clear. Something inside her, some part of herself as wise as the ages, knew she had to do

this, that she would forever regret it if she didn't at least try.
Yes, the action could be an irresponsible mistake—but the
greater mistake lay in doing nothing at all. She stood at a
crossroads: one way led to life, albeit unknown, and the
other way to drying up until she simply blew away with the
wind, like dust that nurtured nothing.

"You don't need to be afraid to eat at this place 'cause of
its name—the Last Chance," Mr. Wolcott teased after the
waitress walked away. "The food's the best in the county."

His eyes were straight on hers in a most disarming fashion. "Oh…" she said. "I'm just not hungry." He was only
kidding, Ellie, she told herself.

She took in a breath to ask him about the price of the
land. But before she could speak, a man stopped beside their
booth to greet Mr. Wolcott. Mr. Wolcott made the intro-
ductions, then Ellie waited while the two men discussed
some cattle and a welding job the man wanted Mr. Wolcott
to do. Ellie strove to look patient, even politely interested,
though she'd already forgotten the man's name and really
had no idea what they were talking about. In her mind she
rehearsed what to say to Mr. W. Wolcott. She really feared
the price he would quote for the land. How would she convince him to sell to her at a lower price?

Her gaze moved surreptitiously over his brown hair,
tinged golden by the sun, and his thick, burnished mustache, which drooped at the corners of his mouth. He was
an immediately likable man, and there was an old-
fashioned, courtly manner about him, Ellie thought,
amused. The air of a gentleman of the old west.

His face was deeply tanned with creases at the corners of
his mouth and eyes, evidence of years spent in the sun. The
eyes were a distinctive gold-brown. He wasn't truly handsome—he was much too rugged for that—but there was
something about him…. Uneasy with the thought, with the
odd feelings stirring inside, she let it go.

She guessed his age at somewhere between thirty-five and
forty, much younger than the image she'd formed of the
man who would own the land. And he was experienced. In
many areas, she thought dryly. Would he need to sell? If he

did, it would help her. But the impression she received from Mr. W. Wolcott was that of a strong, self-confident man who needed very little.

Finally, after what seemed forever but was barely ten minutes, the visiting man touched the brim of his western hat to Ellie and gave a polite goodbye. Ellie found herself once more staring into the golden-brown eyes of Mr. W. Wolcott. She formed the words to ask his price.

The waitress appeared, setting down her iced tea and taking time to familiarly joke with Mr. Wolcott. Again Ellie waited.

When the waitress stepped away, Mr. Wolcott rested both forearms against the edge of the table and looked at her, patiently waiting for her to speak.

"How much do you want for the land and the house?" she asked then, her words coming in a rush. His eyes rested on her again in that disarmingly blatant fashion.

"One hundred thousand."

It was worse than she'd figured, but Ellie refused to let any emotion reflect on her face. She worked for courage to dicker over the price.

"That's pretty steep, considering real-estate prices at the present," she said, keeping her eyes on her glass as she added sugar to the iced tea.

"Not too steep. It's worth it." He stirred his chili. "It has a large pond and seventy acres planted in excellent grazing pasture."

Ellie knew it was a good place; that was why she wanted it. She sensed him grinning just below the surface. He knew what he was doing. He knew so much more about this sort of thing than she did.

She pressed her lips together. If she couldn't match him at the dickering, she'd just have to be honest.

"I have sixty thousand in cash, now, to spend. I can squeeze sixty-five if I have to. That's all."

"Banks give loans," he said after a minute, again averting his gaze to his chili.

"Not to single women," she replied. He glanced at her rings, then met her gaze. "I'm a widow," she said and saw his eyebrows rise in surprise.

He looked at her a long moment. Ellie held her breath. *Please, please let him say yes.*

"Lady, I'm sorry, but sixty thousand would barely pay for the land, not to mention the house—it's a package deal. And I'm not the local goodwill society."

Ellie sat there. What could she say? What could she do? The banks had refused her; her father would never help with this, nor would her brothers, and Galen's folks, well, there was no tie there. There was only herself.

She picked up her purse, very slowly, very gracefully. She wouldn't let this man see her stabbing disappointment; she wouldn't let anyone see. And she had to get out of there before the lump in her throat turned to humiliating tears in her eyes.

"Thank you for talking to me, Mr. Wolcott," she said, forcing the words quietly and calmly past her tightening throat.

He just looked at her. After one glance into his perceptive eyes, she turned away and concentrated on maintaining her pride as she slipped from the booth and walked away. Her heart was breaking, an actual physical pain.

Failure. She'd failed.

She squinted as she looked through the glass door to the bright sunlight outside, made painfully brighter by the tears in her eyes. She reached for the doorknob.

Try again. Don't give up.

The words reverberated within her. She remembered suddenly a quote by Winston Churchill: Never give in. Never. Never.

There had to be something she could do, one more thing to try.

She turned and headed back to Mr. Wolcott's table, an idea bursting within her brain.

Wade, thinking maybe he should have talked to her more about the farm, had watched her walk to the door. But, damn it, he argued with himself as he played the spoon around in the chili, sixty-five thousand was robbery! No matter what the market situation. He was the kind of man who shared with his neighbors and helped when he could—but he wasn't in the business of supporting widows. Besides, she didn't belong on a farm so far from the city.

And he didn't need her there, he thought emphatically. He knew trouble when he saw it: a woman alone, his house less than a quarter mile up the hill. He'd end up down there doing work she had no business getting into in the first place. He didn't need the aggravation.

He took a swallow of his soft drink, then glanced toward her one more time. *Well, I'll be damned*. Mrs. Eleanor McGrew was walking toward him.

The surprise caused the fizzling liquid to ball in his throat, forcing his eyes to water. He coughed, almost choking at the burning sensation. Wiping his eyes, he continued to watch her weave between the tables toward him. She bore the expression of a woman ready to do battle.

Respect for her kindled. She had courage, he'd give her that. He suspected it'd been hard for her to talk to him in the first place. It probably had taken all she had just to walk into the cafe. She wanted that farm bad, he realized.

Maybe as bad as he had eight years ago, he thought, memory pricking like a dull needle.

His gaze locked on hers, and her blue eyes didn't waver. He thought he recognized excitement there. He'd felt like that himself when going after something he wanted.

She stood a moment looking at him, then slid into the seat, never taking her gaze from his.

"Perhaps we could make a deal," she said. Her chin tilted upward and her shoulders were set very straight. "I'll pay you sixty thousand now and the rest over the next six years."

"You mean I could finance you?" Wade said, watching her blue eyes darken.

"Well . . . yes."

He thought about it. His first thought was, hell no! He had his life set easy and smooth, exactly how he liked it. He didn't need any ripples. And he knew this woman would bring him ripples. He'd end up down there fixing this, helping with that. He didn't need it. He didn't want it. All he wanted was to get rid of the place and not be bothered, to let go of memories long dead.

But looking at her, he said, "Why do you want this place? Eighty acres is a lot of land."

"I want to make it pay for itself . . . cattle, hay . . ."

"Hard work." He looked at her. "You ever done this before?"

"I grew up on a farm."

The emphatic no remained on the tip of his tongue, but the words that came out were, "Why should I finance you when a bank won't?"

She sat there a moment, and he could see her marshaling forces. "Because you aren't a bank," she said, gesturing with her hand. "You have more sense than a bank. You can see me as an able-bodied human being—not a woman—and can believe I'll pay you."

She was very convincing; he'd have to give her that. And sharp, too. He put down his spoon, leaned back and looked at her. He chuckled. "Mrs. McGrew, I'd be a fool if I said I didn't look at you and see a woman." He allowed what he meant to show on his face and in his voice. "And I'm no fool, believe me," he promised.

But he must be, he thought, because he still hadn't told her no. And he continued to look into her sky-blue eyes.

Confusion played across her face and pink again tinged her pale cheeks. Wasn't she used to men paying her this kind of attention? She should be, Wade thought.

Then an edge of pleading swept her features, and Wade realized his heart answered, even if he did try to remind himself that this was a business proposition. Maybe he was a sap, but for the life of him, he didn't want to be the one to disappoint her. She waited, seeming hardly to breathe. Wade pulled at his mustache, thinking.

Times were hard; buyers hadn't exactly been busting down his door. It was a good investment for him; he'd be rid of the place. And there was no reason to assume he'd have to be down there helping her out all the time.

Ellie willed him to say yes, then willed him to say anything as long seconds passed, and still he remained deep in thought. She hadn't wanted to lower her pride, hadn't wanted to practically plead for the land, though she knew her expression did just that.

But she wanted that place. She put every bit of femininity in her soul into her eyes. And she didn't care if it was dirty pool. She'd been born a woman. It had proved to be a handicap often enough; no reason why it shouldn't be used to an advantage when possible.

The man's slow manner was infuriating. He raised his eyes to regard her from beneath his thick eyebrows. Her heart pounded. He didn't look as if he was going to say yes.

What he did say was, "I think we need to go out and look at the place." His lips spread into an oddly reluctant and tight smile beneath his thick mustache as he reached for his red cap. "You need to thoroughly inspect the house, walk the land. You may change your mind after you see it up close."

"I don't need to look at it," Ellie said. "I've seen enough. And I'm not going to change my mind."

The next instant Mr. Wolcott's hand, quite a large hand, closed around hers. "We'll go look at the place," he said firmly and tugged on her hand. "I think you should look at the inside of the house. You should never buy anything you haven't thoroughly inspected," he added, almost as if to a child.

Ellie didn't care for his almost patronizing manner. And she didn't care for the fact that she knew he was right. There was no getting around it, however, because Mr. Wolcott simply ignored her objections. Adjusting the cap over his hair, he called to the young woman who'd earlier been sitting with him. "Gayla, keep my chili warm. I'll be back."

Putting a hand on Ellie's elbow, he directed her out of the cafe. She looked up at him, somewhat amazed at his height. She'd known he'd be tall but hadn't been prepared for the length of him. As if a single-minded man, he kept his eyes on the doorway.

Ellie blinked in the bright light and hesitated, thinking of her car across the street.

"We'll take my truck," Mr. Wolcott said, inclining his head toward a deep blue pickup truck parked in front of the cafe. He opened the door for her to slip into the passenger seat, and as she ducked beneath his arm, she felt a strange warmth at his nearness. An uncomfortable warmth. She became singularly aware of the light scent of his after-shave and of the apparent rock hardness of his shoulder and chest beneath the fabric of his shirt.

Quit being silly, she told herself, trying to dismiss the odd fancies. But when Mr. Wolcott slid into his side of the seat and smiled at her, she knew she felt . . . something . . . again.

The air-conditioner blew full blast and the gravelly voice of Waylon Jennings sang from the radio. Ellie averted her gaze from the man beside her and looked out at the fields and pastures. When she realized she was keeping time to the music with her foot, she stopped. She slid her gaze over to Mr. Wolcott.

He smiled at her. "I enjoy Waylon's music, too."

So he'd seen her—and had seen her stop. Ellie wasn't quite certain why it bothered her. She just didn't like to reveal much of herself. And she especially didn't like revealing herself to this man.

Oh, please God, let him sell me the farm.

They pulled into the drive, and Ellie fairly jumped from the pickup. She stared out at the land. The doubts that had been mounting on the drive out now vanished as shadows before the sun. This place was good; it was right for her and the girls. Surely Mr. Wolcott would say yes.

He easily reached the key hidden high on the porch rafters and handed it to Ellie. It was hard for her to unlock the door, her hand shook so from anticipation—and from Mr. Wolcott's close attention.

She went into each of the rooms, Mr. Wolcott following along behind, watching.

The house was old and plain and years of fine Oklahoma grit coated everything. Cobwebs clung to every corner, every nook and cranny. The linoleum in the one bathroom and in the kitchen cracked and peeled. Water stains on the ceiling in the living room indicated a leak in the roof, and several sills showed signs of rotting.

But the house was solid. The oak flooring creaked very little and even shone beneath the layer of dust. The walls needed only a fresh coat of paint. Built into a small hill, the house sat atop a basement garage that Mr. Wolcott said opened into a storm shelter, something of a luxury for the area. The garage was even dirtier than the upstairs, but looked solid, at least to Ellie's eyes. She didn't think it would've made any difference to her anyway. She wanted the house and the land.

When she found the entry to the storm shelter, she raved delightedly over it. Then she opened it. With superhuman effort, she stifled a scream as a spider dropped right in front of her face. She looked to Mr. Wolcott and realized he'd heard the escaping gasp. Refusing to give him satisfaction, she entered the old shelter and looked around the damp, dirty and buggy place. It could be cleaned, she thought determinedly.

Mr. Wolcott took great care to point out the aging furnace that blew air only from the hallway and the water heater that had seen better days.

Back in the kitchen Ellie gazed uncertainly at the stove. She'd always had electric. This was...gas of some sort. She thought back, trying to remember the one their family had had when she was a child.

"Propane," Mr. Wolcott told her without her saying a word. "The furnace is, too. That's what that big silver tank's for outside."

She felt his keen regard and refused to let him think she was disappointed. Which she really wasn't—just suddenly aware of all the work to be done.

"I was going to fix this place up about eight years ago," Mr. Wolcott said. "Did install the new kitchen cabinets and refinished the floors but never got to the rest."

Ellie nodded. She went to look out the back door.

"There's no air-conditioning," Mr. Wolcott said in a low voice from behind her. "And the water's provided from a well. You'll be in trouble if the pump goes out."

She turned and looked at him. He leaned against the kitchen door frame, the muscles of his body, as hard as the wood of the frame, resting loose and easy. He looked at her, assessing her.

"Just trying to tell you what you're in for," he said. "Do you know anything about this sort of stuff?"

"I was raised on a small farm about like this one, Mr. Wolcott. I know it was a long time ago, but it isn't totally unfamiliar."

"You had a man around the house then, I'm guessing."

"Yes," Ellie said. She searched his face. "If you think this place is so bad, why do you insist on the price?"

"This place is worth what I'm asking. To the right buyer."

"A man."

"I hate to say it for what it makes me sound like, but yes."

"The house is solid," she said, a statement, not a question.

"Yes," Mr. Wolcott agreed. "It is that, from the bottom to the top."

She turned back to look out the door. Her eyes feasted on the view before her. Then she turned slowly to face Mr. Wolcott. "I'll not change my mind, Mr. Wolcott."

His gaze rested on her, thoughtful, assessing, and then almost like a sensuous caress. Her stomach knotted strangely, and she averted her eyes, moving to run a hand over the tile counter someone had lovingly laid years before. But she could still feel his gaze upon her.

"Let's go look at the grass," he said with an odd suddenness. The low timbre of his voice reverberated within her.

They walked, Mr. Wolcott barely inches from her, out past the backyard and down through the pasture. Ellie looked down at the grass in which her thin leather flats stood. Her heartbeat threaded with longing. All her plans for the future started racing helter-skelter through her mind.

She and Mr. Wolcott bent to run their hands through the stems. Mr. Wolcott pointed out and named several different kinds of the grasses. Ellie recognized some and not others. They walked on through a thinning in the woods that led to the pond, an actual stream-fed pond, unusual for the area.

Mr. Wolcott walked close enough for his arm to repeatedly brush hers. Ellie found herself extremely aware of it and wondered why. When she had to step over a large fallen log, his hand reached out and gripped hers, an oddly intimate gesture, especially when he showed no sign of letting go. Self-conscious and chiding herself for being fanciful, Ellie pulled her hand away. He gave no sign he even noticed.

"Several years ago, I ran seventy head of cattle on this acreage," he said, gazing off at the pasture. "But though this grass is good, that was overloading it. Can't cut for winter hay when you do that."

Ellie listened to his words, moisture running between her breasts and gathering around her waist, her mind filling with images of her own plans. There were questions on her tongue, but she couldn't ask them. Her dreams and plans were too uncertain, too fragile to speak of yet. She was taking one step at a time. This land, this farm was the first step.

Oh, the man was infuriating! Why wouldn't he say whether or not he would sell? But she didn't want to press him, for fear his answer would be no.

They drove back to Advance, and Ellie again found herself standing in the bright summer sun with Mr. Wolcott. She looked up at him, squinting as she did so, waiting for him to speak. She didn't intend to ask again.

He tugged at his mustache. "Twelve percent interest?" he said, cocking an eyebrow.

Her breath left her. Was he saying yes? But oh . . . she'd not planned on so much interest. She hadn't even thought of how she would pay the balance due. She'd only been bargaining for more time.

Keep your mind on that, Ellie, she told herself. Think about the rest later.

"If you'll extend the time to eight years," she said after doing rough calculations in her mind. Calculations which were probably way off the mark because she was far from a whiz in math.

He gazed thoughtfully at her for a few seconds. "If you get behind, I'll take the land back."

"That's hardly fair. What about all the money I've already paid you?"

"The land, my land, is the only collateral you can use," he said, pausing to make his point. "The bank would do the same."

It was true; Ellie knew. And the bank wouldn't give her a loan.

"You could always sell the land, then pay me what you owe," he offered. "Maybe even make a profit."

"I won't want to sell," she told him evenly.

It occurred to her then that Mr. Wolcott, in his way, was saying yes to the deal—without looking into her situation, her finances. The realization caused her heart to thump.

"Then you'll do it?" she said, trying to keep the excitement from her voice.

A smile shone first in his eyes, then stretched slowly across his lips. He extended his hand. "I think we've got a deal, Mrs. McGrew."

Ellie took his hand and shook it firmly. Her heart had swelled to nearly bursting. *She'd done it!* She had herself the beginnings of her dream. Oh, thank you, God, her heart sang, *and thank you, Mr. Wolcott.*

His gaze lingered on hers. He had a thoughtful expression, and Ellie suddenly realized he wasn't thinking about the land or their deal. She looked away, wondering at his expression, at the feelings suddenly stirring within her body.

Confused and self-conscious, Ellie averted her gaze. "Should I write you a check? Now? I . . ." She left off and dug into her purse, looking for her checkbook. She really didn't know how this was handled. She'd owned, or rather had made payments on, one house in her life, and Galen had handled the purchasing of it.

"A check is fine," Mr. Wolcott said, then giving a half smile, "but there are a few legalities we'll need taken care of."

"Oh." Ellie stood there, uncertain of what to say, what to do. She hated for him to see how ignorant she was of such things.

He touched her elbow, turning her down the sidewalk. "I have an attorney friend right down here a few yards," he said. "We'll visit him and see all about it."

"How much will this attorney cost?" Ellie said. For how many years had she gone and never thought about the price of things? Now she had to; there was only herself to do it.

They continued to walk along the sidewalk, Mr. Wolcott's boots sounding heavily on the concrete beside her. "Depends on how much he has to do," he said, looking down at her through squinted eyes. "This shouldn't be much. He did the title work when I bought the place."

"Oh," Ellie said again.

She entered the attorney's office with more than a little trepidation and exited forty-five minutes later deep in debt, but highly elated. Once more she'd faced a new experience; it was behind her now, and she clutched in her hand the papers proclaiming her right to the land.

"Now it's all legal," Mr. Wolcott said as they stood once more on the sidewalk outside. "And you didn't even have to pay the bill." Referring to the fact that Brad Young had charged him thirty dollars for the service, he gave her a dryly amused look.

"Well, he was your lawyer—your friend," Ellie pointed out. "And I took his word about the title."

He chuckled. "So he is . . . don't worry about it. He's bonded." He paused and thoughtfulness filled his eyes. "You have yourself a farm, Mrs. McGrew."

"Yes," she said, not bothering to hide the wide smile that came from deep within her.

He grinned down at her, and she saw the understanding—more, the empathy—written in his eyes. For a long moment Ellie found herself staring into those warm eyes and feeling the immense pleasure of sharing an emotion. By heaven, it was the most wonderful feeling in the world to finally possess something you've dreamed about so long and so hard.

She stuck out her hand. "I'd like to thank you, Mr. Wolcott."

He accepted her hand and gave it a firm shake, saying, "You're welcome. And call me Wade. We're going to be neighbors."

A coolness struck Ellie. "Oh?"

"I live in the house up the hill from your place," Mr. Wolcott—Wade—said.

The coolness turned to a striking, pleasant warmth. "I'm Ellie," she said, backing away. "Well...goodbye...see you soon, I guess."

"Wait..." He dug into his shirt pocket. "This is yours now. It's the only one," he said, pulling out the house key and throwing it to her.

To Ellie's amazement, she caught it. "Thanks." Excitement and pleasure and fear all mingled, causing her to turn quickly and stride toward her car. Her feet hardly seemed to touch the ground. With her heart pounding as if to jump from her chest, she sought to calm herself. Wouldn't do at all to have a heart attack.

She drove home, thinking about the girls and their reaction...thinking about her parents' reaction...thinking about the man she'd just met and the way he'd looked at her, and about her reaction to him. Her spirits flip-flopped from highest peaks to lowest valleys, from thrill to fear. If this was what it was like to feel alive, she wasn't at all certain she'd chosen wisely.

Chapter Three

They sang "Happy Birthday" to her. The candles—all thirty-four of them—blazed atop the cake like a bonfire.

"Make a wish, Mama," Poppy cried excitedly, her blue eyes sparkling nearly as much as the candles.

Ellie closed her eyes and wished for the words to tell them all of her activities that day and of her plans, plans that would bring great changes to all of their futures.

She waited until everyone had finished the birthday cake and ice cream. She told herself she didn't want to interrupt the festivities, but deep inside she knew she was just being a coward. She felt saved by the presents that needed to be opened—and took her time doing so, her mind dwelling more on the present she'd given herself. For one split second, she envisioned the girls and herself just moving off and not telling anyone. Maybe they'd never notice.

Her parents gave her a lovely new leather purse with matching wallet and key ring. "That one you carry, Ellie, is all worn out," her mother said. "I should think you'd be ashamed to show it around."

There was a small, cross-stitched sampler from Sara, a picture of a house with the words Home Sweet Home stitched beneath. One look at Sara and Ellie had the wild suspicion that her daughter knew about the goings on of the whole day. Absurd, she told herself—and yet it would be easier if Sara did know.

Ellie knew then she should have told the girls her plans before this. It was wrong not to. Guilt raised its ugly head alongside her apprehensions.

Rae gave her a genuine marble rolling pin—Rae loved pies—and Poppy a dish towel with her small, pudgy hand-print traced on it.

Then it was over. Poppy scampered off to watch television, Rae right behind her. Sara pulled out a book.

Ellie nervously ran a hand over her hip and looked at her father sitting comfortably in his easy chair, whipping the evening paper out in front of him. Her mother appeared from the kitchen, bearing two glasses of iced tea. She set one glass on the table beside Ellie; Ellie hadn't asked for iced tea. She thanked God neither of her brothers had driven in for the birthday celebration. She would have only her mother and father to contend with at the moment.

She watched her mother go to the couch and sit down, noting the grace with which she moved. Still a beautiful woman, her mother took great pride in maintaining her figure and her skin. Her hands showed no traces of the work—washing, gardening, livestock handling—she'd done earlier in her life. She had a maid now, and her hands rarely touched dishwater. She creamed them faithfully at night; looks, prestige were mainstays in her life.

Oh, Mama, please try to understand. Your way isn't mine. Have some faith in me.

Then, quietly, Ellie called a reluctant Poppy from in front of the television set to come sit on her lap and indicated Rae should sit on the arm of the chair. Sara, by her normal sensing mechanism, sat on the floor and rested an arm on Ellie's knees.

Ellie made her announcement, her voice soft and steady, as if talking about having purchased tickets to the dinner theater. She wished very much she could have had time to tell the girls alone.

She should have told them before this, Ellie thought in anguish as she looked at her girls. She'd made a huge mistake right at the outset. How many more would she make? Oh, it was much simpler the way it had been: being a puppet on a string, letting others rule her life. She made no mistakes then.

If one never did anything, one never made mistakes.

Sara looked stunned, Rae suspicious, and Poppy thoughtful. Ellie kept her eyes on her girls, their reaction her first concern.

Poppy began asking questions, naturally, one right after the other. "Will we have to travel for days, Mama? Do they gots TV? Do they gots cartoons?"

"Have, Poppy," Ellie corrected automatically, turning her gaze to Rae.

Rae's suspicion ebbed and was replaced by cautious delight as she continued to watch Ellie's face. Ellie smiled at her daughter, saying with her eyes: yes, you may have a dog, and a cat, and a horse.

Then, her gaze rested on her eldest. It was Sara she was most concerned about. And Sara she couldn't read. That in itself was a good clue to the extent of her daughter's shock and upset. It was Sara's way to retreat behind a closed wall of indifference when angered, confused or upset in any way.

"You've got to be out of your mind," Ellie's mother said. It was exactly what Ellie had expected her to say, right down to the inflection of a wounded banty hen that her mother gave the words. Her thin, aristocratic face mottled with emotion, she stared at Ellie. "Now, Ellie, this thing will pass. You've been having trouble lately, I know, but we're here to help."

"Where did you get this outlandish idea?" Her father demanded, staring at her over his now crumpled paper.

"It's not so outlandish, Daddy. Galen and I dreamed and planned on moving to the country. We'd even started saving before he died."

"Galen's gone," her father said bluntly. "Things have changed."

"And I've changed. I see no reason why I have to let the dream go. I know it won't be as wonderful, won't be as easy, as it would have been with Galen, but it can be good." She wanted so much for them to understand. "And it will be good for the girls, too."

Her mother's gaze pierced her. "Now I don't know how you can believe that. They have everything they need or want right here."

"We can have something of our own out there. Something the girls and I can build together."

"You haven't spent what Galen left you for this place, have you?" Her father said, his gaze assessing her. When she nodded, he swore. "What are you going to live on, Ellie? This is madness."

"The money was slowly running out anyway, Father. We live in a rented house, a place above our means, even with the good money Galen left. I've been dipping into the principal for several years. At least now I own something."

"You could have seen about buying a place close by, Ellie." Her mother cast her a reproachful look. "Then you and the girls would be near if you needed help. And we would've been glad to help with the financing. You know you didn't need to worry about the money. This—" she waved her hand "—what will you do if you need help?"

"It's not the end of the earth, Mother. It's only an hour away."

"And now what will you do for money?" her father asked sharply.

Ellie took a deep breath. Her plans in this direction weren't set. There were so many things she needed to do first. And she hesitated to speak of her thoughts for the future, for she knew her father and everyone else would think her crazy. She didn't want to hear their remarks.

"I can get a job," she replied slowly, feeling as if she were sinking into the chair. "We'll own the place, and it will provide a lot for us."

"You couldn't have had enough to pay for a place as big as you say." Her father's voice rose.

"No, I made a down payment." Her voice came weakly.

"And what will you pay the rest with? What kind of job can you get to pay for it and still have enough money left to live on?"

Ellie knew she had to rally, had to appear stronger, or they would take all her plans and dreams and rip them to shreds.

"I'm grown now, Father. I can do things on my own." She forced strength into her words and looked directly at her parents. "I can budget. I know I'm not the world's best, but I can manage quite well. And the land will provide us with a living—I know it won't be a fortune, but it can be adequate." She stuck out her chin. "Just because Galen's gone doesn't mean I should let my life go, not anymore."

Her mother's chin quivered. "I don't think you know what you're letting yourself in for, young lady. You don't remember, you never had to work on the farm. But I did. And I remember."

"I don't know, Mama," Ellie said. "But I want a chance to find out on my own."

Her parents faced her and she faced them. It was eight o'clock. Ellie decided to give them until eight-thirty to have their say, to get it all off their chests, though she doubted thirty minutes would be enough for her mother. And she strove to remember they were saying all these things because they loved her and wanted the best—what they thought was best—for her and the girls.

She listened to their arguments and knew she must look crazy to them. All the arguments made such sense. She was a woman alone, with three girls. Here, she was protected, the girls were protected; out there, anything could happen. What did she plan to do for money? She'd never had to handle finances on a large scale. What about the work? And winter made the work even harder. Did she know how it felt to go out and break the ice from the water so the animals could drink? And besides the work, what would she do about house repairs?

They saw she would not budge. She sensed their anger, their helplessness, their anxiety, and she hurt for them. But she would not change her mind. She could not.

Ellie smoothed the sheet over Rae and Poppy as they lay in the double bed they shared. "Down," she said, pushing the large, extremely fat tabby from the bed. "I'm putting Maynard out tonight, Rae."

Rae frowned anxiously. "But, Mama, he might not come back if you do that." Maynard was a stray cat they'd acquired two months ago and had to keep out of sight if their landlord showed up unexpectedly, which he was wont to do, because they weren't suppose to have any pets.

"Maynard knows full well where he's going to get his next meal," Ellie told Rae. Maynard chose that moment to extend his tongue and lick his lips. Rae lay back, defeated, and Ellie sat on the edge of the bed.

"Do you think Grandma and Papa will ever get over being mad at us?" Rae asked.

"Grandma and Papa are not mad at you," Ellie said firmly. "They're upset with me. And it's only because they're afraid for me—for all of us. And just because you get angry with a person, doesn't mean you don't love them. You usually get most angry with the ones you do love." She knew it had upset the girls to see the confrontation between herself and her parents. "Grandma and Papa love us very much."

"I know," Rae said.

"I don't not like you when you make me eat my spinach," Poppy volunteered in her shrill, reedy voice.

"Tell you what," Ellie said. "This fall you and I will grow spinach in our own garden."

Poppy thought about that. "I'd rather grow chocolate cake," she said, giggling.

Rae was off in thought, ignoring her sister's foolishness. "Is it true we'll have to break ice for the animals in the winter?" She asked.

"Could be," Ellie said.

"Then I'll have to break the ice for my horse." Rae was positive she would get a horse.

"Yes, you will," Ellie told her and gave her a kiss. "Because you'll take care of your own horse. Now go to sleep." She kissed Poppy and then paused a second to smooth her daughters' silky hair and to look into their faces. "We have a big day ahead tomorrow."

"Oh . . ." Poppy clutched the sheet under her neck. "I don't think I can sleep. I'm too excited."

"Well, just don't kick me," Rae said. "At the new house I want my own bed."

Ellie turned out the light and walked into the hall. She stopped and tapped on Sara's closed bedroom door and heard Sara's faint, "Come in." Sara, dressed in a pink gown, sat cross-legged on the bed with papers—pictures, Ellie recognized—spread out in front of her. Ellie sat on the side of the bed.

"You found them, didn't you?" Sara said. She glanced at Ellie, then looked back down at the pictures. They were cutouts, assorted sizes and shapes, from various magazines. Ellie knew they were something special to her eldest.

"I didn't mean to. I was trying to capture a cricket that simply wouldn't shut up. I knew he was in the bookcase. The pictures fell out of *Nancy Drew and the Hidden Staircase* when I pulled it from the shelf."

"I cut these out over three years ago," Sara said. "I used to look at them and pretend it was our house, our garden, our swing in the tree." She shrugged her thin shoulders. "It was just that, well, I didn't like it here then. You were busy with Poppy. And you didn't laugh anymore. I thought about what it would be like if Daddy were still here and we'd gotten the place you and him used to talk about. I remembered how we used to take those long drives and look at places."

"I remember, too. I'd forgotten—until I saw those pictures." She cupped Sara's chin in her hand and smiled at her. "I'm sorry for the years I've wasted, for the selfish way I've let everything go in my life, for the times I haven't been here for you. I can't change them now—I can't even truly

apologize for them. I was doing the best I could. Which is
what I'm still trying to do." She searched Sara's eyes. "I've
made a decision for us all. One I think will be good for us.

"I know I made a mistake not to have talked to you and
Rae and Poppy about all this. And I'm not saying that I'm
doing this just for you girls. I have to make these changes,
Sara. For me. To keep strong, to keep living and growing.
And in that way I hope this change will be best for you girls,
too, because if I'm stronger and happier, then I can be the
best mother I can be." Ellie watched Sara for some sign of
what she was thinking.

"Mom, I know you'd never do anything you thought
would hurt us," Sara said. "I know that you almost always
put us first."

"You do?" Ellie hadn't meant to let the words slip out.

"Of course. I'm a kid, but I'm not stupid." Sara grinned.
The sadness in the smile tore at Ellie's heart.

She realized then that she'd been the same age as Sara
when her own parents had moved their family to the city to
begin their new concrete-supply business. She'd not been
stupid, either. She'd accepted the move and had tried to
adjust because it would have been pointless to fight something beyond her control. And she'd known then, as she did
now, that her parents wanted the best for their children. She
hadn't wanted to move, yet she'd also looked forward to the
exciting change. And her world had widened.

"We won't know until we get moved and settled in for a
while if you'll like living out there," Ellie said. "What I'm
banking on is that you will. That this will be a step ahead for
all of us."

Sara looked at her a long second. "I'm going to miss
Annie and my other friends...my school."

Ellie touched her hair. "I know you will, honey. But
you'll make new friends." It sounded terribly trite.

Sara looked away, closing herself off. A sharp pain
touched Ellie's heart. She knew there was nothing else she
could say. She could only hope that, with time...

"Good night," she said and gave Sara a parting kiss on
the cheek. Still, Sara would not look at her.

Alone in the quietness of her bedroom, Ellie undressed and slipped into a summer nightgown. Maynard, who was supposed to be outside, came and rubbed against her ankle. Ellie reached down and stroked his thick fur.

She straightened and looked around the low-lighted bedroom. It was large enough to contain a queen-size bed, two chests of drawers, a cushioned chest at the end of the bed, a small woman's secretary and chair, and a comfortable boudoir chair just right for curling up in. The room also had an adjoining bath.

Where, she wondered, would she put all this stuff at the country house? Her bedroom there had to be a good fourth smaller than this one. And had no adjoining bath. That was going to be fun—four females sharing one bathroom.

The top of her desk shone warmly in the lamplight, drawing Ellie. Very slowly she walked over, sat before the desk and lifted the checkbook laying there. She opened it and looked at the figures. Her gaze moved to the tablet nearby on which she'd worked out a bare budget. She felt as if she were walking a high wire between two tall buildings; there was precious little room for mistakes—or emergencies.

What had she done? The thought came sharply to her mind.

This was the first time in her life Ellie had made any decision entirely on her own. When still in her teens she'd gone from the protection of loving parents to that of loving husband. Then, at Galen's death, her parents had immediately stepped in again. It was almost as though she'd never left home.

They'd handled the funeral and all legalities. They'd attended to the sale of the house and had moved Ellie and the girls into a substantial rented house in their own prominent neighborhood. They'd seen to getting Galen's insurance settled, his clothes cleaned out, Sara into school, and had even opened a bank account for Ellie.

Ellie remembered so little of those weeks following Galen's death. And there were huge blocks of time in the following four years that she had no memory of, either.

Somehow she'd begun shopping where her mother did and had joined the clubs her mother belonged to. She thought now that the only thing she'd done by herself in those years was to have Poppy, a child Galen had never known he fathered. And that only because she'd felt so strongly about wanting to be alone in her labor—stubbornly, if she couldn't have Galen, then she'd have no one—that she'd actually screamed at her mother and the nurses to get out and leave her alone. She'd given birth, not waiting for the doctor, to a baby daughter Galen would never see.

It was said money talks, and Ellie thought it had fairly shouted at her one day last year. Looking over her bank statements, she'd been alarmed to see the dwindling accounts. Galen had left hefty insurance and a substantial savings account, but it seemed the interest the money drew wasn't quite enough to pay the monthly bills. So Ellie had been dipping into the principal, which left less interest.

In the weeks following that day of awareness, all of her senses had seemed more acute. She'd heard her mother tell her what detergent to buy and her father remind her it was time for an oil change in the car—small, everyday things any woman with half a brain could manage on her own.

She saw that one of Sara's friends, a girl of fourteen, smoked cigarettes. Sara's grades had dropped to Cs, and she spent more time listening to something called heavy-metal music and talking on the telephone than she did speaking to her family.

She saw that Rae was a frustrated animal-control officer—wanting to adopt every stray around—and that Poppy watched enough television to know the jingles of the ten most-run commercials.

And Ellie saw herself: an attractive woman; it was surprising, but true. She was a girl no longer. And her mind had dried up from spending too long living within herself. She was a woman over thirty who still allowed her parents to treat her as if she was twelve. Any aspirations she may have had were buried so deeply she wondered if they existed at all.

And she was a lonely woman who, though she'd never mention it to a soul, longed to feel a man's loving touch. She longed to have a man with whom to share her life, her troubles and her joys. She longed to curl against a man's warmth, to hear his heartbeat in the darkness, to have him kiss her and take her to him. It had been good with Galen, the only man she'd ever known in that intimate fashion, and she'd couldn't forget the rapture. Sometimes, only lately, she felt such a longing that she cried in the night, muffling her sobs in the covers.

Her life had stretched before her like a dry sandy road heading off into the desert. She would get a job of some sort, one requiring no qualifications. She'd see the girls into college, into marriage, and she'd remain in the same house—someone else's house—attending the Friends of the Library meetings, the Garden Club, the Woman's League. And she'd lie in bed alone every night until she didn't care anymore about being alone.

The whole picture had scared the hell out of her.

She felt buried alive.

So she'd begun to ask herself what she wanted—for herself and the girls. And one of the first things she'd realized was she would do best by putting some distance between herself and her parents, or they'd never let go their hold—and she wasn't certain she could be strong enough to insist.

This knowledge had reawakened the dream she and Galen had had so many years before of a place in the country. She'd begun studying, planning and searching. Today she'd taken the first step, the major step in building what she hoped would be a better, more rewarding life for her small family.

"One day at a time, Ellie," she muttered to herself. She started to turn out the light but stopped. She walked to the dresser and opened the jewel box sitting there. She raised her hand and looked at her wedding rings. The memory of when Galen had proudly showed them to her swept through her mind. Closing her eyes, she slipped the rings from her finger, then placed them into the bottom of the box and closed the lid.

Her thoughts turned to Mr. Wade Wolcott, and she felt a sudden jangling sensation inside her body. Not an unpleasant sensation, yet one evoking apprehension.

The man she'd be interested in would be a man like Wade Wolcott, she thought, turning out the light and slipping beneath the sheet. She'd forgotten to put Maynard out and he tugged at the spread. She shooed him from the bed, only to hear him purring heavily as he settled down atop her slippers on the floor.

She recalled, with pleasure and pride and a mingling of anxiety, the purchase of the house and land, her land.

What, she wondered, would Wade Wolcott say to her ideas? Thinking of him set her mind in other directions. She recalled the way he'd looked at her, the way she'd felt. It dawned on her, the knowledge seeping in quickly, that he'd looked at her the way a man does when he sees an attractive woman and is interested.

Oh, he did not, her mind protested. *Why, I've got three daughters; I'm an old married woman.*

But she wasn't married anymore, her mind contested, and he didn't know about her daughters.

She recalled that light in his eye. Mr. Wolcott was definitely a bit of a flirt, and he'd been trying to flirt with her. He was attractive...a manly sort of man. His eyes had a way of looking at her; his muscles were hard and lean. For the very briefest of seconds, Ellie imagined his rock-hard body pressing hers. A warmth and throbbing started deep within her.

"Good grief!" she whispered, then thought: I have to stop this. I won't get any sleep.

She jabbed the pillow beneath her head and forced her eyes to close, but her mind refused to settle down.

She admitted, somewhat in awe, that her body had responded to Wade Wolcott's manner. She'd felt stirrings of desire. Of course, it didn't mean anything, other than that she was too long without a man.

Then she realized this was the first time she'd felt desire for a man in five years—and she observed the fact with awe.

She had never met anyone quite like Wade Wolcott. He was a man unto his own, she mused, turning on her back and staring into the darkness. It was pleasurable and even a bit exciting to think she'd be seeing him again. She chuckled, wondering what he would do when he found out she had three daughters, one in her teens. Her heart squeezed. He'd more than likely show no more interest. Of course, that supposed he'd been interested in the first place.

Either way, she'd find out, for she'd be seeing him again soon.

Chapter Four

We're going to live here?" Sara's voice echoed with disbelief and her eyes mirrored the same emotion as she stared at the house.

They stood in a line, the four of them, beside the car. Ellie's elation sank as she took a second look at the house. It appeared much less inviting to her today in the light of cold reality when she viewed it through her daughter's eyes. She'd known she'd been seeing it through rose-colored glasses before, but now she was starkly aware of the fact. The dull gray sky didn't help the appearance of the place any.

But it was done now, Ellie thought briskly. She stepped out and strode toward the house, in the lead for the girls to follow. "It just needs some fixing up," she said, forcing enthusiasm into her voice. "You wait and see what it looks like when we're finished." She smiled brightly. "And just look at the view! All of that is ours—all eighty acres."

She knew none of them dared grumble in the face of her optimism. Together they thoroughly investigated the house, the barn, the yard. With proud delight, Ellie pointed out the peaches fattening on the gnarled old trees.

They walked down to the pasture and into the woods. The girls loved the land, Ellie saw with joyful relief. Even Sara seemed pleased. All three girls ran through the grass, and then Ellie joined in, feeling the years roll from her shoulders. She determined not to mention or think about snakes. At the pond, Rae found the first real live turtle she and Poppy had ever seen outside the zoo. When Rae begged for them all to go swimming, Ellie's first impulse was to say no. They had no swimsuits, after all, and there was a house to clean.

"We can go skinny-dipping," Rae ventured.

Ellie hesitated and looked at the hopeful faces of her daughters. Even Sara seemed game for the idea. Then, laughing, Ellie sat down and began taking off her shoes. The house would wait. Hadn't the main idea of getting this place been to have a way to draw closer to her girls? The pond was sheltered in the trees, private. It would be such wonderful, illicit fun.

Poppy insisted they all hang their clothes on the branches because that was the way it was done in the movies. They splashed into the water; it was lukewarm, but refreshing nonetheless, and extraordinarily delightful as the warm summer air caressed bare flesh.

Ellie grimaced when her toes connected with the muddy bottom, and she pushed out into the deeper water. Rae delighted in the mud squishing between her toes, and Sara screamed as Rae forced her to touch her feet down. The bright sunlight peeked through the clouds and sparkled on the dark water. The girls laughed and splashed and took turns hugging Ellie. Their skin touched, their gazes met, and Ellie felt as close to each of them as she had when they were born.

It was very near paradise until a large—giant, Ellie thought—red dog came running through the break in the trees, barking. At first, in shock, all Ellie could do was stare. Then the beast came right into the water toward them.

Ellie grabbed frantically to gather the girls, but they were scattered. There was screaming and splashing. The dog kept coming, and Rae began to swim toward it!

"Rae!" Ellie yelled just at the moment the dog reached her. Then Rae was laughing and hugging the dog, and the big monster was licking her face.

"Duffy!" It was a stern male voice. "Duffy!"

Even as she jerked her head around in the direction of the call, Ellie recognized the voice. Wade Wolcott. He was well down between the trees, walking toward the pond.

And here she was without one stitch of clothing!

Ellie sank lower in the water and wondered what in the world to do.

"Hope Duffy didn't scare you," Wade called out. "He's part Lab, part setter and just plain loves the water. He heard the laughing and wanted to play, too."

Wade stood less than fifty feet away, a western hat tipped back on his thick hair at a jaunty angle, hand on his lean hip, boots only inches from the water's edge. Poppy had joined Rae and the dog in play, and Wade, smiling, watched them. Ellie gave thanks for the murkiness of the water she'd been none too thrilled with moments before. Why in the world did he just stand there as if nothing was wrong?

"Nice day for swimming." He spoke quite conversationally.

"Mr. Wolcott," Ellie said, fury at her predicament and at the fact that Wade Wolcott seemed not in the least fazed burning in her chest. "Do you intend to stand there all day?"

"Why...no, ma'am." He seemed taken aback, his brows knotting in puzzlement.

She sucked in a deep breath. "Mr. Wolcott, I...we have no clothes on!" It was infuriating to have to tell him. If looks could kill, she intended hers to go so far as to bury.

His eyes widened, and his gaze moved hesitantly from her to Sara to the knot of splashing water and pale bodies around his dog. Then his gaze flickered to the clothes hanging on the bushes nearby, seeing them for the first time. She detected his blush even at the distance that separated them.

And she also detected a vibration, like a cord of energy, that surged through the air. Even in this moment, she was vitally aware of the man, extraordinarily so.

"Excuse me, Ellie...Mrs. McGrew." He backed away. "Duffy, come. Now," he called in a stern voice. The big dog, recognizing the firm command, turned.

Poppy and Rae, finally sensing the strain in the air, let the dog go and moved back quietly into the water.

Wade stood there a moment, keeping his eyes directly on his dog. And then, mockingly, he turned his gaze to Ellie. She felt she could see his eyes shining gold even through the distance separating them. Very slowly, he touched the brim of his Stetson. "Nice to see you," he said. "I'll pay my respects again at a more convenient time."

He had the nerve to saunter away. A polite person, Ellie thought hotly, would at least have the decency to be embarrassed enough to want to get out of there fast.

"Who was that, Mama?" Sara asked from behind her. "Mama?" Sara prodded, before Ellie found the breath to answer.

"That was Wade Wolcott, our neighbor, the man we bought the farm from."

"He sure has a neat dog," Rae said.

Ellie realized she'd been standing with her feet on the oozy pond bottom. She'd been too distracted to even notice. *And it was Wade Wolcott's fault!*

She knew embarrassment made her unreasonably angry. The man hadn't done anything wrong, after all. The stupid idiot hadn't noticed they weren't wearing swimming suits, and why should he? But he'd looked at her as if he could see clear through the water! Looking down at its dark surface, she made sure he hadn't.

"No privacy anywhere," Ellie mumbled under her breath and stalked from the water. "Poppy, get up and rinse that mud off your knees. Come on, girls. It's time we get to work."

Wade Wolcott just upset her, that's all. He just plain upset her. And she sure didn't need that now. How was she ever going to face him again?

* * *

Wade chuckled as he pulled his pickup to a stop in the driveway behind Ellie McGrew's car. He tried to stifle it but didn't meet with much success. He'd chuckled like this as he'd walked all the way across the field, through the fence and back up to his house that morning. He'd been embarrassed, yes, but it was so darn funny, Duffy jumping in on them like that, and Ellie being caught without a stitch on.

He'd laughed about it the rest of the morning, aggravating Birdie, his housekeeper, who'd wanted to know what was so all-fired funny. He didn't dare tell. He had the distinct suspicion Ellie would never forgive him if he did.

He couldn't help staring at her, forming an image in his mind of what her body looked like; he was a man, after all. And she was a fine-looking woman, he thought, not for the first time.

He sat now and stared at the stone house, wondering about the three children who'd been with her in the pond. Girls, had been his impression, yet he wasn't certain about all of them. Did Eleanor McGrew have three daughters? Somehow the idea seemed oddly unsettling.

He stepped from his truck, curiosity pulling him.

The sounds of voices and laughter floated from the house. The windows were wide open; the front screens, removed for cleaning, sat alongside the house.

As Wade approached the front porch, a torrent of dirty water shot out the near window, missing his chest by a hair's breadth, and that only because he'd quickly stepped back. The gray water landed in the yard with a resounding splash, spattering mud on his boots, his favorite, Rio Mercedes boots.

"Oh!" A young girl's face, with wide, familiar blue eyes, stared at him. Her lips formed a stricken O. An empty bucket dangled from her hand.

She disappeared, then reappeared at the doorway as Wade stepped up on the porch. "I'm so sorry," she said hurriedly. "I didn't know you were there."

"I didn't think you did it on purpose," Wade joked, wiping one boot then the other, on the backs of his denim-clad legs. Boots cost a hell of a lot more than jeans.

The girl had long, dark blond hair, plaited in one braid down her back. Her face was square and pale and tinged with freckles. She was skinny, with small, adolescent breasts showing beneath her T-shirt. He was struck again by her large blue eyes. A bit nervous from such keen appraisal, he asked for her mother, certain that this girl was Ellie's daughter. She looked too much like her to be anything but.

"Oh, she's in the kitchen." Still not taking her eyes from him, the young girl stepped slowly backward instead of turning around. "Mama," she called.

Wade wondered what was bothering her. On the chance that he could be scaring her, he gave her one of his most charming smiles. She gave a half-smile in return.

"Mama?"

Light rapid footsteps sounded, but instead of Ellie, another girl stepped from the kitchen. "Mama says to quit...yelling." The girl's speech slowed when she saw Wade. "She's downstairs. She'll be up in a minute."

This girl was a smaller version of the first, complete with those enormous blue eyes. Her wheat-colored hair hung in double braids and her freckles were more pronounced. She came to stand beside the first girl and to stare at him, too. Wade began to wonder if he'd sprouted horns through his hat. Couldn't be his fly was open, because they kept their gazes on his face.

The smaller girl responded to his smile. "You have a real nice dog," she said. "Did you bring him?"

Wade shook his head. "Too big and rambunctious to haul around in the truck. He's better off at home."

"Can I go see him sometime?"

"Sure. Just step up the hill and call him—Duffy's his name."

"I know. I heard you call him that this morning while we were swimming."

A mischievous look came into the girls' eyes, but Wade refused to let the blushing he felt erupt on his face. *Where in the hell was that woman, anyway?*

He caught the sound of her voice and footsteps and knew she was coming up the stairs from the basement. At last, he thought.

Then, lo and behold, instead of Ellie, another girl, this one even smaller, maybe five at the most, appeared from the kitchen. And there was no mistaking this one, either. Though her hair was flaxen, the color of an angel's halo, her eyes were blue as a summer sky—just like Eleanor Mc-Grew's. This one didn't act scared, though Wade thought he might prefer that to the unabashed curiosity on the tiny girl's cherubic face.

Good grief, the three girls did belong to Ellie McGrew. *Three girls!* One part of his mind told him he'd known she'd have children; he'd even seen them. But now, with them standing there in a line looking so much alike, the fact struck as a cold, hard reality.

And then, finally, Ellie appeared, making Wade feel as if he'd had too much to drink and was seeing double—or rather quadruple.

"Why, hello, Wade," she said.

In a brief second, a thousand and one impressions flew through his mind. He saw Ellie's blond hair, the moisture beading around her hairline and curling the wisps that edged her face. Her pale cheeks were flushed with heat and exertion, and perhaps embarrassment. Her lips parted slightly. The peculiar energy that happened between certain men and women flowed strong between them as he met her gaze. Wade felt his body react to it, an imperceptible tightening in his chest and swelling in his loins.

"Good afternoon," he said and cleared his throat. Finding himself twirling his hat, he stopped. "Guess this isn't a convenient time, either. Just wanted to stop and see if the electricity has been turned on and to say hello."

"You arranged for the electricity? I wondered when we came and found it working." She was watching him closely, and Wade felt surprisingly nervous. He didn't know why, wasn't used to it and didn't like it.

"Yes. No problem. Office's just up the street from the shop."

"Well, thank you very much . . . Oh, these are my daughters. This is Sara." She touched the tallest girl's head. "This is Rae. And this is Poppy. Girls, this is Mr. Wolcott."

With the exceptions of age and size, the females before him were as alike as four peas in a pod. Their blue eyes continued to stare, making him distinctly uncomfortable. The stirring of male attraction he'd experienced minutes before shriveled and died. He'd come as a polite neighbor to pay his respects, and he'd done that, he told himself. He was getting out of here.

"I'll leave you all to it. Good afternoon, Mrs. McGrew." He used the formal address—backing up, as it were, deliberately. "Girls." He nodded, turned and walked out the door, pulling it securely closed behind him.

Then Wade left—fled may have been a better word. Not that he was proud of his feelings or his actions, but neither was he ashamed. He was employing pure, practical common sense. He'd been a footloose bachelor for thirty-eight years, and he had a bachelor's instincts. The instincts that told him Mrs. Ellie McGrew could bring him a lot of entanglement and a lot of trouble.

But, of course, she wouldn't, he thought adamantly, walking in long strides toward his truck. Because he was staying clear of her—and her three daughters. They were a ready-made family. Mrs. McGrew wouldn't see things between them the way he would. He'd been very careful not to extend the neighborly "If you need anything, holler." Wade thought they'd do a lot better to stay distant neighbors.

Where in the hell had that woman gotten the insane idea to buy the place? How would she fix up the house, do whatever it was she wanted to with the land, with only girls to help her? Well, Mrs. McGrew had a mind of her own, he supposed. She had to have known what she was taking on. *And it wasn't any of his affair.*

He opened the truck door with a jerk and slipped behind the steering wheel. Just as he was about to pull the door closed, he heard a piercing scream, followed by a jumble of screams.

It wasn't to his credit that he hesitated, he supposed, but he wanted to leave.

He couldn't. The next instant, flinging his hat to the seat, he jumped from the truck and ran for the front door. The screams had turned to yells. He burst into the house and followed the yells to the kitchen.

"What the hell?" He murmured the words, his eyes searching the room, trying to figure out what was going on.

The kitchen was a frenzy of confused motion and reverberating sound. One of the girls lay sprawled on the floor in a puddle of water. The tiny, curly-banged one stood to the side, peeking from beneath a towel she held over her head. Ellie and her eldest daughter stood side by side groping with something at the sink, while water sprayed up and out—to the ceiling, to the counters, to the floor and into Ellie's face.

"I see him, Mama. I see him!" The girl on the floor yelled, slipping and sliding toward the cabinets.

"Don't you touch that mouse, Rae Ann!" Ellie hollered. "Oh! . . . get me a wrench, Sara!"

"What's a wrench?" the girl cried.

Taking a deep breath, Wade plunged through the melee. He ducked his head against the spraying water, stepped over the girl on the floor and around the tiny one with her tent. He took the stairs to the basement three at a time and raced through the dimness of the circuit box. Checking the markings, he found the one he sought and flipped it to the off position.

Immediately it was as if he'd also switched off the noise above. Water gurgled loudly in the silence.

"That man..." he heard a small voice say as he mounted the stairs. At the doorway he found all four pairs of blue eyes staring in his direction.

"I..." Ellie shook her head. Bewilderment filled her eyes. Water beaded on her face and streamed down her hair. Her soaked shirt clung in all the right places, Wade noticed, then scolded himself for the observation.

"The pump's turned off now," he said, walking to the sink. "Just switched it off at the electrical box."

"Oh..." Ellie nodded.

"Water hasn't been turned on in a long time." He reached to check the faucet handles and Ellie and her daughter moved aside. "Pressure was too much for them."

"I saw this mouse," Ellie said, still obviously dazed, "there on the counter, just as I was about to turn on the water...I don't know...it scared me. I jumped, I guess, when I twisted the handle and water just...sprayed everywhere. And I couldn't get it turned off. I thought maybe by turning on the other handle I could get the pressure cut down, but it just sprayed, too."

Wiping a stray wet strand of hair from her face, she looked down at her body. Her shoulders slumped.

"Well, it got rid of the mouse," Wade said. Her pitiful expression touched him, and he wanted somehow to lighten her load. She rewarded his effort with a slow smile.

"Yes, it did." Then she chuckled, and the room filled with laughter.

"I didn't get wet, Mama. See—I gots me a cover." Beaming, the littlest girl gave a playful dance.

"Have, Poppy." Ellie wiped a hand down her hip and said, "Please, let me offer you a soft drink as a thank-you. Outside, where Sara and I can dry in the sun."

He looked into her eyes. Wide and blue as the sky in winter, they twinkled merrily. "Sounds good," he replied. He tried to ignore the warning bells sounding inside him.

They sat outside on the edge of the porch. The hot, humid wind brought the scent of honeysuckle from the bush on the fence. And it brought to Wade the sweet female scent of Ellie, who brushed her pale hair in the sunlight, allowing the wind to blow it dry. Her full breasts pushed against the thin material of her summer shirt with every stroke of the brush. Feeling it to his credit, Wade schooled himself to spare her only scant glances, though he had to admit she was worth full attention.

He ended up fixing the kitchen faucet for her, though to give Ellie her due, she did put up a small argument, insisting she could get a plumber. But he was already there, he told both Ellie and himself, and the job wasn't much. She proved to be a good pupil, following his every move with the faucet, insisting she could do the bathroom one herself.

Two hours later, after fixing the kitchen faucet, working on the water pump, instructing Ellie on basic plumbing repairs and how to light the pilot on the water heater, Wade's better judgment came to the fore and he hurried himself out of there.

It had turned out exactly as he'd feared, he thought, irritated with himself. He should have had better sense. How was he going to get out of this mess?

He had his life the way he wanted it. He owed a sizable ranch and two profitable businesses in town, which gave him more than adequate income. He had plenty of time both to occasionally check on his employees and to indulge in his favorite hobby, flying kites. He didn't want any encumbrances. He'd passed the age for family-type relationships.

Tomorrow, he vowed, was a good day to drive over to Amarillo and spend a few days with Suzie, an old friend who always greeted him with a welcoming smile, a delicious meal, and a warm bed, if he so chose, to fill the empty place within him. What was especially nice about Suzie was that Wade didn't feel pressured to choose the bed. That made their relationship of the past eight years free and easy, without strings on either side. It was time for some rest and relaxation.

Ellie drove home in the lingering twilight of summer. She was bone-tired and ached all the way down to her toes. But it was a good kind of tired, because along with it came the supreme feeling of accomplishment.

She and the girls had cleaned all day. The oak floors of the house shone again, windows sparkled, and the old bathtub came close to gleaming. Ellie felt terribly proud of herself. She'd actually taken the bathroom faucets, in both the sink and the tub, apart and put them back together again. Just think, she said to herself, yesterday I didn't even know how.

Remembering her plumbing work turned her thoughts to Wade. She recalled his eyes, the way they seemed to naturally hold a smile, to say that nothing in the world was so serious that it couldn't be laughed about.

Memories of the day floated through Ellie's mind. Vividly she pictured Wade standing bold as brass at the edge of the pond, and her, stark naked, only yards from him. She could laugh about it now. Then she remembered his face when he'd met her daughters. That had struck Mr. Wolcott hard.

Her heart dipped. She'd expected him to act just as he had, she told herself. Now, instead of an attractive single woman, Mr. Wolcott saw her as a woman with three children. And if he hadn't heard the screaming, he never would have come back after he'd met the girls. He'd stayed to be neighborly. A gallant man of the west, she thought with a soft sigh. And she wasn't such a fool she couldn't see he'd been eager to get away when he could. Though she tried to tell herself maybe she'd just imagined that.

Was she being foolish to suspect he felt an attraction to her as she did to him?

She recalled his eyes, the way they had looked at her the first time she'd met him, and even again today—at the pond and then in the living room, just for an instant. What magic was it that caused some men and women to react this way— sort of like seltzer being shaken?

For five years she'd looked into the eyes of many men: department-store clerks, teachers, ushers passing the church collection plate, the butcher at the meat counter, three very handsome men her mother had arranged for her to go out with. She'd never had so much as a heart palpitation. But now, when she looked into Wade Wolcott's golden-brown eyes, Ellie felt as if he reached out and touched her. Or wanted to. Quite intimately. And, she admitted with an honest and very tired sigh, she liked the sensations he aroused in her.

Again she wondered if it could be possible for Wade to have similar feelings.

She shook the wondering aside. It didn't matter. Men like Wade Wolcott didn't lean to relationships with a woman who had three kids. Few men did.

Which was just fine with her, too, she thought emphatically, because she didn't need any involvement with a man like him. Then she chuckled inwardly at all her silly thoughts.

Light beamed from inside the house when Ellie pulled the Cutlass into the driveway. She knew her parents were there, waiting. They had their own key—it had always made perfect sense before, but now Ellie found herself irritated by it. She felt the lack of privacy.

When she got out of the car, she slammed the door behind her. "Are we home?" she heard Rae mumble, reminding Ellie of the girls' presence. She didn't want to lose her temper and have another confrontation with her parents in front of them.

A needless confrontation, she told herself. They were her parents; their constant presence and authority had always been a comfort before. Of course they didn't understand her taking what must seem a sudden bent toward self-sufficiency. Ellie herself had trouble understanding it.

She went into the house, leaving the girls to follow. Her mother and father sat in the lamp-lit living room, drinking coffee.

"We had no idea you'd be this late, Ellie," her mother said, giving her a keen, disapproving appraisal. "Why, it's after nine. We were worried."

Ellie stood hesitating in the entry, acutely aware of her red and scratched hands, her tangled hair and ragged, dirt-streaked clothes. It was a stark contrast to her mother's crisp poplin dress, coiffed hair and sparkling rings on satiny hands.

Then Ellie remembered this was her own home—at least for the moment. "You needn't have worried, Mama." I am a competent adult, she thought, but she didn't say it. Anyway, she had a feeling her parents might question that fact at the moment. "We stopped for pizza on the way home."

The girls were crowding in behind her. Throwing her purse and keys on the nearby table, Ellie said, "Help Poppy, Rae. You two bathe and get to bed." Rae started to protest, but Ellie silenced her with a glance.

"Come give Papa a kiss first, girls," Ellie's father said. "And tell us about your day." To Ellie it was like a countercommand of her orders, but she knew very well she was exhausted and feeling a bit unreasonable.

Sara slumped into a chair and Rae and Poppy went to sit on the couch between their grandparents. Ellie kept walking on into the kitchen.

"Did you keep these girls working all day, Ellie?" Her mother called after her. "Why, they're exhausted."

I'm a veritable slave driver, Ellie thought, choking back the flippant remark. At least Sara had done more than listen to rock music today, and Poppy more than sing television commercials. And Rae—Rae'd been her usual curious, resourceful self; she'd had a ball. And they'd been doing it all together, something for themselves.

She had just pulled a coffee cup from the kitchen cabinet when her mother pushed open the door. "Ellie? I was talking to you." She stood there, regal and commanding.

Ellie felt herself shriveling and fought against it. "Mom, the children are fine. They learned something about themselves today." She poured coffee into the cup. All she really wanted to do was to throw herself in bed.

"Ellie, we want to talk to you."

Ellie moved from the counter, past her mother to the door and went through it. She'd never been so rude to her mother in all her life, but she was exhausted and simply didn't want to talk about anything right now.

Her mother followed close behind. "Whatever can you be thinking of, Ellie, taking those girls out to...that place? Away from their home, family and friends?"

All eyes in the living room moved to stare at her. "Girls," she said softly, looking very firmly to her youngest two. "It's time." With dragging steps and soulful eyes, they left the room. Lowering herself into a chair, Ellie sipped her coffee before replying, knowing that until she said something, until they'd all been through it again, her parents were not going to leave.

"That place, Mama, is all mine—all ours. It may not be this nice—" she gestured with her hand "—but at least I can choose the paint I want for the walls, can even tear down a wall if I want." She cast them a look that pleaded for understanding. "I need to make my own life now."

Her parents both stared at her sternly. "You know, Ellie," her father said at last, employing the tone he'd used when she was a child and had misbehaved, "I will not help you if you get into trouble. I can't sanction what I consider irresponsible behavior."

"I don't expect you to help me, Dad," Ellie said. She had at one time, but not anymore. "And I don't believe I'm behaving irresponsibly. I'm being quite the opposite—I'm being responsible for myself and the girls for the first time in five years."

"Do you call going swimming nude, allowing the girls to do so in a place where they could be seen, could even have been attacked, responsible?" Her father gave the words a distinctly lewd connotation.

Ellie's mother sucked in a very loud breath and placed her hand to her throat. "You did what?"

Her father eyed her. "The girls told me about the incident. Thank goodness they thought it all very innocent."

"And it was!" Ellie's voice rose. She glanced at Sara and considered sending her from the room. But Sara was getting old enough to be included, she decided reluctantly.

"It was an accident that Wade happened along. We were swimming on our own property, in a pond secluded by trees. For heaven's sake, people, especially children, have been skinny-dipping for years. And I rather believe Mr. Wolcott has seen nude females before," she added dryly. She immediately regretted it.

"Ellie!" her mother said, quite shocked. "What kind of man is this—and who is he?"

Ellie sighed, squeezed her eyes shut, then opened them. "Mother, I didn't mean anything by it. I simply meant the man is an adult, after all. And Mr. Wolcott is the man I've purchased the land from. He owns the neighboring ranch, as well as a machine shop in Advance. I'm sure he's a fine member of the community."

She looked at her parents. She knew under normal circumstances they'd find the episode terribly funny—that this wasn't truly like them at all, this aggressive attack. But they simply didn't know how to cope with this unwanted change in their life, a change they couldn't control. Ellie's hardened heart cracked. Ever since she'd been born, they'd been responsible for her, had virtually led her life for her. Now they couldn't do that, and they simply didn't want to accept it. It was as terrible a loss to them as if she'd died.

And they were never going to understand; it was unfair of Ellie to expect them to. She wasn't helping matters any by arguing with them. She had to make her stand, completely, unwaveringly. Which would, she hoped, help them to accept what they couldn't understand and feel more comfortable with the change. And she must make an effort to include them, no matter how much they backed up in their hurt and anger.

"You're only thinking of yourself," her mother said, on the verge of tears. Her voice rose. "And you're acting in a way we never brought you up to be—irresponsible, headstrong and a bit fast and loose, missy. I don't know what's going on with you," she said in a way that suggested that it might be something immoral. "Are you carrying on with this man?"

Ellie felt the hardness seep back into her heart. How could her mother say such a thing in front of Sara?

"Why, Mama?" Ellie said. "Because I want a home of my own, for us, in the country? People do it all the time. I'm only one in a million." Good grief! Why couldn't she think of something calm and rational to say?

"Ellie." Her mother pulled herself up very straight. "I want you to consider leaving the girls with your father and me. At least until you can provide them with a settled atmosphere.'' She raised an eyebrow. ''I think you need to give this thing time.''

Ellie's gaze flew to Sara. ''No, Mama.'' She spoke very quietly, trying to remind herself that her mother was desperate. ''The girls and I are a family.'' Her voice softened. ''Please come out to the farm. Mama. Daddy. It's not much, and I know you want more for us, but come and see. It's not so far that you can't drive out and visit. We're not going that far away.''

Everyone was quiet.

''I think your mother has brought up a good idea,'' her father said. ''Their school is here, their friends. This is their home.''

Ellie said nothing. She didn't think she needed to.

''Mama,'' Sara broke in, and Ellie jumped. ''I want to stay here.''

At first Ellie couldn't speak. She'd never imagined Sara would entertain such an idea. Lord, what could she say to this? This was too important to make a mistake.

''No,'' she managed at last. Surely Sara didn't mean it. Surely she wouldn't want to live away from her.

''But, Mama, I don't want to go to school out there. I won't know anybody. Not anybody at all. My friends are here.''

The next instant, Rae and Poppy burst into the room. ''I want to go with you, Mama. I do. I do.'' And then everyone was talking at once.

Ellie just sat there, holding Poppy, who'd thrown herself in her lap, and stroking her hair. Rae shouted at Sara and Sara shouted back. Ellie's parent's both appealed to her. And still Ellie sat, until gradually they all quieted, realizing she wasn't answering any of them.

''Now, Poppy, shush,'' Ellie said finally, when she felt she'd gathered her breath. ''Of course you'll go with me.'' She looked at her parents, at Rae, and lastly at Sara. ''I know your friends and familiar school are here. But you will go with me. We are a family. We stay together.''

In that moment, Ellie realized that it was the first time she'd ever had to say no to a serious wish of Sara's. Sara was always so giving, so undemanding, so practical. She never asked for much.

Sara looked at her, and Ellie saw almost no emotion at all. Sara was withdrawing from her. *Oh, baby!* Ellie's heart cried out.

She rose, still holding Poppy.

"Good night, Mama, Daddy. We've had a long day. And we'll begin moving things out to the house tomorrow. Will you help me, Dad?"

His face grew stern. "No, I will not. This is your wild idea. You find a way to handle it." He turned and stalked out. Without a word Ellie's mother followed him, her back ramrod straight with anger.

Chapter Five

Nine days later the McGrew clan, complete with Maynard the cat, moved into their house. Ellie stood amidst the jumble of furniture and boxes the moving men had plunked into the house without bothering to ask where anything belonged. She sought the kitchen toaster but had failed to mark the box in which she'd packed it—now she gave it up for lost and simply looked around. The mess was enough to try the strongest person's soul. Feeling herself beginning to sink under the weight of all that needed to be done, she fought the panic.

One thing at a time, Ellie. *One day at a time.*

Her eyes swept the walls, bright and clean with new paint; the new linoleum she'd laid with Sara's help was smooth enough for sliding. The house held a fresh smell, and a promise that touched Ellie's heart. In that moment came the warming sound of the children's laughter, the beat of pop-country music from Sara's portable radio and the fragrance of a southern breeze. A fresh breeze she would feel and smell every day, she thought. At last she had her very own home, a home of her choosing. And it would be all that she made it.

"Mama..." Rae's voice sang out from the bathroom. "There's no hot water."

Ellie stood there a moment, wishing, hoping, she'd been mistaken in what she'd heard. But Rae called again. "Mama..."

She found Rae with her hands in a sink full of gray water. A dirt streak stained her small freckled nose. "Me and Poppy forgot to clean our closet," she said. "It's pretty clean now, but I've been running the hot water for a long time, only it hadn't gotten hot." Her words came in that singsong rhythm children employed when speaking bad news.

Ellie stared at the water, then moved her gaze to the hot-water handle. It appeared there wasn't ever going to be time around this place to allow for a good, wrenching panic.

"Well—" she reached for a towel and handed it to Rae "—just finish washing in the cold water, and I'll go check the water heater."

The pilot light was out on the water heater. Ellie, on bended knees, stared at where it was supposed to flame. Wade had showed her how to light it. He'd showed her how to check the gas and turn it on if needed. He'd showed her how to turn it off. But there was no one who could give her the courage she needed in this moment to strike the match and hold it in the right place.

Don't be silly, she told herself, stomping back up the stairs to the kitchen for matches. She stomped purposefully back to the basement with box in hand. She knelt in front of the water heater, her mind seeking to recall the instructions Wade had given her.

Fear and pride warred within her, but fear won out. She simply couldn't decide if she had the steps right. And every time she thought of striking the match, the fearful image of the house blowing up filled her mind.

She could ask Wade to come and help, she thought hesitantly, rising and stepping out the garage door, looking up the hill toward his house. His blue truck sat in the drive beside his house. She'd like to ask him, like to see him. Her heart smiled at the thought.

You don't need to do that, she argued with herself the next instant. You can't be calling on him for every little thing. Now go back in there and light that stupid pilot, she scolded herself.

She marched purposefully back inside and knelt down in front of the water heater, her fingers poised to strike the match. Only she couldn't. Fear knotted her stomach.

"What's the matter?" It was Sara's voice.

Ellie turned to see her three daughters looking at her from the stairway.

"The pilot light's out," she said with a large sigh. If she did something wrong and the house blew up, she could kill them all—or at the very least lose the only house they had.

"Sara, you and Rae run up to Wade's and ask him to come down to help us with the pilot light," Ellie said.

"No." Sara shook her head. "I'm not going up there."

Ellie looked at her daughter's stubborn, set face.

"I'll go, Mama," Rae said, already starting down the steps toward the garage door.

"Me, too," Poppy said, following.

Ellie waited beside the water heater. She didn't want him to find her watching eagerly for him. She did feel a bit eager, she thought hesitantly as she smoothed at her hair. Oh, quit being silly, she cautioned. He won't think you pretty, won't think you anything except the mother of three girls. And helpless at that. It occurred to her to wonder if he would even come.

Her heart beat a tad faster and anticipation nipped at her.

She heard his heavy footsteps on the gravel driveway and his voice before he came into view. Venturing a smile, she searched his face when he walked into the garage, Rae and Poppy dancing around him, chattering. "The pilot's out again," she said. "I'm not certain how to light it."

His gaze, unreadable but cold, held hers for a moment. Ellie turned to shoo Rae and Poppy upstairs. She wished vehemently in that instant that she had not called on him.

Without a word, Wade took the box of matches from her hands. Bending, he tinkered with the water heater, then lit a match. Ellie held her breath, her mind still picturing an explosion, or at least a giant fire. But the pilot lit neatly.

The next instant he amazed Ellie by shutting off the pilot. She looked at him.

"You do it now," he said, extending the box of matches toward her, his voice very firm, his eyes daring her.

Ellie took the box of matches. She fiddled with the knob the way Wade had done. Gripping her courage, she struck a match, set it to the pilot and with relief watched it flame.

"You'll need to have someone come out and clean this thing," Wade said gruffly. He was close enough for her to catch the warm, male scent of him. "I'd recommend Barker from the other side of town." He turned his brown eyes to her. Something within Ellie tightened. "The Barker brothers are the best in plumbing and electric around, should you need them."

"Thank you," she said with correct politeness.

She moved to rise. Wade did, too. They stood very close in the small space beside the water heater, chest to chest, eye to eye. Though his gaze and expression seemed cold and aloof, she felt something from him reaching out to draw her to him. They didn't touch.

Then, giving a quick nod, Wade stepped away and strode from the garage. Ellie watched him go, then walked to the garage door and stared after him as he strode up the hill toward his house. He couldn't seem to get away fast enough.

He hadn't wanted to come, she knew. He'd done so much for them already, she never should have asked him to come now. Obviously he thought her a burden, was regretting selling her the farm. A widow he'd end up baby-sitting. Humiliation stung her heart.

She would never ask him for anything again! she vowed hotly. She'd rather blow up the house than have to swallow her pride. The thought of being a burden to Wade Wolcott—or anyone—was unacceptable. She herself had embarked upon this lunatic idea, and she herself would just have to learn to do things. She could and she would. And without further assistance from Mr. Wolcott, who so obviously didn't want anything to do with her!

She gripped the garage door frame. Yes, he obviously didn't want anything to do with her—but there was an attraction between them. Surely she didn't imagine it. Just a moment ago, with him standing only inches away, she'd felt a heat vibrate between them. His eyes had rested on her, had slid down to her breasts. Her body warmed now as she remembered. He was a man, all man, and he made her feel all woman.

She shook her head, turning back to the house and mentally away from the thought. There was nothing between her and Wade Wolcott. She wasn't only a woman—but a mother with the responsibility of three young girls. Thoughts of what was between her and Wade, of what could be between them, had no place in her life. Accept it, she told herself firmly, and added that no doubt she was blowing it all out of proportion.

That night she sat in the kitchen, the house quiet at last. In what she termed the perverseness of nature, the cooling night breeze had stopped. Outside it was comfortable now, but the air within the house still sweltered. For a brief moment, she thought longingly of the central air-conditioning they'd had at the house in the city. Then she tore her mind from the memory. There was no money for an air-conditioner. Maybe, she thought, giving a dispirited sigh, she could find a used window fan.

The bills and bank statements lay spread on the table, their varying colors glaring beneath the kitchen light. She'd been adding and dividing, and trying to find more money where there was none.

In disgust she tossed down her pen, then lifted and fluttered the front of her blouse from the dampness of her skin. It was so hot that she perspired even when the only muscle working hard was her brain. She reached for her glass of iced tea. A piece of paper came up with it—the final electric bill from their rented house. She'd accidentally set the glass on it. Unsticking the bill, she waved it to fling away drops of water, then tossed it to the table where it seemed to mock her. She took a swallow of tea and discovered the ice had melted.

Ellie plunked the glass on the table, then stood up angrily. She moved to look out the window only to find her own distorted reflection in the eerie blackness.

In three weeks the girls would begin school. But, Ellie realized, there was going to be no way around it: she would have to get a job before that.

She detested the idea. She'd never left her girls alone like that. And so much of the burden of responsibility would fall on Sara, who had enough to bear at the moment.

But Ellie could think of no other way.

The desperate need for money lay like a weight of iron on her chest. She clenched and unclenched her hands.

As was the way when one dark thought entered, a dozen more followed, whether they had anything in common or not. She thought about how much it would cost to get the girls new shoes. Their clothes were more than adequate, but Sara needed new things. It was important to a teenage girl to have new, "in" things at the beginning of a school year, especially when starting in a new school.

Ellie worried about Sara, about failing her daughter. She had to go carefully now; teen years were hard. Sara had lost her father. Who knew what kinds of scars lingered from that? And now Ellie had disrupted the secure home Sara had known, plunking her out here where she didn't want to be.

A painful rent tore through Ellie. Just that morning, with the moving men loading the furniture on the truck, Sara had again brought up the subject of living in the city with her grandparents. Like a last desperate effort to regain something she'd lost.

It was like a knife slicing Ellie's heart, a wound further twisted by the fact that she knew her mother had spoken to each of the girls and had advised Sara to ask again. Behind her back, her mother had done this.

"No," Ellie had told Sara as calmly and quietly as possible. "I can't do it, Sara. We're a family." Inwardly, she prayed for Sara's understanding and for the words to explain.

"You don't care about me!" Sara exploded at her. "All you care about is yourself and your wants!" Tears clouded her blue eyes and spilled down her pale cheeks.

"I do care," Ellie said, pain choking the words in her throat. "I'm doing what I think is best for all of us." She reached to embrace Sara.

But Sara stepped away. "Did you ever think you could be wrong?" she shouted, then stomped off before Ellie could reply.

"Yes," Ellie murmured now, remembering the bitterness that had etched her daughter's face. "Oh, yes, my darling."

Tears filled her eyes and she blinked and blinked again, looking around the new kitchen. Her spirit felt as if she'd been swished around in one of those old-time washers, then pressed through the wringer.

Why, oh why had she ever embarked on this lunatic idea? She wanted more for her girls, more for herself. But was this the way?

She'd made a big, irrevocable mistake in buying the farm. The admission fell loud and heavy in her mind. She heard the ticking of the kitchen clock, the pounding of her heart in the quiet house as she faced her mistake.

She was simply not equipped to suddenly leap out into life as she'd done. It had been a fantasy, enticing her along. And desperation had driven her to change her life. A life in which she'd been trapped. Now she was living hard realities.

But there was no way to go back. There was nothing to do but go on and try to turn the mistake into a victory—or at least a draw.

Somehow, she thought, looking again at the papers spread across the table, she had to make enough money to cover everyday expenses—to buy the girls some school clothes and Sara something special—so she wouldn't need to dip into the money left in the bank. That money she considered almost sacred, set aside for the purchase of cattle and to make the first payment on the farm due Wade the coming spring. She intended to have the payment for Wade come hell or high water. She had no idea where future payments would come from—and right now she refused to worry over it.

But where would she get a job? she thought, discouraged. What could she do?

For the past fifteen years she'd kept house and raised three girls. It sounded boring and inept. But Ellie had never considered it so; she'd chosen to be a homemaker at the outset. And, she thought with lofty anger, how many people could do the things she did? Make coffee, fry eggs, write notes, defuse disputes, and all one-handed while soothing a crying infant with the other? Why, she was an underpaid secretary, diplomat, maid and repairman all in one.

The anger seeped away, replaced by sinking despair. She turned out the light, leaving the bills still spread across the table, and walked slowly to her bedroom. She lay awake in the darkness for a long while, her mind casting about for places to apply for work. Throwing an arm to the summer-warm sheet beside her, she ran her hand up and down. The bed felt exceedingly empty this night. She wished there was someone, a man, to talk to about her worries. Her mind pictured Wade, his body bare and muscles rock hard, as she knew they'd be, lying in the empty space.

Over and over she told herself to stop such nonsense. She had herself, and only herself.

The next few days were spent settling in: unpacking boxes, filling the attic with things that simply would not fit in the house, hanging pictures, arranging furniture. Ellie and the girls met the mailman and one of the Barker brothers, whom she'd called to come check the water heater and the furnace. Two more cats were found in the barn, to be friends with Maynard; Rae was ecstatic.

Ellie made a point of telephoning her mother every morning at their usual time of eight o'clock, though it cost her several dollars each time. Her mother remained distant, unrelenting, refusing all offers to come for a visit.

Not finding it an emotion to be proud of, Ellie was somewhat relieved. She simply couldn't cope with her parents and their feelings right now. She had enough problems of her own. Time, she prayed, would work things out. When one of her older brothers telephoned from Tulsa and immediately began berating her for what she was putting their parents through, Ellie amazed herself by hanging up on him. She'd never hung up on anyone in her life.

Well, she hadn't done a lot of any of this in her life, she thought dryly.

The times she ventured from the house on errands, she scouted for places to apply for work. There seemed few. Gearing up her courage, she inquired at the local electric-company office, an endeavor that left her ego in shreds. She couldn't operate a computer or one of the electronic typewriters, much less type.

On Sunday Ellie bustled the girls up and out, complaining all the way, to the small, white-steepled church a few miles down the road. There they met the preacher and his wife, several distant neighbors, and they saw, much to Ellie's surprise, Wade Wolcott. With him sat the dark-haired young woman Ellie had seen him with on their first meeting at the Last Chance Cafe. After the service, he politely, if distantly, took the time to introduce Ellie and her girls to the young woman. She was Gayla Lutz; Ellie found she liked the smiling, flamboyant woman immediately. That night at bedtime prayers Rae asked for a horse the color of Gayla Lutz's hair.

Except for that morning at church, they saw Wade Wolcott only from a distance—either driving in or out from his house or, wonder of wonders, flying a kite. In fact, several kites. On one occasion he'd had two triangle kites up at once. He flew triangles, box kites and some kind of kite with multicolored, yards-long tails.

Rae and Poppy had been enthralled when they'd first seen him flying a kite and had grumbled loudly at Ellie's refusal to allow them to go up and see.

"He doesn't need your help," she'd told the girls, steeling herself against their crestfallen expressions. "He's a bachelor. He likes his privacy."

But she, too, had watched his kite dip and sway in the wind. She, too, had felt drawn and curious. It was surprising, hard to believe, that the big, rough man had such a hobby. She remembered his ruggedly handsome features and his brown eyes shot with that curious shade of gold. Eyes that had regarded her so very closely, seeming to see something no one else saw, something Ellie held privately and preciously to herself.

Monday evening, at eight o'clock, Ellie finished washing dishes and went purposely to hang her new swing on the side porch—a swing she'd assembled and painted herself. Balancing on the railing of the side porch, with one hand hooked around the post, Ellie hung the last chain of the swing to the hook in the roof.

"There!" She murmured to no one in particular as she emitted a long, tired breath and jumped from the railing. Her body protested the action.

For a long second she gazed with pride at the swing, then she sat down, sideways, with one arm resting along the back and one leg extending across the seat. With her other sneakered foot she pushed against the floor to set the swing in motion. It felt good, magnificent, actually. Now her home was complete.

The sun was far to the west, a summer sun that wouldn't set for nearly another hour, though cicadas had begun their nightly orchestration and martins darted through the cooler air, feeding on mosquitoes. The girls' voices and the murmur of the television drifted softly through the open window. For a few minutes, at last, Ellie felt her muscles relaxing as she rocked the swing to and fro and looked at the land around her.

Then her gaze came to rest on Wade Wolcott's house up the hill. It stopped. Wade sat there, situated where the sun slanted through and illuminated his figure on the front porch. Though up the hill nearly a quarter of a mile, Ellie could clearly see his lean form, his blue jeans and plaid shirt, his booted foot propped up against the front railing—and his head turned toward her.

Quickly she turned away, more comfortable with no greeting on either side, as if he wasn't there. Her heart raced with small, swift beats. Her body warmed, just as it did whenever she looked into his eyes. She didn't want to have this feeling—didn't want anyone to know she had such a...lustful reaction to anyone, much less Wade Wolcott.

Why did he have to be there, she thought with irritation, just when she finally had a few peaceful moments alone? Good grief! All these acres and acres and she had to be in sight of another person! Why wasn't he inside watching re-runs on television like everyone else? *Had he watched her the entire time she'd fumbled with hanging the swing?* She hoped not; she'd been anything but adept and graceful.

Oh, she knew what was wrong with her—and it had darned little to do with Wade Wolcott, other than that he was a man, she told herself. Her problem was that she was a healthy adult woman and sleeping alone. It was a very natural and normal reaction, her physical human side making itself known—after many years of dormancy. She wondered, wearily and flippantly, if she were doomed to a life of celibacy.

At that moment, and thankfully so, Poppy poked her cherubic face out the screened doorway. "Hi, Mama," she whispered.

Ellie held her arms out in welcome, glad for something to take her mind away from the foolish, irritating thoughts. "Come swing," she said, speaking equally as softly as Poppy.

Poppy's round face broke into a wide grin, and she flew over the floor and virtually threw herself into Ellie's open arms. Her pink overalls were smudged with dirt, her curly bangs damp with perspiration.

"I was waiting for you to finish," she whispered breathlessly. "It's pretty, Mama. Let's not tell—at least for a bit. Let's save it just for us."

Ellie chuckled and pressed Poppy to her, inhaling the childish, summer muskiness of her, and softly swung the swing. After a few minutes, Poppy pushed free of Ellie's cuddling to look around from their perch on the porch.

"Mama," Poppy said an instant later, "Mr. Wolcott is up on his porch, too."

Though her muscles remained relaxed, Ellie felt her insides stiffen. "Oh?" she said.

"Yes." Ellie could feel Poppy's attention focused on the man up the hill. "His dog is there, too." Poppy's face, in the golden glow of the western sun, held an avid interest. "Wonder why he's not flying a kite."

"Dogs don't fly kites," Ellie teased.

"Oh, Mama!" Poppy giggled.

"The wind dies down too much at this time of night to fly a kite," Ellie explained then. She stopped the swing. "Come on, time for you to get a bath. You positively stink."

"Let's wave to him, Mama."

"No...come on now," Ellie said, walking ahead, not wanting to give Poppy time to say anything more.

Wade saw Ellie stand and move from the swing, then all he could see were her legs, long, summer-bare legs, as she retreated into the house. The little one, Poppy, lingered, though, and she looked up his way. Though he couldn't see clearly at this distance, he could easily remember her smiling, round, pink-cheeked face. Her tiny hand came up in a wave.

Wade hesitated only a split second before waving in return. The little one waved again, hopping from one foot to the other, then in a flash she was gone. For a few minutes, his gaze lingered on the small house below, the stone walls washed a golden-red by the sun. It took him those minutes to realize the small girl's friendly wave delighted him. She was something, with her sparkling blue eyes and the preposterous things she said.

She and her sister had come up several times when he'd been flying his kites. Shyly at first, but without any prompting, he thought dryly, they'd come forward and asked if they could try. Those two were game for just about anything, he believed, and not afraid of much, even his attempts to put them off with brisk, short-tempered humor. Once the littlest one had rebuked him for swearing. He laughed now, remembering.

When he'd watched Ellie struggling to hang the swing earlier, he'd adamantly refused to allow himself to go down to help her. He wasn't going to fall into that trap. No matter how much he thought about the pleasant picture of her long legs up close.

No sirree. He'd made his point that he wasn't to be considered a ready handyman, and she'd understood. No sense rocking the boat. He'd stay up here, and she'd stay down there. Best thing all around.

He turned his mind back to a difficult kite design he sought to perfect. He sat there, contentedly sipping a beer and mulling over the problem until well after darkness had settled over the porch. It was his favorite time of day.

Chapter Six

What was she going to do? Ellie felt her heart beat faster, panic rising in her throat. Over the past four days she'd been to eight businesses seeking employment; only three had allowed her an application—and for one of those she'd actually lied, saying she'd had previous experience as a receptionist. Still, the message was: Don't call us, we'll call you.

There was nowhere else in the area left, and Ellie didn't see how she could work in the city, so far from the girls. And even in the city she'd have trouble finding a job. The economy was bad, so many people out of work—and according to those applications she couldn't do anything.

She'd pulled the Cutlass into a parking space along the main street, only half aware of what she was doing. Mechanically, she rolled down the window, allowing a blustery wind to sweep inside, bringing fresh, hot air and dust. A tear made a stinging trail down her cheek. Ellie slowly wiped it away, her thoughts filling with despair. She couldn't find a job, Sara was resentful of her even trying and Poppy's little lower lip quivered at the mention of Ellie being away every day for hours.

And she didn't want to leave her girls. They were all going through so many abrupt changes; the girls needed her at home.

But there was precious little choice. She had to get work of some kind, and soon. She just had to.

A truck pulled into the space beside her, and Ellie averted her face, reaching for a tissue in her purse. Checking her image in the mirror, she wiped the moisture and mascara smudge from beneath her eyes. She stared at herself and searched the recesses of her soul for scraps of faith and hope. There was mighty little to be found.

Blinking in the bright light, she looked around her as if seeing where she was for the first time. The red and gold lettering of the Last Chance Cafe adorned the window directly in front of the Cutlass. Thinking longingly of a cup of coffee, Ellie got out of the car and entered the cafe. She thought herself too tired and forlorn to be self-conscious about being among strangers in a strange place, and when her gaze fell, first thing, on Wade Wolcott sitting at the back of the cafe, she suddenly wanted to turn and run. Especially when he raised his head and looked at her.

What did she care? she told herself emphatically. He had a right to sit there and look at whomever he pleased, in whatever way he pleased. And she had her rights, too, she thought, turning her gaze to the lunch counter.

Ellie stood there an instant and swept her palm down her hip, an unconscious and decidedly sensual gesture Wade recognized as habit. Then, seeming to have her mind on things miles away, she went to the counter and sat on a stool.

Wade's gaze slipped from her hair downward, noting the blouse falling over her full breasts and the soft material of her dark skirt swirling loose and full around her long legs. Mrs. McGrew was apparently given to soft, flowing fabrics, he thought.

For a bare fraction of a second he considered going over to speak to her. Then, amazed and irritated with himself for staring at her and thinking such thoughts, he shook out his newspaper and turned his attention firmly to the printed words. There was absolutely no reason for him to speak to Ellie McGrew.

At the clunk of the china saucer hitting the counter in front of her, Ellie started and found herself staring at a white cup being filled with coffee. All thoughts of Wade Wolcott vanished as she looked up into the lively green eyes of Gayla Lutz.

As always before when Ellie had seen her, Gayla's face was flawlessly made up, making her look exactly like a china doll. Her exceedingly pale skin was in stark contrast to her long and voluminous auburn hair. Large silver hoops hung from her ears, giving her the air of a Gypsy.

She smiled, one of her vibrant mauve-colored eyelids closing in a half wink. "You look like you could use a pick-me-up," she said. "This pie's the best in the county—made right here fresh every night."

"Thank...you, Gayla." Ellie managed a small smile. She didn't care to eat anything, but thinking of the younger woman's feelings, she stuck a fork into the pie. To her dismay, Gayla propped a hip against the stainless-steel cabinet on the other side of the counter, apparently intent on staying and talking.

"You know this is a small town?" It was half statement, half question. Gayla raised a carefully shaped eyebrow. "Everybody talks about everybody, especially anything or anyone new. They don't mean no harm—actually mean to help."

Ellie smiled at Gayla's earnest expression. "I think it's a fine town, fine people."

Gayla smiled broadly again, and her earrings bobbed with the motion of her head. "Well, I heard you'd been out to the Henderson aerial spraying place looking for a job," Gayla drawled. She reached for the coffee pot to refill Ellie's half-empty cup. "Todd Henderson told me. He was awfully sorry, but they have his wife and sister to help with the telephone and office work. Why pay someone?" Her face turned earnest again. "You have trouble finding a job, Ellie? Anyone would around here."

The whole turn of the conversation took Ellie by surprise. But after a moment of staring into Gayla's earnest and open face, she gave a long sigh and nodded.

"Yes, you can safely say I'm having trouble in that area." Giving in to the overwhelming urge to prop her elbows on the Formica-topped counter, she drank deeply of the coffee, using it as a small placebo for her problems of the moment.

"This is good," she told Gayla, forcing a smile for the friendly younger woman.

"Thanks." Gayla absently wiped the counter. "What do you do?" she asked.

Ellie considered the question. "Well...for the past fifteen years I've kept house and raised three girls." She looked into the dark coffee and brooded over her answer.

"Guess you've tried a lot of places around here, huh?" Gayla said.

Glancing up from the cup, Ellie saw sympathy written in the younger woman's eyes—no, it was more empathy, as if Gayla really understood.

"All of them," Ellie said.

"Which isn't saying much."

Ellie shook her head. "And I just hate to go into the city. It's too far away from the girls. If they should need me..."

Gayla was shaking her head in agreement. They both fell silent, Ellie feeling suddenly awkward. She'd eaten only three bites of the pie, but simply could not finish. It was time to make a graceful exit, and as she dug into her purse for money to pay the bill, she tried also to gather the remnants of her pride.

"I have a job open here, if you'd like it," Gayla said as Ellie laid her money on the counter. "It's not full-time at first, just about two hours in the mornings and again in the evenings, five days a week. But when one of my girls goes back to college, you can work lunch, too, if you want. And the tips aren't half bad." She looked at Ellie, her eyes wide and frank.

"You run this cafe?" The question popped from Ellie's lips before she had a chance to reconsider; she found the fact amazing.

Gayla laughed good-naturedly. "Yeh, ain't it a kick?" She looked thoughtful. "I'm pretty good at it, even if I do say so myself. I think it's because so many of my customers are men, and I do like men." Again, she gave a playful wink.

Ellie listened and watched Gayla, her amazement rising. She didn't know when she'd met anyone as refreshingly candid.

"So, want the job?" Gayla asked.

"I...I've never been a waitress." Ellie felt hope and doubt at the same time. Her mind raced ahead like a rushing stream tumbling over rocks as she considered the aspects of the idea. That Gayla was obviously very friendly with Wade and that he seemed quite at home at the cafe also entered into it, although she wasn't exactly certain how, only that it made her hesitate. "I have no experience."

"You said you have three girls, have been raising them for the past fifteen years."

"Yes..."

"Honey, don't you put their food on the table every morning and night?" Gayla raised her etched eyebrow. "Don't you remember who likes what? And I'm imagining you didn't have those girls by yourself. You knew how to serve your husband his meals and soothe his ego at the same time. I think that qualifies as experience."

Ellie had never looked at it in that light—but she could as Gayla spoke. Why, she thought, she could serve people and do it well. And she did know how to deal with other people, with their likes and dislikes, amiable and fussy.

"You'll do all right, Ellie." A slow smile came across Gayla's lips. Ellie looked into her eyes and realized she didn't have to say what she was thinking to this unique young woman. Between them existed a rare telepathy, and she knew she'd found her first friend in town—her first friend in a long time.

"If you're willing, I guess I should certainly give it a try," she said quietly.

On the drive home her mind whirled. *A job—she'd found a job!*

Just outside town, she noticed her vision blurring. With shaking hands, she pulled the car to the side of the road and burst into full sobs. She was terrified of going to work, of leaving the girls, of any change in her already changed life. She didn't know if she could handle it. She was so very glad to have gotten a job at last—and she dreaded telling her daughters.

She worried lest someone should drive by and see her— the new woman in town—carrying on in such a fashion. It seemed to take all her strength to get control of herself, but at last, recalling every platitude and positive quote she'd ever heard, she managed to stop crying and trembling. She wiped her eyes, then dabbed her face with powder, hoping to conceal some of the effects of the outburst. But there was no hiding her red-rimmed eyes, and Sara, at least, would notice. Well, her daughters, no doubt, had discovered long ago that their mother wasn't perfect, she thought, pulling the Cutlass onto the road again and heading home.

"Oh, I hired your new neighbor, Ellie McGrew," Gayla said in an offhand manner. She'd come to sit with him as she always did after the lunch rush had died down some. She'd come to flirt; Gayla flirted with anything male, and generally Wade flirted back, considering it harmless enough.

But this time the flirting nature died within him. He stared at her.

"You did what?"

"I hired Ellie McGrew. She'll work the morning and evening shift right now, then take on the lunch shift when Melanie quits to go back to school."

"Why in the hell did you do that?"

Gayla's eyebrows shot up as she recognized his displeasure for the first time. "We need someone to take Melanie's place. Ellie needs a job."

"She doesn't have any experience."

"How do you know?" Gayla's expression turned uncomfortably curious.

"I know. She's a widow with three daughters. She hasn't worked a day in her life."

"What do you call being a wife and mother?" Gayla shot back sharply.

"We need someone experienced at waitressing," Wade insisted, averting his eyes from Gayla's.

"The woman needs a job. And I think she'll do very well. For Pete's sake, she's taken on moving out here alone, fixing up that house. I imagine she can learn the art of waiting tables." Her manner and voice turned quiet. "You pay me to run this place," she said. "You unhappy with what I'm doing?"

Wade looked up to find her green eyes boring into his. Further protests evaporated from his tongue. Gayla had a sharp mind beneath her wildly feminine exterior. If he made a big to-do about this, she'd more than likely get some crazy idea there was something between him and Ellie. He shied away from any thoughts about the whole situation.

"No." He took a breath. "You're right. You're the manager." He gave her a deliberately playful smile and wink. "You know more about this stuff than I do. Just wondering, is all." Wade stood up from the booth and reached for his cap, which lay on the table. He stopped. "Does she know I own the Last Chance?"

Gayla observed him a moment before shaking her head, a puzzled expression sweeping her face. "I don't know . . . I didn't say anything. Wasn't important . . . was it?"

Wade shook his head. "No, just wondered." He turned to step away.

"Wade?" Gayla said, stopping him. "You ever going to ask me out?" She was serious for a change. Her china-doll face looked exceedingly young.

He shook his head. "I'm too old for your ways," he said, giving her a warm grin and slipping into an exaggerated southern drawl. "You keep your eye out for one of these young fellers that keep hanging around here, looking at you like they'd like to have you for breakfast."

She seemed to accept it. "Okay." She smiled. "See you later."

"Sure thing."

He walked from the cafe, relieved that he and Gayla had gotten things straight at last. He'd always considered himself a pretty plain, no-nonsense sort of guy, but he'd allowed this flirting matter with Gayla to go on the fuzzy side way too often. He'd wondered if maybe she took his flirting more seriously than he intended. They'd cleared the air now; no need for misunderstanding on either side.

As he reminded himself often, his life went on exactly as he liked it: free and loose, no demands that he didn't willingly take on.

Now why in the hell had Gayla gone and hired Ellie McGrew?

It was a good thing Ellie was an early riser, because her shift at the Last Chance started at six-thirty. She rose, dressed and headed for her porch swing with a cup of coffee well before six. Deliberately she refrained from looking up the hill. But still, she somehow sensed that Wade Wolcott sat there. It seemed crazy, but she thought she could feel his gaze.

Finally she shifted in the swing to cast a covert glance up to check. And there he sat.

Determined to refuse to let it bother her, she turned her head and pushed the swing into gentle motion. She had too much on her mind already to be concerned over such a silly irritation.

Gayla had told her to wear anything she liked to work, anything comfortable. The cafe would provide an apron. Sara had advised Ellie to wear her new blue jeans, and feeling a bit juvenile, Ellie had complied. Now she was glad she had. They were comfortable—and, surprisingly, made her feel pretty and feminine, even a bit sexy, though a nervous twinge came along with that amusing thought. A pale blue blouse with embroidery on the collar and soft leather flats completed her uniform for the day, and she was highly pleased with herself.

Don't get carried away, Ellie, she reminded herself, then argued that she needed every scrap of self-confidence she could get at the moment. She'd been eighteen the last time she'd had a job outside her home. And that job had been filing and general handiwork around her father's office. Nepotism in the highest form.

Her heart fluttered. Well, here I go, she thought, finding herself nervously pushing the swing harder.

There came a small sound from within the house, and Poppy poked her head out the door. With tiny hands rubbing her sleepy eyes, she ran to squirm into Ellie's lap. Ellie held her youngest close, seeking comfort from the contact. Suddenly she didn't want to leave their home, not at all. But then, she never had wanted a job like this. It was an unavoidable necessity.

"Mama," Poppy said, whispering and squirming to peek around Ellie's shoulder. "Wade's up the hill on his porch again, too."

Turning her head, Ellie saw Poppy jiggle her hand in an eager wave. Glancing up the hill, she was amazed to see Wade wave in return.

She stood up. "Poppy—come on, we have to get Sara awake before I leave." She lifted Poppy in a quick motion and strode away from the swing.

No doubt, Ellie thought, and not for the first time, she'd see Wade Wolcott often at the Last Chance Cafe. Something quivered inside her. Why should it bother her? She'd wait on him like she would anyone else. He'd be just another customer.

Why did the thought ring so very false?

As she drove into town, she found herself repeatedly thinking of Wade, her thoughts chasing each other around and around like frantic squirrels. She was nervous, afraid of facing the unknown. And thinking of Wade Wolcott didn't help at all. Something happened inside her every time she saw him, every time she even thought of him. She scolded herself because she knew exactly what that something was: it was human desire. It had nothing to do with Wade at all, she told herself. She was simply lonely, her body aching for the pleasures it remembered. She could and would handle it with sane, adult reason.

But when she entered the Last Chance Cafe and the first thing she saw was Wade Wolcott leaning against the end of the counter, she couldn't seem to gather one cohesive thought.

Wade watched Ellie's eyes widen and her palm sweep at her shapely hip as she paused uncertainly. Her surprise he recognized, but he also sensed some other emotion, though he couldn't put his finger on what it was. The next instant she'd recovered her composure and walked toward the counter. Wade noted her hour glass shape, shown to good advantage, he thought, in the soft blouse and slim-fitting denims. She looked away from him, glancing around, seeking Gayla, no doubt. Wade averted his eyes to his cup as he took a drink of coffee.

There was the occasional clink of china, the crack and pop of sausage sizzling on the grill in the kitchen and the low hum of voices, four early morning customers, regulars Gayla and Cori had already served. The low hum dropped even lower as the men noticed Ellie, a beautiful new woman in their midst.

"Mornin', Mrs. McGrew," Wade said when she reached the end of the counter.

He was purposely bland, but inside he chuckled, savoring the information he knew would come as quite a surprise to Mrs. Eleanor McGrew. Observing her face carefully, though unobtrusively, he tried to imagine her reaction when he told her this particular bit of news—that the owner of the Last Chance Cafe was none other than himself.

"Good morning, Mr. Wolcott." She was pleasant enough, though she didn't smile. Her wide blue eyes met his gaze, and something tightened inside Wade. Her complexion was smooth, tawny colored like a soft apricot, showing she'd been out in the sunshine much more than when he'd first met her. It was the kind of skin a man longed to stroke.

"Lookin' for Gayla?" he asked, jerking his gaze back to his coffee as he again raised his cup.

"Yes." Ellie nodded.

"She's back in the storeroom. Be out in a minute." Without looking directly at her, he inclined his head and said, "You can put your purse in the office."

She cast him a curious glance, then stepped around him and into the small office. Quickly Wade took an apron from the hook near the swinging kitchen door and waited.

When Ellie reappeared, he held up the white cloth apron. "Here's your tools—order pad and pencil're in the pocket." But instead of handing it to her, he stepped quickly behind her and dropped the apron's front loop around her neck.

"I . . ." She fumbled with adjusting the apron, obviously flustered at his actions.

Extremely pleased with himself, Wade relished every moment of the subtle teasing, until, as he tied the apron strings at her back, he became oddly uncomfortable. He was suddenly all too aware of her sweet, warm scent, of the silkiness of her hair only inches from his face, and of her body's vibration just beneath his fingers. And it suddenly occurred to him the four other people in the room were almighty interested in what was going on.

He hurriedly finished tying the apron and stepped a safe distance back. She did something for the apron, he thought as she turned around, but he was careful not to allow that thought to register on his face.

"Thank you," she said, looking downward and running her hands in an exploratory fashion over the cotton fabric. She glanced up, met his gaze, then looked nervously away. "Guess I'd better go ask Gayla what I need to do first."

"She'll be here in a minute," Wade told her. "I'll begin by showing you how to brew coffee—that's one of the most important items on the menu."

He saw her cast him another curious look before he turned and walked to the coffee maker. He continued to feel the odd need to keep a respectable distance between himself and her, but thoroughly enjoyed anticipating her reaction when she found out exactly who she was working for. Instructing her in the simple rudiments of a commercial coffee maker, he prolonged the moment of truth.

He had an instant of concern as he saw her face, so pale, so intent on what he said—so obviously nervous about the prospect of her job. Maybe he shouldn't tell her today; maybe it would be too much for her.

But she'd find out sometime, and more than likely today. There was no getting around that.

Gayla appeared from the kitchen.

"Hello, Ellie." Gayla smiled broadly, her gaze moving from Ellie to Wade then back again. "I see the owner has already got you started."

Talk about timing, Wade thought dryly, watching Ellie's blue eyes widen as she turned to him.

"Didn't you know?" he said easily, relishing the shock on her face and pained by it at the same time. "Guess there's no reason why you should—but I own the Last Chance."

His words seemed to hang in the air as all motion seemed to stop. Realizing she'd opened her mouth, Ellie closed it. Whatever she'd been about to say had evaporated from her mind.

Embarrassment surged through her, anger right on its heels. She didn't want to be indebted to Mr. Wolcott any more than she already was. Feeling her face grow furiously hot, she averted her eyes from both Wade and Gayla, unwilling to have either of them detect her discomfiture.

"Well, he may own the place, but I'm the boss," Gayla quipped as she turned with a flurry. "So don't pay him much mind. Come on back to the kitchen, and I'll introduce you to Cori, our morning cook."

Following Gayla, Ellie was distinctly aware of Wade's gaze upon her back.

If she'd only known, she thought, she never would have taken the job. She owed him for the land, for the help he'd given when they'd moved in. She didn't want to be further obliged to him. And now here she was, working in the only place she could get a job—a job on a handout—and she had him to thank for it!

Oh, and he found it all so terribly funny! He'd just been waiting to tell her. Well, she hoped she'd crushed some of his expectations with her low-key reaction—she hoped, but was unsure. She knew he'd seen her shocked expression.

With these thoughts filling her mind, she smiled and greeted the woman Gayla introduced as Cori and then another waitress, Janie, who burst breathlessly through the back door. Ellie tossed thoughts of Wade and her own pride away as too cumbersome at the moment. It took all she had to concentrate on Gayla, who showed her where things were and rapidly fired instructions at her. More than once Ellie suspected she was totally over her head, and she was certain of it when it came time to step out and tend to customers who'd begun filling the cafe for the morning rush.

Chapter Seven

It seemed to Ellie as if a starting cannon had fired, signaling everyone to pile into the cafe at once. The place filled with the hum of conversation and laughter, smiling faces, scowling faces, cowboy hats and ball caps, the scents of tobacco and coffee mixed with hot grease and baking biscuits. It crossed her mind that she'd never seen so many men in one place at one time; she felt as if she were in a sea of them. Tall men, short men, handsome men, homely men, men in blue work shirts and several in suits. A few women also came, women who were obviously regulars and worked alongside the men.

Then there was no more time to think, only to react. She listed orders shot at her like bullets out of a machine gun, deciphered mumbled sentences and one-word orders, carried trays meant for weight lifters and sidestepped Janie and Gayla, who also whizzed among the tables.

Gayla was a wonder, taking orders, serving, joking nonstop and keeping an assisting eye out for Ellie, all at the same time. "Here's John's coffee, Ellie." "Jelly's in the third cabinet." "Wait . . . the scrambled-egg breakfast is for Rupe, not Willy. Willy might just throw it in your face."

There wasn't even time for Ellie to wish she could lie down and die, much less time for her to consider Wade Wolcott's presence—but she did.

He'd retired to a booth in the back, the same one at which she'd first met him. He read the morning newspaper. Several people came and went at his table, visiting, and Gayla brought him breakfast. Though Ellie barely looked at him, didn't know if he looked at her, she could feel his presence, almost like something tangible in the air. She tried hard to be competent because she couldn't stand for him to think, to know for certain, that she was so inept.

As abruptly as the rush began, it ended. Ellie's two hours were over, leaving her feeling more like she'd worked forty-eight straight. She stood behind the counter and looked around the room, catching her breath and almost unable to believe the previous two hours.

"You did fine," Gayla told her, patting her arm and casting her that now-familiar wink. "Tired?"

Ellie nodded; she couldn't muster enough energy to even answer. She leaned against the stainless-steel cabinet and looked around the cafe. Janie waited on one of the several tables still containing customers.

"We'll have customers dribble in now until lunch, when the rush will happen all over again," Gayla commented, following Ellie's gaze. "The morning is the biggest time, with the farmers, ranchers and businessmen beginning their day. Lunch is a riot, too, but dinner is nice—full but not crazy."

Ellie hoped so. At the moment she felt every one of her thirty-four years. She didn't think she could go through this twice in one day—she wasn't certain she would.

She saw Wade rise from the booth. She averted her eyes immediately, though she was fully aware of him walking toward them.

"Do you stay here from morning to night?" she asked Gayla. Out of the corner of her eye she saw Wade move behind the counter to the coffee machine.

Gayla shook her head. "I'm always here for breakfast, sometimes skip lunch and usually return to close up after dinner."

Wade stepped over to them. That slow smile slipping across his face, he held a cup of coffee toward Ellie.

"Congratulations, Mrs. McGrew. You survived breakfast at the Last Chance."

His approving expression pleased her, though she was uncomfortable with the pleasure and the attention in front of Gayla. She averted her gaze to the cup he offered. "Thank you," she murmured.

"Why don't you sit down and have some breakfast?" he asked.

Taking a sip of the coffee, Ellie shook her head. "No...thanks...I have to get home." Even as she spoke she stepped around him. With another quick sip of the coffee, she slid the cup in the sink and slipped off her apron.

"I'll be here this evening, Ellie," Gayla said. "You rest this afternoon. You'll get used to it in time."

Ellie nodded. "Thanks...see you."

She practically fled the cafe, she thought, and dryly chuckled at herself. She drove home automatically, her mind whirling. She considered quitting; she never would have taken the job if she'd known Wade owned the Last Chance. Then she asked herself why his owning it should upset her.

He'd been nice that first day when he'd helped them at the house. But when she'd called on him for help with the water heater, she'd known beyond a doubt he hadn't liked it. He'd made it plain she should call a plumber or an electrician in the future, not him. When he'd sold her the land, he'd probably worried about her constantly calling on him for help.

And if he'd had anything to say about Gayla hiring her, he probably would have put an instant stop to it.

But today, this morning, he'd been amiable enough.

How strange.

Not strange, she told herself. He'd been polite, and she knew that about him: Wade was a gentleman of the old southwest. Few of them left. Men who treated a woman in a courtly way, out of respect for womanhood. He'd shown her no more courtesy than he would any other woman.

Why did she care anyway?

And how could she quit after Gayla had been so kind as to give her a chance? It was close to home, to the school if her girls should need her.

Pulling into her driveway, she realized she didn't remember anything between backing from the parking place in town to reaching home. Thank God she'd made it without an accident.

Sara or Rae had thoughtfully left the garage door up, and Ellie drove into the dim interior. Taking her keys from the ignition, she sat there, feeling somewhat as if she'd been run over by a locomotive. She'd left the house with the sun balancing on the eastern horizon. Now it was high in the sky, yet still far to the east; it was barely nine o'clock.

"Mama! Mama!"

Raising her head at the familiar call, she saw Poppy, still in her short pajamas, hopping down the stairs, Rae right behind her. Slowly Ellie opened the door and swung her legs from the car. The next instant Poppy pressed into her lap— and to add one more amazement to the morning, Ellie found herself crying as she hugged her littlest to her.

Poppy pulled back and placed a chubby palm on either side of Ellie's face. Her blue eyes were saucer round. "Mama, did you miss us so much?"

Ellie smiled then. "I missed you very much," she said. Brushing away the foolish tears, she hugged Poppy once more and reached for Rae's hand. She ran her gaze over Poppy, then Rae, then Sara, who'd quietly joined them. "It was just something so new to me, that's all." Her smile widened as she looked again at Poppy. "Just like those first few days when you started preschool."

"And you're not as young as you used to be, huh?" Poppy said, imitating not only words heard often, but Ellie's tone as well. Rae gave her sister a swift, disapproving nudge.

Lifting Poppy from her lap, Ellie smiled wryly. "That's true." She reached for her purse. It jingled loudly and dropped with unaccustomed weight. "Oh—" she smiled at the girls "—let's count my tips."

Catching her eagerness, Rae and Poppy ran up the stairs. Sara lingered at her side. Ellie was heartened to feel a loving warmth, one that had been missing often of late, vibrate between them. She draped an arm around Sara's shoulders and together they went up the stairs to the kitchen.

Bowls, cereal boxes, coloring books and crayons covered the kitchen table. Sara helped clear a place, and Ellie sat down to pull out her coin purse. She emptied it, coins pinging and bouncing on the oak surface, bills floating down softly.

For a moment, she sat back and looked at the pile. Though small, it was more than she'd imagined. She'd been way too busy to attempt to count any of it that morning.

"I had about a dollar and seventy-five cents already in here," she said, sitting forward to begin counting. She set that amount aside.

The girls stood close. Ellie counted. And her heartbeat began to pick up tempo. Not a fortune by any means, but...

Dropping the last quarter into its pile, she sat back dumbfounded. "Thirteen dollars and fifty-five cents," she said. She couldn't believe it, and her eyes remained on the small pile.

No, not a fortune, but more money than she'd anticipated. Her mind raced ahead with calculations. She'd been far from adept on that, her first, morning. She'd been slow, had confused and fumbled orders, which a few of the customers hadn't appreciated. But she would get better—and it stood to reason her tips would improve. Twice a day, five days a week. And Gayla had said Ellie could work lunch in two weeks. Adding her estimated tips to the small salary Gayla paid her, she would make enough to pay the bills.

Oh, no, there would be no more thoughts of quitting.

Hallelujah! she thought, giving her daughters a wide grin and seeing them smile in return.

A cautionary voice entered her joy—she would make it provided she could learn to be a competent waitress, provided she could keep the job, and...provided she could control her feelings around Wade Wolcott.

The fact that Wade could fire her and the question of what exactly her feelings for him were came to mind at the same time.

"Think I'll be able to get my horse soon?" Rae asked, thankfully tearing Ellie's mind away from both thoughts.

"I think we're one step closer, honey," she told her.

"Mama," Poppy piped up, "are we poor now?"

At that Ellie laughed full and loud, delight flooding her spirit.

"No, darling." She looked at each of the girls in turn. "I'd say we're about the richest people I know."

Poppy squirmed her way into Ellie's arms. "You're talking about love, huh, Mama?" she said, her reedy voice disapproving. "I meant money."

As Ellie hugged Poppy, her gaze strayed to the small pile of money on the table, then moved to look through the window at the meadow beyond. She imagined cows grazing in that meadow, her own cows, money on the hoof. It was time to start looking for stock to begin a herd. She had no idea how to go about it—but then she'd had no idea how to go about buying a house and a farm or moving, either. But she'd learned.

The girls scampered off to clean their rooms. To play was more likely, she thought with a smile as she raked the money from the table into an empty jar. She stared out at the meadow again.

It was a lonely business, she thought then, very clearly, this doing everything herself. Oh, it was freedom, all right, but empty. How much more it would be if she could share it with someone, a man, a mate. Look what I did today, honey—I bought this land. I searched and I chose it and it's good. I worked today, my first job, and I did okay.

How wonderful it would be to sit on the porch swing and share coffee with her man and talk about things they'd each done that day, sharing joys and heartaches. How much easier it would be to share her concern over the rift with her parents, her problems with the girls or even a simple thing like having a headache. Galen used to massage her shoulders and then they would end up in bed, loving each other.

An overwhelming yearning stole over Ellie, bringing an almost physical pain. She clutched the kitchen sink, willing it to pass, because she could think of nothing else to do.

It was a fact that she didn't have a man to share her life with. She had to face it, had to stop any kind of yearning because it was simply too painful. With purposeful motions, she strode to the table, gathered the dirty dishes and plunked them in the sink. She turned her mind to the things she had to do at the house before getting back to the cafe. Making time for a quick nap was a necessity.

Four days later Ellie purposely awoke earlier than normal, earlier than she had on the preceding three days. This one morning she intended to have the porch swing and all the scenery around completely to herself—without the observing eyes of one Mr. Wade Wolcott.

At barely five-thirty, with the eastern horizon growing bright and herself already dressed for work at the cafe, Ellie carried a steaming mug of coffee out on the porch and eased her body into her precious swing.

The air was morning cool and summer fragrant, fresh. She inhaled deeply, raked strands of hair from her neck and pushed the swing to rock. Her gaze, eyelids half closed in beautiful contentment, skimmed over the earth before her, then moved smugly up to the Wolcott house, pleased with herself for eluding him this one fine morning.

It came as a swift, hard, and definitely unwanted jolt to see Wade Wolcott sitting reared back in a chair on his porch—just as he'd been every single morning since Ellie had moved in.

Damn, was Ellie's first thought. Her second was: *Double damn!*

For the past three mornings, Ellie had come out to sit in her swing only to discover, with sharp disappointment, Wade sitting up on his own porch with his perfect bird's-eye view of her. With each morning, Ellie had gotten up a bit earlier in an effort to avoid him, until this morning she'd decided to make it the very break of day. *And still, there he sat!*

No one, she thought angrily, absolutely no one got up at this hour to sit on a porch. This was her time of day, she railed inwardly. How dare he invade her morning. Didn't he have cows to tend or something, if he insisted on getting up at this hour?

Though well aware her thoughts weren't exactly the voice of sound reasoning, she couldn't seem to cool her anger.

Turning directly east, she pushed the swing back and forth, sipped her coffee, tasteless now, and determined to ignore the fact that Wade sat up the hill within sight. She hoped he hadn't seen her staring at him, hadn't noticed her. And she was as angry at him as if he'd done this all on purpose.

It was as if she could feel his gaze upon her, as if he stood right behind her. The hairs on the back of her neck stood up. She would see him this morning, came the whisper into her heart. Just as she had seen him the previous mornings at the cafe. And the pull was becoming stronger between them.

It seemed, all the time now, as she worked she felt Wade's gaze upon her. Once she turned to find him leaning against the stainless-steel cupboard, staring at her. She was so unnerved she'd almost dropped the dishes she carried.

Once a boisterous young man had made some suggestive remarks. She'd considered him harmless enough, was handling the situation, but Wade had suddenly appeared, lifted the man from his seat and showed him to the door. There was something in Wade's eyes then, something Ellie hadn't been able to describe, but something she'd been able to feel.

The way he looked at her made her very aware of herself as a flesh-and-blood woman—not a widow, not a mother, but a full female. When she met his gaze, she was forced to meet the sexuality within herself.

She didn't need that, she thought. Not now. She didn't have time for it, didn't want to face it because she not only didn't understand it but hadn't the least idea how to deal with it.

So thinking, she rose from the swing and went into the house.

Wade stared at the empty swing, imagined he could hear the banging of the door from the small stone house down the hill. The bright white swing still swayed from Ellie's abrupt departure.

He gave a dry chuckle, mocking himself, because he desired a woman he had no business desiring.

She liked early mornings and sitting on the porch. And he was pretty sure his being up the hill on his porch bothered her. If he'd been close enough to see those sky-blue eyes of hers, no doubt they'd have been spitting fire.

Wade didn't know what told him his presence bothered her. Instinct, the energy that vibrated between them, drawing them together without words. He just knew. And after the second morning he'd guessed she was getting up and out on the porch earlier and earlier in the hope of avoiding him. Some perverse twist of his character made him go out on the porch a bit earlier every morning just to see if he was correct.

He drank deeply of his coffee and chuckled inwardly. He'd been right; he knew he had. And something in the way she'd moved this morning told him she was madder than a hornet.

He leaned his head against the tall-backed wooden chair and wondered why he cared, why it should matter if she thought of him at all.

He wouldn't be going into the Last Chance for breakfast this morning—nor for mornings to come. He was finding himself too damn attracted to Eleanor McGrew for his own good.

The following Saturday, Ellie slept past nine. It was wonderful. Her body was gradually getting used to the demands of the waitressing job, didn't actually ache now after one full week of work, but each evening she felt drained of every ounce of energy.

Slipping into a thin cotton robe, she fluffed the damp hair from her neck. Today she intended to get into town and purchase a window fan. The heat hung unbearably heavy in the house at night, causing Ellie to take forever to fall asleep, even though she was totally exhausted every night. Thankfully the girls slept with the abandonment of youth, apparently immune to the heat.

Ellie paused and looked into the mirror. She knew it wasn't only the heat robbing her of a decent night's rest. It was emotional and physical loneliness…frustration. Fairly slamming the hairbrush to her dresser, she pushed the thought away and reached for pins to secure her hair off her neck.

Sara, her nose in a book, barely grunted a good-morning. Their warm moment of the previous week had turned out to be just that—a moment. Sara had again retreated into anger disguised as indifference. And the closer the first day of school came, the worse it got. Ellie knew it was fear of a strange school propelling Sara. And she also knew there was very little she could do to help her daughter—except to be there for her.

She allowed a soft touch to Sara's hair before moving into the kitchen, where she set coffee to brewing. As she pulled bacon from the refrigerator, Rae and Poppy burst into the room and raced to the back door. The floor shook with the rapid pounding of their feet.

"Come and see," Poppy cried, allowing the screen door to bang in her wake.

Curious, Ellie did just that. Stepping out the back door, she saw Rae and Poppy stop in the yard. With eyes shielded against the bright sun, they looked upward. Ellie followed their pointing fingers with her gaze. In the summer-blue sky flew a huge, bright scarlet kite, the biggest Ellie had ever seen. Though quite distant, a good half a mile into the sky from where Wade stood on the hill, the motif of a golden unicorn was clearly visible. The kite danced in the strong, gusty south wind, its four gold and scarlet ribbon tails twitching like those of an angry cat.

"Mama," Poppy cried, her gaze still on the kite, as Ellie approached, "can we go up and see?"

Ellie automatically shook her head, though regrettably as she observed Poppy's eager face.

"Oh, please, Mama," Poppy implored. "Wade said... ouch!" This came at a poke from Rae.

Ellie raised an inquiring eyebrow. "Wade said what?" She bent to look Poppy in the eye.

"See what you did." Rae folded her arms and rolled her eyes skyward in disgust.

"When have you two talked to Wade?" Ellie looked from one to the other of her daughters. She knew they'd been up to something they weren't supposed to be by the expressions on their faces.

Poppy's bottom lip quivered. "Mama, he didn't mind us going up to see. Honest. He even let us fly his kite some." Her angelic blue eyes widened. Then she stepped forward and raised a finger to smooth Ellie's eyebrow. "Don't be mad, Mama. Make your eyebrow come back right."

Ellie choked back a smile. She knew full well her habit of arching her right eyebrow when disapproving; and clever Poppy knew how to disarm her. Her face and eyebrow relaxed and a smile slipped out. Poppy wiggled onto her knee and hooked an arm around her neck.

"I repeat," Ellie said then, firmness returning, "when did you two see Mr. Wolcott?"

"You said Wade," Poppy pointed out.

"All right—Wade. Now when and how much have you two been going up there—against my orders not to?" Ellie lifted her gaze to Rae, the older of the two, the one Ellie held responsible.

Rae shuffled her feet. "Just a few times—when he was flying his kites."

"Since when?" Ellie demanded.

Rae shrugged. "Since a couple of days after we moved in." She didn't meet Ellie's gaze.

"A few days after..." Ellie couldn't believe it; she'd had no clue. How had these little scamps gotten away with such a thing?

Rae looked earnest. "He didn't mind at all, Mama. Really. And it just happened. We were in the woods by the fence once, and he came out to fly this really neat dragon kite, and..." She left off and stared at her sneaker as she rubbed it in the grass.

"And you didn't see fit to tell me, Rae?"

Again Rae shrugged.

"We didn't want you to tell us we couldn't," Poppy said flatly. "And he makes them, Mama." She spoke eagerly, pointing to the kite now flying in the sky. "He's been working on that one for weeks."

"He makes them?" Surprised, Ellie glanced from Poppy to the kite, then looked to Rae for confirmation.

"Yes," Rae said excitedly, sensing Ellie weakening, no doubt. "And he designs them himself. He said this is the biggest one he's ever tried. He had one pretty big last week, and I'll bet we got it up near a mile—maybe two," she elaborated. Her gaze moved to her sister. "Then Poppy made it fall into the trees."

"I did not!" Poppy protested immediately. "The wind..."

"When was this?" Ellie cut in.

"Oh...the day you did grocery shopping after work in the morning," Rae answered hesitantly.

Ellie nodded, remembering that Wade had left the Last Chance early that morning, before she had. She eyed her daughters, debating how to handle this situation.

"You've both disobeyed me," she said after a moment.

Rae looked away, and Poppy's lower lip quivered. She reached to smooth Ellie's eyebrow again, but Ellie moved her head away. "What should I do about this, girls?"

After several long seconds, Poppy answered. "I think you should admit you were wrong. Wade doesn't mind us going up there at all." She peeked at Ellie from beneath long lashes.

Slowly Rae lifted a hopeful face. Ellie wasn't at all certain what to say.

"He really doesn't mind, Mom," Rae said softly. "And we are sorry. We didn't mean to disobey you. It was just..." She let the words trail off.

"So much fun," Poppy finished after a second. "And we were together, Mama. We didn't go alone. And he's really nice, Mama." Her expression sobered. "And we were very polite."

"Oh?" Ellie suppressed a smile.

"Yes. Wade said we were so damn polite it got on his nerves." She shook her golden head disapprovingly. "I told him he shouldn't swear, especially around children." She giggled. "I like him."

"You do, huh?" Ellie said at last, cracking a rueful smile. She sighed. "Okay. We'll let it go." She looked at the eager hope breaking across their faces. "And you can go up to see him and his kites—but don't overdo it, or I'll have to put a stop to it."

"Can we go now?" Rae asked eagerly.

"Can we, Mama?" Poppy echoed.

"Breakfast..." Ellie started to shake her head, but all thought of practicalities broke as she looked at their hopeful faces. "Yes, go... but be home in thirty minutes for breakfast," she called after them.

They flew away across the grass even before she'd finished speaking. Their braided hair gleamed in the sunlight; their short, tanned legs pumped furiously, joyously. Rae stopped to help Poppy through the barbed-wire fence. Looking up the hill, Ellie saw the monstrous dog, Duffy, running down the drive to greet them.

She thought then that Poppy didn't in the least know what it was like to have a father. And Rae barely remembered. Oh, there was their grandfather, but he'd never done much beyond joking and pulling their braids. And, for the moment at least, the girls were separated from even that small contact.

Their world was one of women—as was Sara's, and Ellie's own, for that matter.

It wasn't good for a girl to be without a father, Ellie thought, an angry ache settling into her heart. If only Galen...

No! She wouldn't dwell on if-onlys. That changed nothing. The facts were as they were. The girls had only Ellie herself. She'd just have to keep trying her best to be both mother and father.

Maybe, she thought, turning and walking slowly back to the house, when she got things straightened out, she'd look around for a man who would be a good father to her girls. It couldn't hurt to look.

When Wade's image popped into her mind, she shook her head. Wade Wolcott was a fine, handsome man, but certainly a far cry from father material. Ellie had the feeling he wasn't husband material, either.

While making breakfast, she cast an occasional glance out the window to see the figures up the hill, one tall, one short, one shorter. The unicorn still dipped and swayed in the sky, though it appeared smaller the farther up it went. For some odd and very nice reason, Ellie felt her spirits rise when she looked at it. This morning she wasn't tired or rushed, a breeze blew softly through the window, and she had enough money, at least she hoped, to buy a fan in town that afternoon.

Ellie had begun to think of money in chunks: enough money to pay the electric bill; enough money to buy Sara a smart new outfit; enough money for one roast, for a half gallon of ice cream, a treat of ice-cream cones.

As she'd hoped, her tips had risen since she'd begun working at the Last Chance Cafe the previous week. Mornings she did better than evenings, her tips averaging around eighteen dollars, and growing by a few cents every day. She looked forward to what she would earn when she started working lunches.

Reluctant to ask anyone outright about how to purchase cattle, she listened to talk at the cafe, looked over agricultural magazines lying about and searched the newspaper. Buying cattle wasn't the problem; buying good cattle stock she could count on for breeding was. Which breed? What age? What did she look for in the animal? She had more questions than answers and was afraid, actually certain she was going to have to ask someone. Only she didn't know just whom to ask and was hesitant for fear of looking foolish.

You'll have to get over that, Ellie told herself emphatically.

She'd considered asking Wade, and considered it again now, then tossed the idea aside as too risky. She couldn't risk being near him. And he apparently felt the same, because she hadn't seen him at the restaurant for three days.

It was for the best, she told herself.

Thinking this, she jerked open the refrigerator door and reached in for the carton of milk. Childish voices and laughter floated in from beyond the back door, feet clomped upon the steps.

"I was getting ready to call you two," she said, whirling around to greet Poppy and Rae with a wide smile. When her gaze fell on Wade standing in the back doorway, the words and the smile died on her lips.

There he stood, all six and a half feet of him, filling her doorway, one daughter tugging at each of his hands. Fleetingly Ellie thought she detected a hint of hesitancy on his face, but it passed instantly, if it had been there at all, and his charming, easy grin swept his lips. She definitely recognized the intimate survey he gave her and was suddenly reminded she wore only a short thin gown covered by a long thin robe, both white.

"Good morning, Ellie." It was odd, hearing a male voice in her home, the first since the day they'd moved in. Odd, but not unpleasant.

"We invited Wade to breakfast," Poppy announced, quite proud of herself.

"You can sit over here," Rae said, pulling out a chair for him at the end of the oval table.

Wade hung back, his expression definitely uncertain now. "I know it was unexpected..." He allowed the words to trail off.

Ellie met his gaze. She recognized his hesitancy for what it was—deliberately calculated, as a little boy who's out for something and hopes to get it by appearing properly contrite and undeserving.

She smiled. "We have plenty, Wade. Please do join us." The use of his first name came easily.

She told herself it would be rude not to extend the invitation. After all, she tried to raise her girls to be generous and polite. But even as she thought all this, she also recognized the delight in her heart. She'd extended the invitation because she wanted Wade Wolcott there. Because it was exciting, and too tempting to resist. Especially when he insisted on looking at her like . . . like he enjoyed what he saw.

"Go wash your hands, girls," Ellie told Poppy and Rae. "Please, Wade, sit down. I'll get you a cup of coffee."

While she poured milk for the girls she briefly considered, then discarded, the idea of changing from her gown and robe. She was, after all, covered from her neck to her toes, and to say something like "Pardon me while I change my clothes" sounded a bit ludicrous—and unduly self-conscious.

"Poppy and Rae said you're the best cook in the state," Wade commented, looking at her with lazy eyes. He'd stretched his long legs sideways and seemed very relaxed in the chair.

"I'm sorry, they do exaggerate," Ellie said, bringing the coffeepot and a fresh cup.

Her gaze met his and rested there. His eyes were warm upon her, just for a fraction of time, yet Ellie felt touched, quite intimately.

At the sound of girlish laughter the spell broke. Ellie jerked her gaze away to Rae and Poppy as they rushed into the room, bringing with them all their childish energy and excitement. Sara came behind them, much more subdued.

The hard scraping sound of chairs being pulled close to the table echoed in the room, and Poppy and Rae bombarded Wade with enthusiastic talk about the kite.

"It must have taken a long time to reel it in," Ellie said, extending the plate holding bacon toward Wade.

"Oh, we didn't reel it in, Mama," Rae said. "It's still up there."

"Up there?" Ellie glanced to Wade. "Well...who's flying it?"

He chuckled. "The wind. We just stuck the reel in a holder fixed in the ground. The kite's so high up it'll fly on its own until we get back."

"And we're going back right after breakfast, right, Wade?" Poppy mumbled, a big bite of biscuit in her mouth.

"Right, Petunia."

"Poppy." She giggled.

Ellie looked from her daughter to Wade, amazed at the ease between them. She searched for the words to show her appreciation yet let him know he didn't have to continuously cater to her daughters.

"Thank you for showing the girls your kites, allowing them to fly them," she said. "They really enjoy it." She looked back at Poppy and Rae. "But you two have chores after breakfast. And I'm sure Mr. Wolcott has things to do that don't involve you girls hanging at his heels."

"He told us to call him Wade," Poppy said, her blue eyes wide.

"I'm going to fly the kite a while longer, Ellie." Wade's voice came unusually soft and deep. "The girls are welcome to come up and join me."

"Long as we give him room," Poppy chimed, an impish grin on her glowing face.

Ellie didn't have anything to say to that. She was uncertain about exactly how she felt; she only knew that here she sat, for the first time in five years, in her robe, hair still uncombed, sharing breakfast with a man.

Chapter Eight

Wade sat at the table in Ellie's kitchen, a room transformed from the one he remembered: bright, warm, inviting. The walls were papered in some small, pale, flowered pattern; the light-colored linoleum was shiny enough for a television commercial.

Glancing around, he felt an odd tug of wistful regret and for an instant remembered the plans he'd had for the house eight years before, but he pushed it away. That had been then, this was now.

He looked at Ellie sitting only a foot to his left, close enough for him to repeatedly catch her womanly fragrance, and wondered what in the world had possessed him to come.

Ellie's pale hair was pinned on top of her head, stray wisps brushing her temples. Although the kitchen light was bright, it complimented her face, unlike the harsher lights at the cafe, which magnified the fine lines at the outer corners of her eyes. And the strain that usually held her face when she was working tables was also absent. Her skin stretched creamy smooth, flawless, her cheeks tinged a healthy pink.

She smiled often at her daughters, several times at him, with a smile that transformed her from plain to striking and that reached out and touched a person. Wade felt it happen to him. He fairly itched to stroke her cheeks, to bring his lips to hers. It felt damned unnatural to act completely unaffected.

Unable to keep his eyes off her, he resorted to quick, small glances, so as not to appear to stare. Still, energy surged between them. He felt it, knew she felt it.

And again he asked himself why he'd come. He didn't want to get involved with her.

Wade reiterated the thought very firmly as he looked around at the surrounding females, at the cozy breakfast table, at the oldest girl, who continually glared at him, saying little, and at Ellie herself, dressed in a fully concealing though mighty thin robe.

Since she'd begun working at the Last Chance, she'd seemed quite determined to keep her distance from him, he thought. But then, women sometimes did that just to throw a man off guard. The females Wade had known had always been eager for a permanent relationship. He would've been less than honest if he didn't admit Ellie's attitude puzzled him. With her having the three girls, he'd have thought she'd be coming right after him.

But even now, though she'd gracefully invited him to breakfast and, if Wade could be so proud, seemed actually pleased to have him, she kept an invisible wall between them. One that he could feel as clearly as he could feel the energy drawing them together.

He didn't wait long after finishing his meal, didn't linger over a second cup of coffee, but rose to go, giving polite compliments to Ellie even as he stood. He'd enjoyed a great meal, but to have done so had been a mistake, one he didn't plan on repeating.

"Would you like to join us?" he asked the older girl, Sara. He'd wondered if her sour attitude had to do with feeling left out. She quickly squelched the theory.

"No," she said shortly, her blue eyes openly hostile. "Thank you," she added a full second later after a firm look from Ellie.

Ellie rose and moved to the door with them. "It is still there," she said, as if not quite believing, her gaze fixed on the kite high in the sky.

Wade grinned. "Makes a person feel downright useless."

She smiled that warm smile, only a glance for him, but a long, loving look for the smaller girls. "You two can go for one hour. Then it's home and chores."

Wade had an irrational feeling of being left out. Until he glanced over his shoulder to see Ellie still standing in the doorway, the breeze playing with the hem of her white robe, her gaze fully on him. She wasn't smiling.

He had the sensation then of a shift in the earth. It seemed unnatural to try to deny the pull between them. Desire. He thought the word, putting a name to the pull.

"Did you say something, Wade?" Rae asked, and he realized he'd mumbled aloud.

"Storm clouds—think I see storm clouds coming." He gazed toward the western horizon, not really seeing.

"There's no clouds over there," Poppy said, slipping her tiny hand into his and tugging.

Wade shrugged. He was getting fanciful in his old age, he told himself. He'd known a lot of women, and he'd stayed away from a lot of them. Nothing different in this instance.

Ellie determined to consider the morning Wade had joined them for breakfast as next to nothing. So he'd had breakfast with them—it hardly constituted a close relationship. It had been a courtesy, nothing more. She continued to keep her distance from him while working at the Last Chance, and he certainly made no advances to her.

Wade and Gayla appeared to get on quite well. Not that Ellie cared, but their behavior did seem a bit much. They never missed a chance to touch, and Gayla came more alive whenever Wade entered the cafe.

But gradually Ellie saw that Gayla reacted the same way with several other regular customers—handsome single men who made a point of flirting with the younger woman. And it seemed that Gayla was the one taking every advantage to press herself, her hands, her shoulders, up against Wade. Only one time did Ellie see Wade initiate the contact, and that was to move Gayla away from the hot coffeepot. Not that he didn't appear to greatly enjoy Gayla's attentions. And not that it was any of her business, Ellie reminded herself. But she couldn't completely ignore things what went on right beneath her nose.

She couldn't ignore Lee Ramsey, a lonely man who needed her to take a few extra moments at his table to listen to him repeat the small happenings of his day and his yesterdays. She couldn't ignore Sue Mellon, a young, single, pregnant woman, who needed to be instructed in good nutrition and convinced she hadn't committed an irrevocable sin. Or elderly Edna MacDonald, who couldn't read but didn't want anyone to know, so Ellie always repeated the dinner menu for her in such a way as to gradually be teaching Edna to read—menus, anyway.

These were her regulars, as she called them, her neighbors, and she was beginning to love them. Steadily, she and the girls made a place in the community. The clerks at the grocery and the bank called her by name, Jim at the gas station remembered what oil she needed in her car and she and Gayla often had nice chats by phone on the weekends, when Ellie didn't work.

No longer willing to bear the expense, Ellie had quit telephoning her mother every morning. She couldn't plead for their acceptance forever, she decided. It was gratifying when one evening a telephone call came from her parents. Slowly they were mellowing.

A new window fan, caught on sale, made sleeping at night a pure pleasure, sensual even, with the cool air it generated brushing her skin. Who needs air-conditioning? Ellie quipped to herself.

And it was a big day when she and the girls traded in the Cutlass for a four-wheel-drive pickup. Though a used model three years old, it had low mileage and its tan and brown body shone like brand new. The truck received accolades from Sara, who used slang terms like "rad-style" and "boss." Ellie assumed, by the admiring looks Sara gave the truck, that "rad-style" meant very good. Rae, the perpetual tomboy, raved about it being four-wheel-drive, and tough. Poppy said simply, "Bet Wade will like it." Ellie sighed happily at finally doing something of which everyone could wholeheartedly approve.

The first two days of school had been murder at the house, with Sara practically snapping the head off whoever dared speak to her, but with every passing day, she became more confident. She was making friends and was less lonely for her old ones. Rae, of course, had no trouble, except for her longing for a horse. And Poppy did more than meet changes, she embraced them, a ray of sunshine wherever she went.

Overall, Ellie found herself pleased, content and very much alive. She was doing okay, she judged, taking into account the huge mistake the entire endeavor had been in the first place. She was progressing, inch by inch. If at times she felt an undefinable longing and wished some of the men would flirt with her the way they did with Gayla, she tightened the reins on her emotions. She wasn't the first woman to go through life alone; she wouldn't be the last. She'd handle it.

A week after the girls started school, Ellie began working lunch as well as breakfast and dinner. It was a long haul. Gayla expressed concern over Ellie working so hard, but Ellie was close enough to Gayla to tell her frankly that she needed the money. It was reassuring and kind of nice when Gayla said Ellie had become their most valued waitress.

The first day she worked lunch, she found herself looking out the window nearly every other minute, beginning at twelve-fifteen, when Poppy should have been arriving. At twelve-twenty, she began praying.

Kindergarten met half days; Poppy went in the morning. The school was only three blocks away and the town small and friendly, but still Ellie worried. She'd never allowed Poppy to walk alone anywhere before.

"What's wrong?" Wade asked, his sudden appearance at her shoulder startling Ellie. "You're jumpy as a cat." He, too, looked out the window, as if to see something.

Ellie sighed. "Poppy—she's supposed to come here straight away after her class lets out at twelve." She chewed her lip and again looked out the window in the direction Poppy should come from, unheeding of the coffee she continued to pour.

"Hey—" The urgency in Wade's voice drew her attention back to the coffee. She'd overflowed and just plain missed the cup. "I'll take it." He chuckled as he reached for a rag and helped her with the mess. "She'll be here, Ellie. She's responsible enough to walk from the school."

"I know..." She really did, but it didn't help "mother worries," as she called them.

Suddenly Wade's hand touched her chin; he raised her face so she looked straight at him. "She'll be fine," he said in a calm, mellow voice.

As Ellie looked into his brown eyes, she felt the energy, stronger than ever, and for a moment all else faded from her world, save his nearness.

Gayla's voice brought her back sharply. "Ellie, I'm sorry, but we're going to have to double up today. Lorene won't be coming in."

Turning from Wade, Ellie quickly tried to focus on Gayla's words. "Okay..." She nodded, reaching for a fresh coffee cup. Gayla's curious eyes rested on her for a fleeting second, then the younger woman pivoted and banged through the kitchen door, calling orders.

Ellie hoped Gayla hadn't gotten some mistaken idea about what had been going on between herself and Wade. Because nothing had been going on. Silly to think of it. She turned her thoughts back to Poppy.

For the next ten minutes her nerves wound tighter and tighter as she waited for Poppy. Finally the bell jingled and there stood her littlest, smiling, carefree. Relief washed over

Ellie as Poppy ran forward, waving a colorfully painted picture.

"Hi, Mama...look what I did!" She shook the picture so hard, Ellie saw only a blue, green and orange blur.

"I'm proud of you, sweetheart."

"I'm going to show Wade."

Before Ellie could speak, Poppy ran weaving among the tables to where Wade sat at his customary table. Without so much as a give-me-leave, Poppy scrambled up onto the booth seat opposite him, waving her painting.

Ellie stood holding Mr. Winston's chicken-fried steak and wondered exactly what she should do. Finally she said to hell with complicating emotional problems and took Mr. Winston his steak.

Later, when Wade rose to leave, Poppy trailed behind him. "I'm going to Wade's shop, Mama," she said with a great deal of self-importance.

Ellie's gaze flew to Wade. She'd planned on setting Poppy in the office with colors and paper for the next forty minutes, until she finished her shift. And what in the world did Poppy mean by announcing such a thing? Wade was...well, he wasn't a baby-sitter.

Adjusting one of his Wolcott Machine Shop ball caps over his head, Wade gave an easy grin. "It's okay." He winked at Poppy. "We'll get an ice-cream cone on the way."

How could she be the wicked witch and deny Poppy? Ellie thought sinkingly. She watched them leave, the extraordinarily tall man with the tiny child following along behind. Poppy was growing close to Wade, and it made Ellie uneasy. Her daughter could get hurt. What happened when Wade tired of Poppy tagging along, of Rae and Poppy pestering him about the kites? Their attention was a novelty, no doubt, at the moment, but it would wear off sooner or later—or Wade would take up with a woman who objected to the girls' presence. What happened to her daughters then?

In fact, came a soft whisper, what would to happen to *her*?

Though she kept a tight rein of common sense on her emotions, Ellie couldn't deny that the attraction she felt for Wade seemed to grow hotter with every passing day.

He came rarely in the mornings now, didn't linger over lunch, but she always watched for him, expecting to see his lean frame sitting in the usual booth. She looked for him afternoons when she went home after the lunch shift, knowing more times than not she'd see his tall silhouette against the sky on the hill, holding a thin white line attached to a kite fluttering in the wind.

The deep, slow timbre of his voice, the intent way he looked at her was enough to cause a slow warming to steal over her. Plain desire. And though he'd kept his distance, Wade felt the same. Ellie knew this as surely as she knew that to give into it would be heading down a dead-end road.

Sometimes she chastised herself for being prudish, unnecessarily hard with herself. She wasn't going to up and die if she gave in to the desire. The world wouldn't stop spinning, a glowing red A wouldn't appear on her forehead for all to see. She even doubted very seriously if God would condemn her. He knew and understood.

What would it hurt? *Who would even know?*

But she knew herself well enough to know she couldn't give in to pure desire without her heart following along. It wouldn't be too long before that heart ended up broken. For she was a settling down type of woman and Wade a free-and-easy kind of man. The two did not mix.

She reminded herself of Gayla, who had a crush on Wade. Then she reminded herself that she wasn't a single young girl any longer; she had three growing daughters to consider. To carry on a hidden affair would mean being deceitful with them: the old double standard of do what I say, not what I do. And to carry on a bold, unhidden affair would confuse her daughters, shaking their world, and the gossip would hurt them terribly.

No, it was not to be thought of, Ellie told herself—at least a dozen times a day.

* * *

Though reluctantly, Ellie ended up going to Wade for advice about purchasing cattle. She had a steady income now, making her feel secure in spending the money set aside in the bank. She had to have help, and there was none better than Wade. Not only did he know the type of range she had, he knew the cattle-raising business. Ellie trusted his judgment, and she simply couldn't afford to make any mistakes. Trying to make money from cattle was risky enough. She knew full well she could lose every penny she invested, but she could also make some. And if anyone could make money, it was Wade.

Once decided, she was nervous, yet a twinge of delight touched her. She was glad to have a sound excuse to talk to him. Just this time, she told herself. And nothing would happen between them.

She slipped into the seat opposite him on a rare day when he'd lingered until the end of the lunch-crowd rush. He looked up from the papers he studied, surprise sweeping his face.

"I need to talk to you, Wade," Ellie began, hurrying the words. "About buying cattle."

He nodded. "Okay—what do you need to know?"

"Everything." She spoke in earnest, but he smiled.

"Think you want to sit here all night, Ellie?"

Catching his point, she laughed lightly, then spoke slowly, trying to voice her exact need.

"I need to know what cattle to buy for my land, the best investment." She paused, aligning her thoughts. "I need to have an idea of how much it will cost, what kind of return I can expect, and who to buy from. I have a pretty fair idea of the work involved, the animals' needs, but I need to make certain."

Wade regarded her a moment. "Well," he said slowly, "I can sell you some cattle, good stock. Herefords. They'll do fine. Their feed requirements are simple enough, as well as inoculations and such." He paused and took a deep breath. "The market's down right now, so it's a good time, but the market has been down for a while. You'll break more than even, but I don't think it's a good investment for you."

"You raise cattle," Ellie pointed out.

Wade nodded. "On a pretty large scale, but I sell at different times, spur of the moment." He grinned. "I know people in this business." He rubbed a hand over his mustache and averted his eyes to the table between them, looking thoughtful. "The days of making good money in cattle are over, I'm afraid."

Ellie's heart tightened. "I bought the land to use, Wade," she said. "Are you telling me I can't make money from it?"

"No." He shook his head. "You can make money. But you want to make the most possible."

"Of course."

Wade nodded. "There are a number of ways," he said, his brown eyes filling with interest. "I think you should consider running angora goats."

"Goats?" Immediately Ellie pictured the old cartoon from childhood of the billy goat butting the farmer and chewing up his house.

Wade chuckled. "They're not what you think." He reached for his Stetson lying on the table. "Come on, we'll go see some."

"I . . . I can't just leave," Ellie began, taken by surprise. "I still have to finish with my shift—and Poppy . . . she's with a friend now but she should be along soon."

Shaking his head, Wade took her hand and tugged her from the booth. "Lorene," he called to the girl behind the counter, "hold the fort here. If Gayla comes in tell her I've taken Ellie out to Andrew's place. And sit Poppy down with a malt."

Just as easy as that, Ellie thought, amused and awed at the same time. Reassured by Lorene's smile and nod, she hurried out of her apron and grabbed her purse. It wasn't her nature to drop responsibilities on the spur of the moment. It made her feel uneasy, yet she found it exciting, too.

Again Wade reached for her hand, grasping it tightly in his, leading her from the cafe, not letting go until he'd helped her up into the cab of his pickup. She slid onto the warm truck seat, extremely aware of his nearness—and that she was going off with him, alone.

With the day warm but not blistering, they left the truck windows rolled down. Wind tugged at Ellie's hair, bringing with it the scent of hot concrete and earth. Her skin quickly grew damp. She sat less than two feet from Wade. The pickup fairly filled with his presence: his warm brown eyes shadowed by the wide-brimmed Stetson, his low, mellow voice, his faint scent.

"Andrew's been raising angoras for three years now—he's Gayla's brother," Wade clarified.

"Oh, she's spoken of him." Ellie tried to recall the bits and pieces of what Gayla had said about her brother.

"She thinks the sun rises and sets with him," Wade supplied for her.

Ellie smiled and nodded. "Something like that."

"Andrew's a good kid," Wade said. "Hot-headed sometimes, full of himself, but okay."

She glanced at him, thinking: sounds a lot like the man in this truck.

Wade must have caught her look, because he grinned suddenly and shot her a knowing look of his own. When his gaze flitted down to her shoulders and lower, it was as if he'd touched her. Self-conscious, Ellie averted her eyes to the fields of cotton bordering the road.

"Andrew and his parents had a spat four years ago," Wade said. "Taking what little money he had, Andrew set out to prove himself to his father. He risked his money and about all he could scrape together from friends to purchase a place of his own. And he's done well. Oil was up then; he managed to buy in on a couple wells on his property. Now he looks after his parents' ranch as well as his own. He raises a few cattle, for the family's consumption mostly, but his main livestock interest is in angora goats."

"I've never heard of them," Ellie said.

"You've heard of mohair?"

She nodded. "But I never really considered where it came from."

"You get mohair from these goats, and also a type of angora. It's used for making fine coats, sweaters, upholstery fabrics and the like. Fabric made from it is used a lot by airlines and hotels because of its fireproof qualities."

As Wade went on to speak of the goats, where they came from and how well they adapted to the Oklahoma climate, Ellie paid close attention. Her mind hurried ahead with speculations. Possibilities. She'd noticed that more and more sweaters for sale in stores in the past two years were a mixture of manmade and natural fibers such as wool, angora and mohair. There was a definite trend toward returning to these fibers.

"The demand is growing?" she asked.

Wade nodded. "You bet."

Ellie knew, from what Gayla had said about her older brother, that Andrew was a year older than Gayla and loved the land, the rodeo and money, in that order.

Looking at him, Ellie decided he was what she classified as a nice young man, though at most he could be only ten years younger than she was. He stood a good six feet tall, with auburn hair the same shade as his sister's, and he bore all the usual traits of a rancher: deeply tanned face, well-worn boots, jeans, Stetson and a wide, tooled leather belt.

As Wade introduced them, Andrew stuck out his hand. "Hello, Ellie," he said, giving a wide smile and a firm handshake. "I've been hearing a lot about you." He gazed pointedly into her eyes and kept hold of her hand.

Gently she tugged it away. "I take that as a compliment—I think," she said.

"Oh, yes, ma'am. I meant it that way." His tone dropped a notch; his hazel eyes twinkled warmly. "I been meaning to come into town and meet you, but I've been busy..."

The roundabout compliment and the sudden realization that he was flirting with her brought both pleasure and self-conscious confusion.

"Thought you'd been romancing down in Dallas," Wade said suddenly. Andrew shot him a frown. "This boy here," Wade broke in with a pronounced drawl, "makes it a point to know about all the females in the county, Ellie."

Andrew sent Wade a quick glance, then again turned his winning hazel eyes to Ellie. "This boy is five years past the age of consent." His smile broadened and he stepped closer, taking her elbow. "Allow me to show you our ranch, Ellie."

That he disclaimed Wade's term of boy wasn't lost on Ellie. And she was both flattered and flustered by the attention. Especially when Wade quickly fell in step close to her other side. Feeling sandwiched between two giants, she had the sudden urge to laugh, both from amusement and from nervousness. Controlling the urge, she forced her mind to focus on the goats. These men could play their games; she meant business.

Ellie had the usual woman's reaction to the goats, Wade thought. She fussed over the "cute" little animal Andrew carried over and readily took to the idea that angora goats were raised for hair, not meat.

Though Wade knew all Andrew had to say, he remained close at hand. To help explain things, he told himself, since all this had been his bright idea.

The wind tugged at Ellie's pale hair, and she squinted in the bright light. She didn't hesitate with the questions, good sound ones, Wade realized. Andrew turned on the charm for her, as he did around all women. Wade couldn't tell the exact effect it had on Ellie, but she certainly didn't seem adverse to the attention. When Andrew offered to supply Ellie with goats on time payments with no interest, it seemed to Wade the young man had gone a little overboard. And he found Andrew's attention to Ellie a bit irritating.

"Thanks, Andrew, but we have to be getting back," Wade said when Andrew suggested cool drinks. He looked pointedly at Ellie. "Poppy'll be waiting for us."

"Yes...thank you, Andrew," Ellie said, warmly.

Andrew smiled at her. "You get in touch with me, Ellie. We'll fix you up with stock. I'm available any time to answer any questions you have."

"Be seeing you," Wade said. Impatient with the drawn-out goodbye, he took Ellie's arm and hurried her toward his pickup. He almost wished they hadn't come out; the way

Andrew looked at Ellie, as if she were a peach ripe for picking, grated on his nerves. The kid had no scruples, needed to be taken down a peg. Ellie was a lady.

He helped Ellie up into the pickup, fully aware she could use the side step herself. He caught her scent, cologne mingled with warm body, then slammed the door behind her.

"Andrew's very nice," she said as Wade drove away from the ranch. "Thanks for bringing me."

Wade allowed a grunt of agreement. Ellie shot him a curious look, but remained mostly quiet on the way back to town, her few comments centered on goats.

That evening Ellie sat on her swing, enjoying a cup of coffee. Rae and Poppy watched television in the living room, and Sara worked at the sewing machine in her bedroom.

Ellie pushed the swing gently and gazed out at the shadowy meadow, her mind going over the events of the afternoon. Excitement charged her spirit. A lot remained to be done, but the McGrew clan was about to go into the angora goat business.

The investment sent doubts churning. How much of her money should she spend? What if it all turned out badly? What would happen then? If something happened to Ellie, the girls wouldn't have even what remained in the savings account.

Well, she countered, if she didn't try this, they may have a bit of money, but not near enough to live on anyway. She had to push herself to try.

With round, curious blue eyes, pink noses and gentle faces, the goats had stolen her heart at once. They greatly resembled sheep, though their thick, off-white curly hair fell longer and was straggly, and they had horns that reminded Ellie of mountain goat horns stretching back from their foreheads. Their bodies were also more finely drawn than sheep, and they seemed to make no sound when they were approached, simply scattering fearfully away.

Andrew had led Ellie and Wade around the ranch, explaining the goats' fencing and food requirements. A plus about goats was that they were sheared spring and fall, thus producing a cash crop twice a year. They consumed brush and leaves off low hanging branches as well as grasses, so Ellie's land would be ideal. Two herd dogs could supervise a herd of as many as a thousand goats easily, he'd told her. Herding and guarding came as a natural instinct to the dogs chosen for the work.

The more he'd talked, the more Ellie had liked the idea. She felt certain she could do this. Surely they'd be easier to handle than huge cows. And they were so cute. The girls would readily take to this endeavor.

"Are you thinking of investing in the goats?" she'd asked Wade as they'd driven back to town.

"I already have," he'd answered, oddly terse. "Half of that goat you were petting back there belongs to me."

His words settled the matter in Ellie's mind. If Wade had invested in it, it had to be a good idea.

Now her mind fluctuated between what lay before her to ready the land for the goats and recurring images of Wade. A new barn was needed; the goats had to be protected from rain for five weeks after shearing, or they could die. It was Wade who told her who to see about a barn and the goat fencing. But Ellie hadn't asked him. She didn't want to ask anything more from him than absolutely necessary. She had started now; there should be no further reason to call on Wade.

"Good evening, Ellie."

Wade's voice sounded out of the evening dimness, startling her. She caught the sound of his steps then, and the silhouette of his tall frame came into view. His boot scraped the porch step. So deep in thought, she'd not noticed the sun had set.

"...evening, Wade." She watched him come up the stairs to the porch. His brown hair shone golden in the light pouring through the living-room window. His hands were stuffed into the pockets of his jeans.

Inclining his head, he said, "Mind if I join you?"

Chapter Nine

Though astounded by Wade's sudden appearance, Ellie managed a polite, "Of course ... please do," and slid over to make room on the swing.

Wade eased his tall frame onto the seat; the swing gave and creaked with the added weight. He stretched his long legs out before him, rocking the swing gently with one boot. Ellie noted signs of a recent shower: damp hair, just shaved cheeks, fresh scent of after-shave.

She couldn't think of a thing to say.

"Nice evening," Wade said. He looked completely relaxed, without a care in the world.

She nodded. "Yes." She realized she clutched her empty coffee cup. "May I offer you a cup of coffee?" The question came out stilted, formal. But it was something to say.

He nodded. "I'd like that." He gave his charming smile.

Ellie had the feeling he found the situation—a situation of his making—amusing. Well, she didn't intend to contribute to his amusement, she thought, determined to relax. She opened her mouth to call for Sara, then closed it. She rose. "I'll be just a minute." She cast him an equally friendly and easygoing smile and went into the house. For some odd reason, she'd rather put off the girls' knowing Wade sat on the porch. She dreaded both Sara's disapproval and Poppy and Rae's happy intrusion.

In the kitchen she quickly checked her reflection in the mirror fastened inside the cabinet door. Her hair resembled a vacant bird's nest, and she tried to smooth it with her fingers. With rapid movements she filled two cups with coffee. She paused at the cookie jar, then changed her mind. She didn't care to appear too anxious to please—because she wasn't, she told herself tersely.

She passed quietly back through the living room, behind Poppy and Rae, who remained enraptured with their television show.

Stepping out on the porch, she looked right into Wade's smiling eyes. "Thanks," he said, taking the cup she held toward him.

"You're welcome." It felt odd to ease herself down beside him. Her arm brushed his; her thigh did, too. A warmth flickered into her blood, and immediately she pushed it away, down, though it refused to go out.

"So, Ellie, are you ready to go into the mohair business?" Wade asked, raising the cup to his lips.

"Yes." Ellie nodded, feeling wonderfully positive. "But I'm not certain how many goats to start with. Andrew recommended one thousand, but that's a bit above my budget."

Wade looked thoughtful. "He's selling them to you without interest," he said, giving a wry grin. "I admit, he'll still make money, even with the low price he's asking, but I doubt if Andrew or anyone else will give you such a deal again. You should probably stretch your budget as far as it will go this first time to take advantage of the deal. They'll let you pay for the barn on time, and each goat will end up paying for itself, and fast, at the price Andrew's giving you."

Ellie listened carefully, yet found her attention straying to other thoughts as she looked at his face, gazed into his eyes.

Suddenly aware that Wade was staring back at her, she jerked her gaze away and returned her thoughts to the conversation.

"I'll call about the barn tomorrow. Do you think it will take them over a week to build it?"

Wade shook his head. "Two, maybe three days."

It seemed fantastic it could be done so fast. "It'll definitely take me longer to do the fencing," she said. She stared at the porch floor, her mind picturing the enormous job of stretching the fence around the entire eighty acres. She'd thought her hands rough and sore now. Putting up a fence surely wouldn't help.

"Just take it one day at a time," Wade said then.

She looked up and realized the bleak thoughts must have registered on her face. "Yes." She nodded thoughtfully. That was a lesson she should have mastered by now. Seeing the understanding on his face, she relaxed and discovered she could talk to him, about the goats, about cattle, about the land, no longer feeling foolish or self-conscious.

Forty-five minutes later, he rose to go. He gave her a wide smile as he handed over the coffee cup. "Thank you for the hospitality, Ellie." There was something she couldn't quite read in his eyes, but that set her heart to beating faster. "Good evening."

"Good evening..." She watched him disappear into the darkness and continued to stare after him for long seconds.

"I thought he'd never leave." Sara's sharp voice brought Ellie abruptly back to the present. Sara stood just inside the screen door, and though shadows hid her face, Ellie sensed her scowl.

"What's wrong, Sara?" Ellie had surmised weeks earlier that her eldest didn't take to Wade. But then Sara hadn't been very happy with anything or anyone since they had moved to the ranch. Ellie had put it all down to growing and changing pains. Now she sensed something more to it.

"All the kids at school say Wade chases everything in skirts," Sara said.

Ellie rose and opened the screen door. "All the kids?" she asked as she stepped inside, carrying the two empty cups.

Sara shrugged, not answering. She followed Ellie into the kitchen. "Leah Corbin said Wade used to date both her sisters and some other woman at the same time." Sara paused, waiting for Ellie to reply.

"Wade is a handsome single man," Ellie said, emptying the coffeepot. "I'm sure he dates a lot of women."

"Well, we don't need him around here," Sara said.

Ellie turned to look at her daughter. "No, we don't...but he's been kind and helpful to us, Sara."

"He's just trying to get on your good side."

"You make it sound like he's after something."

"Are you forgetting Daddy?"

Instinct had told Ellie this was coming. "No, darling," she said, reaching to stroke Sara's cheek. "I'll never forget your daddy. And Wade had nothing to do with him."

"Do you like him?"

"Yes, I do," Ellie said, looking straight into Sara's pain-filled eyes. "But there's nothing serious between us. Wade is simply a neighbor and a friend."

She couldn't altogether blame Sara for looking skeptical, she thought in that instant, acknowledging the hidden longings tugging within her. She searched for the words and the courage to be honest with her daughter, who balanced on the brink of womanhood.

"He is a very handsome man, Sara. I find him attractive. But I also must think with my head and not just my emotions. He should remain a friend. There will be many times and many boys for whom you will have to make the same decision."

She was gratified to see a flicker of admiration in her daughter's eyes. Then Sara said cautiously, "He's going to be over a lot because of the goats, huh?"

"We'll see him some, yes. Since his house is right up the hill, I imagine we probably always will."

Sara nodded and turned, the conversation at an end. "Come see my skirt," she called over her shoulder.

"Be there in a minute."

Leaning against the counter, Ellie let out a sigh. Being a parent was darned difficult these days. She wondered briefly if it would have been easier to have boys.

She thought of what she'd said to Sara about her feelings for Wade. Her words had been as honest as she could make them. She'd sounded quite convincing.

She wished now she could convince herself of her ability to keep those words.

Sara felt threatened. It wouldn't only be jealousy of Wade, but of any man Ellie might see, neighborly or otherwise. And Sara was intuitive. No doubt she'd picked up on the vibrations that filled the air whenever Ellie and Wade came near each other. In this case, Ellie felt, no amount of talking would do. It would take time and action on her part. When Sara saw nothing coming of Wade's presence in Ellie's life, she would relax.

But would she see that? Ellie asked herself, the question popping unbidden into her mind.

Of course she would, Ellie thought vehemently, pushing away from the counter.

The following morning, between her breakfast and lunch shifts at the cafe, Ellie purchased and brought home rolls of goat fencing, staples and enough posts to do a small section inside the acreage. Backing to where she would begin, she managed to shove and roll the heavy fencing from the bed of the truck. Then it was back to the Last Chance to work lunch, then hurry home again with Poppy, change into an old shirt and jeans and begin attaching new fencing to the posts already strung loosely with barbed wire.

This was no job for a woman, she thought thirty minutes later, with the eighth smack of the hammer to her finger. Yet she needed to save every penny she had for the purchase of the goats and the barn; there was nothing extra for hiring help. And women before her—the valiant ones that had settled this western land—had strung fencing and much more. If they could do it, so could she!

When another stroke of the hammer went awry and hit her finger, Ellie yelped, then sat back on the grass and

looked at the fencing through a blur of tears. She'd pro-
gressed no further than the first two stout end posts.

She couldn't do this! If she worked until Christmas, she
wouldn't finish the yards and yards lying before her. It was
as if all her dreams and plans swirled away, with no hope of
gathering them again. Squeezing her eyes shut against a
flood of tears, she voiced a silent cry for help.

Almost as if in answer, Ellie heard a noise in the grass.
Opening her eyes, she found herself looking through blurry
vision at a pair of worn brown boots and two legs encased
in faded blue jeans. Both looked familiar. She blinked,
doubting the reality of their existence. But they remained.
Squinting in the bright sunlight, she jerked her head upward, dumbfounded to see Wade gazing down at her. Her
next thoughts were of how foolish and inept she must appear, sitting there in the grass like a pouting child.

He bent and took her hand, lifting her to a standing position, saying, "Thought maybe I could help you . . . just to
get started," he qualified. "If you'd like me to?"

She blinked and blinked again, hoping he couldn't guess
she'd been in tears. Looking downward, she brushed at her
clothes.

He waited for her answer, his brown eyes unreadable, and
Ellie knew he meant to give her a choice, not make it for her.
She appreciated that; somehow it make the help he offered
easier to accept.

She allowed a grin. "I sure could use some pointers." She
felt sheepish. "And strong arms."

Wade grinned slightly in return. "It's not so hard once
you know how."

With sure movements and an easy manner, he showed her
how to tap the staples into the wooden posts before ham-
mering on them. He'd brought a peculiar looking instru-
ment, made just for stretching the fence taut, he told her,
instructing her in its use. With delight, Ellie discovered she
could actually do it.

The sun bore down hot for late September, making the
high wind a blessing. Poppy came along to inspect the

goings on, then, bored, ran off for a game of tag with Wade's dog, Duffy.

Perspiration trickled between Ellie's breasts and dampened the hair around her face. Her back tightened with the constant bending and tugging. A thousand times she thought she'd been crazy to ever consider trying to farm or ranch or anything of the sort. But with every repeat of the thought came an immediate rebuttal and renewed determination. No use looking back at something she couldn't change. She had to make the best of the situation. For her girls, for herself. And she refused to let it beat her.

Wade seemed to work effortlessly. He smiled and joked often, and though tired, even disgusted at times, Ellie found herself smiling and joking in return.

Wade stopped and removed his chambray shirt. His skin stretched tan and sleek over muscular shoulders, back and chest. After one good look, Ellie averted her eyes. She could avoid looking by keeping her eyes to the fence and posts, but she couldn't avoid the warm smell of him, the mellow sound of his voice or the awareness that tugged deep within her. Wild fancies of making love in the softness of the tall grass flashed into her mind. With difficulty, she shooed them out.

Then, gradually, she forgot all else but her fatigued and aching body. She moved slower and slower.

Securing the fencing to the metal posts required only strength of hand, of which Ellie seemed to have precious little. Though encased in gloves, her fingers ached from using pliers to bend clips that held the fence in place against the metal posts. And at least once on every wooden post she smacked her finger with the hammer. At times puffing with the exertion, she pushed herself to work as hard as she possibly could. This was her place, her responsibility.

Sara and Rae calling from the back step of the house alerted her to the time. Four o'clock, and the dinner shift awaited her. She stood back and realized with a start that they'd fenced nearly to the corner post to the south. All she could think was: thank God.

"I've got another hour free," Wade said. "I'll just finish to the corner."

The eyes Ellie turned to him were glassy with fatigue. She didn't argue, simply nodded, saying a soft, "Thanks." She peeled off her gloves and bent to pick up her hammer and pliers. She had trouble straightening. With a nod and a small smile, she walked stiffly up the inclining ground to her house. Pain showed with her every step.

Wade didn't like it; she'd been too exhausted to even argue with him about his help. He bit back the suggestion she skip her shift at the Last Chance. She was old enough to know what she had to do. It was her choice, her life.

He turned his back, uncomfortable with watching her. "Damn fool woman," he muttered as he continued with the fencing. He thought of himself: "Damn fool man!"

When twilight settled across the land that night, Wade stepped out on his porch, his gaze going directly to the small stone house down the hill. He looked for Ellie, disappointed not to see her. It was the first evening since she'd moved in that she hadn't sat on her swing. He knew she must be exhausted, maybe even in pain. For a brief few minutes he considered going down to check, then talked himself out of it—what business did he have doing such a thing?

He popped the top on a beer and settled down into a chair. Confusion swirled within him, a confusion that had been mounting in the past weeks. It was foreign to him; usually he knew exactly how he felt, exactly in what direction to head.

But somehow in the past weeks, Eleanor McGrew had settled herself into his thoughts. She was there mornings when he sat on his porch, when he saw her for breakfast at the cafe—hell, even before he saw her. She just plain popped into his mind all the time.

It made him feel out of control, not at all certain of what he was going to do. For instance, he hadn't in the least planned to take her out to Andrew Lutz's place, nor had he intended to go down and help her string fencing today. He'd just found himself doing it.

He didn't like the feeling.

And he was angry at her, too. Why in hell had she taken on a job big enough for two men, much less one woman? Why did she have eyes the color of the sky in winter and full breasts that beckoned his gaze? Why did she have to move her hips with that gentle sway and carry a scent that lured a man?

And why in hell had she come to buy that house and work in his cafe where he had to look at her all the time?

She could have gotten a job in the city and put her money in the stock market—ranching wasn't much more certain and constituted a whole lot more work. Especially for a woman.

Still, grudgingly, he admired her determination. She was going after something she wanted. The lady had guts.

He considered for a moment the possibility that he could be falling in love with her. It didn't seem likely, though he frankly admitted himself a poor judge. The one true brush he'd had in his life with love had left a bitter taste in his mouth.

Telling himself he was being as loco as she was, he pushed from the chair and went into the house to work on a kite. His thoughts remained free of Ellie for all of fifteen minutes. And she was there when he retired to bed.

Wade knew he desired Ellie, perhaps more than he ever had any woman—at least more so than he had in years. And he debated what he should do about it. What he could do about it.

The following morning, he watched for her to walk down to the meadow. It being Saturday, he had no doubt she'd be at fencing again, all day, no matter how tired or hurt she was. He would have gone first thing and started on the fencing himself, but he suspected she wouldn't appreciate it. The woman had a lot of pride.

When he saw her, nearing ten o'clock, he gathered his tools and went to join her. Whistling for Duffy to come along, Wade continued whistling as he strode down the hill.

Ellie had known he would come even before she heard his familiar whistling. She didn't turn around. She wasn't certain how to react, or even how she felt. Lord, she was confused. Tired and achy, too.

But some bit of joy touched her spirit. She was glad for Wade's help, for his presence—and, doggone it, for today, at least, she refused to deny it. She would enjoy it.

Squinting in the bright sunlight, she looked at the fence they had strung the previous afternoon. Glared at it was a better term. She thought of all the work that lay before her, and silently vowed it wouldn't best her. Yard by yard, she'd get this done—and she'd be smart enough not to turn down Wade's help, too.

She'd left Sara in charge of seeing the housework done, with her sisters' help. And there was a yard to mow and clothes to wash. It was more responsibility than she'd ever required of her daughters, but Ellie knew it was time she did require it of them. And she had precious little choice.

"Hi," she said, turning to greet Wade when she could no longer ignore his approach.

"Good morning." He grinned slightly, then moved to test the tautness of the fence.

"Thanks for all you did yesterday," Ellie said.

Wade nodded. "Ellie—" he paused, his brown eyes questioning. "Why don't we just get this straight and save a lot of pussyfooting around? I admit, you're one hell of a capable woman. But you can't do this job alone." He pushed his ball cap to the back of his head. "I have plenty of time to help you—and I don't mind, long as you're not set on doing it all in one day. So let's just consider that I'm in on this job until we finish, okay?"

She'd never expected him to say that. But she was glad he had. Immensely glad. She couldn't help chuckling as she stuck out her hand. "It's a deal," she said.

Chuckling with her, he took her hand in a firm shake, his big palm rough against hers. Then, instead of letting go, he tugged her toward him and lowered his head. The next instant his lips brushed hers. Fleetingly, giving Ellie the feel of the feathery softness of his mustache and the velvet warmness of his lips and sending a quick flickering of desire swirling up from the recesses of her body.

He held her gaze. Gold flecks shimmered in the brown of his eyes. Desire reflected there, boldly.

Ellie broke the gaze. "We'd better get started," she said, forcing her voice from her throat.

She struggled to control her fluttering heart. She felt herself running, hiding from the potential the kiss invoked. And she felt foolish, certain she should say something, but unable to think of a rational word. So she simply turned to the work at hand.

She started slowly, but soon found the kinks worked out of her muscles. The sun felt good on her back, the wind cooling as perspiration gathered at her hairline and dampened her blouse. Soon, as he had the day before, Wade removed his shirt—and again Ellie tried to keep her gaze fixed on the wire, on the posts, on the clips and nails. She wondered if he realized this—and how he'd feel if *she* were to take *her* blouse off.

After nearly two hours, Rae, Poppy and Sara came down with a picnic basket of sandwiches and soft drinks. Giving in to Rae and Poppy's pleas, they moved to the shade of a cottonwood tree for a picnic. Sara declined to join them.

"I have stuff at the house to do," she said, speaking shortly.

"She's waiting for a boy to call," Rae teased.

"Sara," Ellie said, "it's nice out here. Stay awhile."

"Do I have to?" Sara glowered, glancing quickly at Wade then back to Ellie.

"No...of course not," Ellie said, disappointed and embarrassed at her daughter's rudeness.

Sara turned and strode quickly away. Ellie watched her retreating back for a moment, then turned her attention to the laughter and teasing going on between Wade and her younger daughters.

Poppy plagued Wade with "why" and "how come" questions. Why is the sky so blue? Why does the inside of Duffy's mouth have black splotches? How come Wade lived all alone?

Though embarrassed by the last question, Ellie listened intently for the answer. She'd been wondering the same thing.

"Because no one will put up with me," Wade answered, teasing.

"I would," Poppy said seriously.

"Thanks, Pumpkin."

"Poppy!" She giggled. "Don't you have a mother?"

"Yes," Wade answered. "She lives in Florida."

"Have you ever been married?" This came from Rae, entering the conversation.

Wade's gaze moved and settled on Ellie. She just looked back, trying to repress a grin, allowing her gaze to tell him he was in this one alone.

Amusement traced his eyes and lips as well. "No," he said. "I almost made that fatal mistake once, but was saved at the last minute." For an instant, Ellie thought she read sadness in his face, but the impression passed so quickly she couldn't be certain.

"What's fatal?" Poppy asked.

"Causing death," Rae answered.

Poppy looked curiously at Wade. "I don't get it."

He tugged her braid. "Doesn't matter anyway, Peanut."

As Poppy and Rae lugged the picnic basket back to the house, Wade stood, then extended a hand to help Ellie up from the grass. Ellie's bones protested, but she refused to let the fact register on her face.

"Thanks," she said, tugging her hand from his, feeling suddenly shy, very aware of being alone with him and of her body's response. Falling in step beside him, she walked back to the fence. The sun shone hotter now; but the wind blew cooler.

Glancing toward the house, Ellie saw Poppy and Rae enter the back door and Sara come out, carrying a sheet to the clothes line.

"I'm sorry about Sara, Wade," she said, pulling on her gloves. She looked at him. "She's not usually rude. She's really a very sweet girl. It's just that the move out here was hard for her...leaving a home she'd known since she was nine, her friends, her grandparents.''

He nodded and bent for a hammer. "Just plain growing up is enough problem for a kid," he said. He gave a wry grin. "I caused my parents all kinds of gray hairs.''

"You?" Ellie gave a wicked grin. "Come now. I'd imagined you perfect.''

He laughed. "Maybe my problem was that I imagined myself the same way." He took hold of the fencing and pulled it against the post. "Actually, my father wanted me to be perfect according to the Navy book of regulations. And my idea of perfect wasn't the same." There was a cutting edge of sadness in his tone.

"They...your parents...live in Florida?" she asked.

Wade nodded. "I have a brother and a sister. We're all scattered. Never were close. My father loved and lived for the Navy, and my mother did the same for him. I left home when I was eighteen, right after high school." He stood back from the fence to catch his breath. "I go home every couple of years. It works out best for everyone that way.''

Ellie wondered about his mother. Didn't she miss him? Ellie couldn't imagine ever being so distant from her daughters. Her heart gave a quick tug as she thought about her current estrangement from her own mother.

Aloud she said, "How long have you lived here?"

"About ten years." He inclined his head toward his house. "The house and the land belonged to my aunt, Netta Halpern. I came out here, visited and helped her get the place straight, then just sort of settled in. Netta and I got along." By the way he spoke, Ellie could tell he'd been very fond of his aunt. "She died three years ago. Left the ranch to me and a nephew up in Tulsa. I bought him out, and here I am." He paused and looked at her. "Now your turn. How'd a city lady like you get out here?"

"Well—" Ellie finished fastening a clip "—I was raised in the country. Down south of Norman. My parents had a farm and Daddy ran a small concrete business. When I was about Sara's age, Daddy sold the farm and moved his business to the city." She gazed at the rolling hills and woods, remembering. "Like Sara, I didn't want to move. Galen—my husband—and I had planned to move out to the country and do a bit of farming. He was an accountant."

"How long were you married?" Wade asked.

"Almost nine years. He died five years ago—a freak thing—blood clot traveling to the heart." She spoke of it in a straightforward manner. It no longer hurt; in fact, she had little feeling about it at all. It was done and over. She didn't realize she'd stopped talking or moving and simply crouched where she worked at the fence, staring, until Wade spoke.

"You must have loved him a great deal." His voice came deep and soft.

She glanced up to see his brown eyes boring into her.

"Yes," she answered. "We'd gone steady since my sophomore year in high school, married when I was nineteen and Galen about to finish college." She stood and gave a small smile. "We were lucky. We had nine good and wonderful years, and I have those years to remember. Sometimes I think there are few people who find the happiness with each other that we did."

Wade nodded and looked away. "You got that right." He worked at a clip.

Ellie was surprised by the personal conversation, and yet not so. It seemed perfectly natural to talk with Wade like this. She watched his face, wondering at his last comment and the hint of bitterness there. She was debating whether to ask about the "fatal mistake," as he'd called it, when he spoke, his voice almost startling in the quiet that had sprung between them.

"I was almost married, once," he said. "I bought your house—" he nodded toward it "—this place. The old couple who'd originally built the house wanted to retire to the city. It was close and a fair price. I didn't think it too good an idea to bring another woman into Netta's home, but I didn't want to be too far away from her, either. She was ailing by then." Ellie caught the pain in his voice.

"What happened?" she asked quietly when he paused and seemed uncertain about going on.

"A misunderstanding. She thought I had a lot more money than I did, and that I'd move away into the city just because she wanted to." He shrugged. "I guess we were both fooling ourselves. I wanted no less than she wanted from me, only in a different direction. And neither of us wanted to give in." He smacked at a staple in the wood post. "She left, had our baby she was carrying aborted."

A dull pain reverberated with his words. And Ellie knew this was a wound Wade carried deep within him. One that, in hearing, had left a ragged scar. She sensed a loneliness in the man. And felt her own loneliness like never before. It was as if a strong and vibrant thread of understanding connected their hearts. Side by side, they continued to work, their minds and motions in rhythm with each other.

Ellie told him about her parents and how they'd always been overprotective of her, how she'd left their care and gone into Galen's. She even laughed. "I guess this is the first time I've ever really left home."

Wade told her how his father had virtually kicked him out of the house. It was join the Navy or leave—either way, he had to get out. He didn't seem critical of his parents. He spoke of places he'd seen, things he'd done.

They talked of the Last Chance Cafe, and Wade told how he'd come about owning it. "A loan situation he'd found himself in," was how he described it. The owner preferred signing over the cafe to paying cash back on the loan. Wade had remodeled, hired Gayla and had been making a profit ever since, if only on his own free coffee.

Their talk turned to the land, Wade's ranching endeavors and then Ellie's plans. They discussed problems with the goats and ways to solve them and estimated profits. Grossly overestimated, Wade joked, but it was fun. They teased and laughed easily. Ellie forgot worries over money, concerns over Sara, and even the ache of her hands and back. The day was balmy, the sky the bluest blue, the strong breeze fresh against her face.

"Why are you doing this, Ellie?" Wade said, pausing to lean against a set of wooden brace posts. His brown eyes regarded her seriously. The wind tugged strands of hair across his forehead.

Ellie paused, too, thinking out her answer.

"I didn't realize it at the time, but I think now I did this mostly to make a break from my parents and the life I'd been living for the past five years." She gave a soft snort. "I was running from it—as hard as I could." She shrugged. "But I was trying to run *to* something."

Encouraged by the understanding in his eyes, she continued. "It was something Galen and I had wanted to do. And one day I realized I still wanted to do it. It seemed grossly unfair not to be able to simply because I was alone now. I guess I rebelled against my limitations, as if by denying them they wouldn't exist." She looked at the land. "I wanted— still want—something substantial for my girls. Something that can provide for them now and later in life. Something we have pride in because we've built it. And I want to do something on my own."

"Have you counted the cost?" His eyes filled with concern.

Ellie shook her head, looked away at the land before her, then back to Wade. "I thought I had, but no...I didn't realize." She gave a small smile. "I think sometimes it's better not to count the costs—or only to figure them as you go along—because if you start out looking at costs, you may be too afraid to begin. And then you never get anywhere."

The warmth and respect she recognized in his eyes touched her. He brought his palm to rest against her cheek. Automatically she closed her eyes and leaned her face into that rough palm, relishing and taking strength from the caring touch of another human being. A very male human being.

A glowing, vibrating warmth began inside her. Ellie opened her eyes to see Wade's gaze hard upon her. His pupils were very small, and suddenly she knew without doubt: she wanted him.

The sharp, staccato beeping of a horn made Ellie jump. Wade raised his gaze to look beyond her shoulder. Turning to follow his gaze, she struggled to bring herself back to the moment at hand.

A pickup truck bumped over the pasture toward them, and the horn sounded again. Ellie didn't know the truck, but as it pulled to a slow stop, she recognized Andrew Lutz behind the wheel.

Chapter Ten

Wade felt his hackles rise the second Andrew stepped from the truck and focused his charming smile directly on Ellie. This reaction to Andrew was foreign to him, and he tried to sluff it off. It wasn't easy; especially when Andrew jumped right in with eager assistance on the fencing.

Ellie was a grown woman, Wade told himself, as the three of them stretched fencing, hammered staples and bent wire. She could handle the situation—any way she pleased.

Again she didn't appear adverse to Andrew Lutz's attention.

When Sara, Rae and Poppy came down with an afternoon snack, Wade found it oddly consoling that Rae and Poppy didn't appear overly impressed with Andrew—and oddly irritating that Sara did. At least Sara smiled and spoke to Andrew. She frowned darkly at Wade. Wade felt like a triumphant kid when Rae brought him the biggest glass of iced tea and Poppy saved him the best piece of apple pie.

At five o'clock, Ellie, her face etched with fatigue and pink with sunburn, announced it was time to quit. "May I offer you gentlemen dinner?'' she said. Wade could tell her hands ached when she stripped off her gloves—but she wouldn't allow it to show on her face. Instead, she smiled. "Sara put a roast on this afternoon. Inside of an hour, I can offer you all the trimmings to go with it.''

"Thanks, Ellie,'' Andrew said with his charming-boy smile. "That's music to a single man's ears.''

She smiled broadly at him, then looked at Wade, her blue eyes questioning.

He nodded. "We'll finish here and be up there in about forty-five minutes.'' He found himself glad when she pressed a hand to his wrist, like a special goodbye, before she walked away toward the house. With quick, firm motions, he fastened fencing to a post, intent on stringing a few more yards before quitting.

With Ellie gone, Andrew apparently figured himself done, stood back, peeled off his gloves and stuck a dip of chewing tobacco in his cheek.

"Wade,'' Andrew said after a minute of watching Wade work, "is there anything between you and Ellie?''

"Depends on what you mean by anything.''

"Well, I don't want to be stepping on your toes, old man.''

Wade knew Andrew was paying him back with the term old man. "Eleanor McGrew is my neighbor,'' he said, giving a hard tug to the fence. He stopped and looked at Andrew. "She works in my cafe. She's a woman alone who needs help with this job. I guess it's always been our way out here to help a neighbor. That's about the size of it.''

Andrew studied him a minute before letting out a small, crooked grin. "Okay—just wanted to know how things stand.''

"Ellie's a lady, Andrew. A grown woman with three daughters.''

"I have eyes, Wade.''

"You're nearly ten years younger than she is, Andy.'' Wade paused in his work and looked at the younger man.

"Nine,'' Andrew corrected, then shrugged. "I'm a grown man with a house and a solid ranching business.''

Wade nodded and said no more. It wasn't his place to butt in. And like as not, Andrew was simply flirting with Ellie. Nothing to make a big deal about. *And what did he care anyway?* Wade asked himself.

With Wade and Andrew's help, the fencing got done. Many times in the following weeks, Ellie returned home from the lunch shift at the Last Chance to find Wade at work on the fence. Several times Andrew was with him. It became almost routine to have both men for dinner at the McGrew house. More than a few nights Ellie stayed up late, baking sweet breads, pies and cookies especially for Wade and Andrew. It was the only repayment she could offer and it helped her keep her pride.

A new galvanized-metal barn was erected in the pasture, stacks of supplementary winter feed were hauled into storage in the old barn and eight hundred angora goats with about seven weeks' growth of hair on them arrived. Accompanying them were two Australian Blue Heeler herd dogs, which Rae immediately christened Mutt and Jeff. Ellie and her girls were in business.

Ellie tried not to panic about the mounting bills from her investment. They would be paid in the spring. She hoped to make enough from the first shearing of the goats, if not to pay for them, at least to go a long way in offsetting what she owed for them and their care.

It had been a hard decision, but after extensive figuring, she'd decided she could purchase eight hundred goats from Andrew. She decided to dip into the money saved for the payment due Wade in the spring, leaving her less than she owed him. But not too much less, she reasoned and, she hoped to make up this money from her waitressing pay. If shearing time came early enough, she'd have plenty of money to pay all her immediate debts. She knew she was walking a very fine line, but decided to take the risk. As Wade had said, the deal with Andrew was simply too good to pass up.

In the following weeks, with the girls' help, she successfully handled her three shifts at the Last Chance and all the chores around the house and farm. The goats thrived, their valuable hair growing thick and long. And Ellie felt more secure. Though she'd chosen a hard road, she was making it.

Both Wade and Andrew dropped by often, checking to see how things were going. Between them, Ellie learned the business of raising angora goats, spotting problems before they arose, handling inoculations and lice and keeping the animals clean.

Andrew was affable and charming, so much like his sister Gayla that one couldn't help liking him, even though at times Ellie found his habit of chewing tobacco unpleasant and his bent toward fun a bit overdone. He was just young, she told herself. A nice young man whom she was glad to call a friend, to whom she owed a lot.

Wade remained distant, though polite, and visited just long enough to inquire as to the state of things. Rae and Poppy continued to join him flying kites on the hill, but those sessions were becoming fewer as cooler wet weather set in. Poppy still joined Wade for lunch at the cafe while waiting for Ellie to finish her shift.

Sara settled into her surroundings and felt more secure. But she didn't like Wade's visits, short as they were apt to be, and she let the fact be known. Ellie knew Sara must have sensed the attraction between herself and Wade, because her daughter's reaction to Andrew was completely different. Sara always greeted Andrew with an easy, welcoming smile, finding no threat in this direction.

Ellie herself wasn't quite certain where everything stood with Wade—not on his side, not on her own.

A bond of some sort, though Ellie found it hard to describe, had developed between them. Gratitude was a big part of it. She never could have gotten where she was without his help. She'd cherished the time they'd worked together on the fence. The physical labor had tired her, yet doing it and talking with Wade, she'd found relaxation and peace from the other strains in her life—if not from the one strain that repeatedly raised its head to mock her, that of her physical attraction to him.

Trapped between the caution of good sense and the irresistible tug of desire, she dared neither to give in to the gnawing hunger nor to turn firmly and resolutely away.

It was during these weeks that one of life's glorious moments occurred. Ellie's parents visited the farm. The girls greeted their grandparents with unbridled delight. Ellie found it harder to act as if the rift had never existed; her heart still bore the scar of hurtful words.

Without any apologies, her parents looked around, interested in every small detail of the house and the land. Apprehensive, fearful of their disapproval, Ellie showed them the goats and explained what she was about.

When her father said, "You've done well, daughter," Ellie thought she would explode with joy. His pale blue eyes looked straight into hers. Ellie returned the look, tears blurring her vision. Her father opened his arms. She went into his embrace and stayed for what seemed a very long time.

"Can I make you a gift of some money?" her father asked as he and her mother prepared to leave.

Ellie looked at him. Pride and a lingering hurt told her to decline.

Then suddenly she realized the pettiness of her emotion. She saw the contrite look on her father's face, became distinctly aware of his growing age. Her mother looked hopeful, the sharp, early winter wind mussing her usually perfect hairstyle.

"I'd like that, Daddy," Ellie said then, all resentment gone. "Rae wants a horse and I haven't been able to afford one."

Pleasure and relief swept her father's face; her mother gazed lovingly at first her husband then Ellie. The rift between them was healed.

Ellie stood in the drive and waved as they drove away. She stood looking at the land around her after they'd gone. Pulling her coat tighter against the biting chill, she sucked in a deep, cool breath. The air tasted of winter.

She had her dream, that of a freer, new life, but at that moment it seemed terribly empty. Her heart squeezed.

She had the land, the house, the type of life she'd wanted for her girls. And she had them, three beautiful, loving daughters. She was not alone. But she felt so. She had no man, no mate, to share it all with.

The Saturday Sara came home with her lovely long hair cut short, Ellie thought she handled herself quite well—considering the fact that she wanted to rant and rave and jump up and down.

Sara had stayed overnight with a friend and arrived home in mid-morning. A hat covered her head. "Mama, I have something to show you," she said, entering the kitchen.

Ellie looked up from where she sat at the kitchen table, studying reports on angoras. "Hi, sweetheart. What is it?"

Sara, her anxious face alerting Ellie to something dire to come, slowly removed the hat. Ellie stared at her daughter's head. The beautiful, sleek, glowing blond hair was gone. Oh, it was still blond, but now it was trimmed at the back, shaped up around her ears and cropped close on top, with bangs just feathering her forehead.

Ellie's voice stuck in her throat. She was fearful of saying anything lest it came out in a high scream. She looked at Sara's apprehensive face.

"Lynda's mom is a hairdresser. She knows all the latest styles. She did it for free." Sara's words came in a rush. "Do you like it, Mama?"

Ellie's mouth felt dry as cotton. "But...it is a good job," she offered, rising to inspect her daughter's hair. Where, she cried inwardly, was her baby's hair? The new haircut made Sara appear so much older. "I liked it long, Sara."

"I know, but I'm almost fourteen, Mom. I wanted a change." Her chin jutted stubbornly. "It is my hair."

"We could have talked about it. I would have gone with you to a hairdresser."

"I just decided last night. Lynda got a new style, too. Haven't you ever wanted to do something on the spur of the moment...something crazy and fun?" Ellie's heart tugged at Sara's anxious expression.

She nodded. "Yes...yes, I have." She continued to stare at Sara's hair, wishing it were a dream.

"Do you like it, Mom?"

Ellie knew she had to speak, had to say something calm, something reasonable.

"It's not really my kind of style, but it looks very nice on you, Sara. Lynda's mother did a wonderful job."

A pleased smile slipped across Sara's lips. She touched her hair. "I like it. It was sort of a shock at first, but it feels good, free like." She whirled around, saying, "I'm going to show Rae."

Ellie stared at the doorway after Sara had gone. Then, very quietly she reached for her coat, pulled it on and headed out the back door. With long strides, hands tucked into her pockets, unheeding of the light misting rain, she walked across the yard, through the gate and into the meadow.

Some of the goats lingered in the shelter of the trees; some had taken shelter in the barn. Those nearby scattered as Ellie came near. Jeff ran out to greet Ellie, accepted a pat, then ran back to his charges. Ellie continued on to the far side of the barn. Reaching it, knowing she was hidden from the house, she leaned upon the cold tin wall and cried with hard, wracking sobs.

Her Sara wore a size thirty-four bra and now looked close to twenty. Where was the tiny baby girl she'd held in her arms? Where were the times when Ellie could soothe every disaster with a kiss?

And Ellie herself was five months away from the age of thirty-five and sleeping alone. Like a knife the thought sliced through her, though she recognized perfectly well the absurdity of the emotion.

She didn't know how long she leaned against the barn and cried, wasn't even aware of her surroundings until a firm hand suddenly fell heavily upon her shoulder.

She jumped and twisted around with the pressure of the hand. Wade stood very close, looking down at her beneath the wide brim of a Stetson.

"You've been out here twenty minutes that I know of," he said. "In case you haven't noticed, it's raining."

She jerked away from his hand. "I don't need your advice at the moment." The sobs started afresh, and she didn't care one bit that Wade stood there watching.

"Why don't you stand in the barn? That way at least you wouldn't get wet."

"I . . . I didn't want to bother the goats . . ." she mumbled through her sobs.

"Bother the goats?" Wade said, his voice incredulous.

Irritated at his presence, Ellie turned away. She didn't want to see or talk to anyone at the moment. She wanted to wallow in her irrational feelings without interruption! Since she'd neglected to bring a tissue, she wiped her nose across the sleeve of her coat. Cold water dripped from her hair and ran down her cheeks, mingling with the tears.

Wade touched her elbow. "Come on up to the house."

The pressure of his hand on her arm strengthened and Ellie complied, allowing him to lead her up the hill. She didn't care, knew only that she couldn't go back to her own house at the moment. She couldn't face Sara, any of the girls, yet. Uncontrollably the sobs continued.

Wade opened the door and led her inside a large kitchen. He took her coat and sat her in a chair at the table. And all the while Ellie cried, seeing everything through a blur of tears. She didn't care if Wade observed her irrational behavior, and she silently cursed the entire world.

Wade thrust a box of tissues at her then left the room. Ellie sniffed and tried to stifle the sobs wracking her chest. She pressed a tissue to her eyes and blew her nose with another one. The sobs came softer but refused to cease. Returning, Wade tossed her a towel. She rubbed it over her wet hair.

Bringing two cups of coffee, he plunked one on the table beside her, then lowered his tall frame into another of the chairs. Ellie felt his keen regard and embarrassment finally seeped in as she began to return to her senses. But she couldn't manage to stop crying.

"What is it?" Wade asked.

"I . . ." Fresh hard sobs started. "I'm going to be thirty-five and . . . and Sara cut her hair," Ellie mumbled through the sobs. "She looks like . . . like some rock star."

Wade said no more and gradually Ellie succeeded in getting herself under control. She felt old, worn and run over by life.

"Drink your coffee," Wade said.

Ellie reached gratefully for the warm cup. She'd not noticed before how cold she felt. After drinking deeply, she glanced sheepishly toward Wade. "Thanks."

"You're welcome."

His gaze remained hard, and Ellie looked down at her coffee. Everyone's allowed to be a fool sometimes, she told herself.

"Hey. . ." She glanced up to see him grinning wryly. "I'm thirty-eight. It ain't so bad."

A small smile sprouted within her. Taking a deep breath, she sighed. "I guess I did sort of lose control of sane reasoning." She breathed deeply again, making certain her sobs would not return. "I just feel so over the hill. When I saw Sara's hair it made me realize that in a few short years she'll leave me—off to college or to get married. She's not my little girl any longer. She's practically grown up, and it was only yesterday that I held her in my arms . . ." The ache returned in full force, but thankfully not the tears.

Wade got up and brought more coffee to freshen what remained in Ellie's cup. Casting him a thankful glance, she drank the hot, dark liquid. Wade again sat in the chair near hers. They were quiet but not uncomfortably so. Ellie's nerves gradually settled.

For the first time she took in her surroundings. A country-style kitchen large enough to contain a couch, an easy chair and a portable television. Newspapers lay in a pile beside the easy chair, slippers near the couch. The room smelled of fried onions and sausage, and a large pot simmered on the stove. An inviting room, it spoke of a man's life, as if never touched by a woman.

"I have to get back to the house," she said after finishing her coffee. "The girls will be worried." She stood up, looked around for her coat and spied it hanging from a standing coatrack.

Before she could move to get it, Wade rose to stand very near. Putting his hands on her shoulders, he turned her to face him. Placing his hands on her cheeks, he tilted her face upward, forcing her gaze to meet his. Ellie's breath stopped in the back of her throat as she gazed into his brown eyes.

"I see a very beautiful woman," he said, his voice firm. "A woman in the prime of her life."

Then his lips lowered toward hers.

Automatically Ellie closed her eyes and parted her lips, her entire being awaiting his touch.

His kiss came sweetly, druggingly, sending the pulse beating in her ears and longing spiraling throughout her body. His mustache brushed soft against her skin, his tongue flicked into her mouth, exploring. Her arms rose and her hands clenched the soft fabric of his flannel shirt at his waist. His kiss deepened and Ellie met him, measure for measure.

Wade drew away. His eyes were glazed with passion, passion Ellie herself felt. She thought she could not only hear his heart beating but feel it as well, although they only touched each other with their hands. His palms moved at her cheeks, and she felt their roughness.

The next instant, Wade pulled her to him and kissed her again, this time rough and demanding. His hands moved hungrily over her body. Exultation flooded Ellie. She pressed against him, delighting in his hard, strong body. With his hands firmly on her hips, he moved against her.

As a person starved for food, she grasped the moment and the feeling and held it to her.

When at last Wade raised his head, they both gasped for air. Wade's eyes were warm and questioning, even mesmerizing. Dazed, she stared into those eyes, then ran her gaze over his face. Tentatively she stroked his mustache. The hairs were thick and coarse. She stroked his cheek, feeling the sharp hairs of a day-old beard.

It would be so easy. And quick, the way they were both feeling. His body warm and hard against hers. The prospect drew her as a parched traveler to a fresh, life-giving stream. Lord, how she wanted him.

But the girls. No doubt they were looking for her right this moment. Probably were out there in the rain, searching the barns.

Fear began small but quickly grew.

Ellie shook her head and dug her teeth into her bottom lip. She was conscious of Wade's breath teasing her hairline, of his warm, virile scent, of his rock-hard muscles beneath her hands.

"I can't, Wade." Her voice came out ragged, almost a whisper. She drew in a long breath and searched for the words. "I'm a mother. I have three daughters depending on me. I can't just let myself..." She left off speaking and forced herself to look up and meet his gaze, searching for understanding in his eyes. "I have to think of what's best for them," she said. "Always. They will always come first."

She found understanding in the shadows of his eyes; at least she thought she did. And boldness, too.

"You can't deny what happens between us, Ellie," he said gruffly.

"No." She shook her head and swallowed, praying for strength. The scent of him was almost her undoing. "I can't. But I can suspect the wisdom of it." It was hard to force her voice beyond the lump in her throat. Desire hammered within her.

"I want you, Ellie. And you want me."

Her breath left her. She did want him. So very badly. But the voice of reason shouted loudly within her mind. There was no forgetting what she wanted for her children. For herself.

"I want something more than that," she told Wade then, her voice coming surprisingly firm. "I want to cherish and be cherished. I want someone who will care for my girls as well as for me." She pushed from his arms. "I can't, Wade," she said, shaking her head. "It won't work...isn't any good for any of us."

"Ellie..." Wade stretched out a hand, then let it fall.

Without a word, he watched her slip into her coat. She was grateful for his silence. Didn't know what she would do should he try to stop her. Then she was running away through the rain, fresh tears streaking her cheeks.

With the children settled into bed that night, Ellie walked through the house lit only by light filtering through the windows from the outside pole lamp near the barn. Taking care to stand in the shadows on the porch, she gazed up at Wade's house. She saw it through the misty rain, the light from his pole lamp making shadows against the clapboards. She wondered if Wade sat on his porch.

She wondered about desires of the body and desires of the heart, about where one ended and the other began, about where they merged and became one.

She wondered what would have happened if she'd stayed with him.

Any man who became interested in her would have to know that she didn't come alone, she thought fiercely. Her daughters were a part of her. It was the way it was, the way she was.

But she was also a woman, came the whisper into her aching heart.

The weight of loneliness and wanting sat upon her shoulders like a huge stone. She was flesh and blood, with flesh-and-blood needs.

They wouldn't be denied, came an insistent warning from her heart.

A bone-deep loneliness filled her. She didn't only desire physical pleasure from Wade, she saw in that instant. She desired his companionship, his strength and support. She desired all that went with love between a man and a woman. He was a very special man.

She couldn't be certain if she loved him, or if her longing beyond endurance for a man to share her life forced her to focus on the only man available at the moment. Her heart recoiled at the thought. She would not cheat herself in such a way.

It really didn't matter, she told herself, sorrow bowing her shoulders. Wade certainly didn't lean in the same direction. And it would never work between them. Wade was . . . well, not a husband or father type of man. He was so different from what Galen had been . . . so very different.

Ellie remained staring at the house up the hill, the longing resting heavily on her heart.

Wade stood holding a cup of coffee, gazing out the dining-room window. Through the mist he could just make out the small stone house below, washed by a fuzzy glow from the outside lamp. Thoughts of Ellie were so strong, he could almost catch the scent of her. Never in all his life had he desired a woman the way he desired Eleanor McGrew in this moment.

Nothing to be done about it, he told himself shortly, as he continued to stare out the window and search for a release for the longing. She'd made it plain, though she hadn't really needed to. He knew Ellie well enough by now to know she'd never indulge in a casual affair, short or long. And he understood her reasons. They were good and sound, too.

Wade found himself wondering if he wanted an affair. Well, he thought angrily, he sure as hell didn't want the alternative. He couldn't see himself as father to those three girls. Sara didn't even like him.

Suddenly the house felt exceedingly empty, and he recalled dinner down at Ellie's. Her house was full—with laughter, with arguing. With love. He envied her that.

She was a good woman. And she was right. Human beings certainly weren't known for always desiring what was best for them. Both he and Ellie were simply going to have to show strength of character in this situation.

It was a firm resolve, but it didn't help him sleep. And he didn't think it to his credit that he found himself thinking up ways to get Ellie into his bed.

Wade left the house late the following morning, intent on skipping the morning shift at the Last Chance and avoiding Ellie. It was cool and damp, threatening rain, with a strong wind bearing down from the north. Seeing Sara, Rae and

Poppy huddled together beside the road awaiting the school bus, Wade stopped to offer them a lift.

"You bet!" Rae shouted, smiling and running forward, followed close behind by Poppy.

They jumped eagerly into the seat beside him, but Sara remained standing, her body rigid as stone.

"Come on, Sara," Wade coaxed. "I have the truck all warmed up."

"No, thank you," she said, turning cold blue eyes toward him.

Wade nodded. "Suit yourself."

At school, Poppy hugged his neck before running off to her classroom. He sat in the truck and watched until she disappeared. He found himself amazed at the way the tiny little girl could make him feel ten feet tall.

As he moved to shift into gear, his gaze fell on a thin young girl alighting from a school bus. Sara. For an instant she turned her face toward him, seeming to look right into his eyes. Then she walked away into the throng of other children.

Even over the distance, Wade felt her hostility. He recognized it as jealousy. Sara wanted him to have nothing to do with her mother; no doubt saw it as a threat to the memory of her father. And he could understand it.

"Oh, hell," he muttered. He didn't need the aggravation. It struck a profoundly sad note within him to think of the pleasant times he'd spent at the McGrew house over the past weeks. Those times had ended. It was best all around.

In the weeks that followed, Ellie saw little of Wade. He generally skipped the morning rush at the cafe and stayed only for a short lunch, rarely speaking to her, though he often waited long enough to speak to Poppy and to take her with him for an ice-cream cone. Ellie was grateful.

"You and Wade have a fight or something, Ellie?" Gayla asked one day.

"No, of course not," Ellie answered quickly, averting her gaze. Gayla had the ability to read eyes quite well. "Why would you think that?"

"Because he doesn't hang around here like he used to—or at least like he has in past weeks." Gayla continued to stare at her.

Ellie shrugged. "Maybe he's just changing his habits."

She was grateful when Gayla said no more about Wade and turned the conversation to the annual Last Chance Cafe Spring Blowout.

"The party is five months away, Gayla," Ellie said, laughing. "Isn't it a bit early for worrying over the plans?"

Gayla shook her head, sending her earrings into a dance. "I love planning it. Why, I start the planning for the next year the very day after the Blowout. We'll have live blue-grass music, wooden kegs of the finest beer, ribs, beans and corn bread—enough to feed the town. And every politician who happens to be running for office that year fights for an invitation. Something like that takes planning."

"How long have you been doing this party?"

"Ever since Wade hired me when he first got this place. He came to me and said he wanted to have a party, one wingding big enough for the whole town. It worked out so well it sort of became a tradition."

Ellie looked skeptically around the cafe. "Where do you put everybody?"

Gayla laughed. "They fill this place, even the kitchen, and spill out into the street for dancing." She inclined her head. "We take out the tables and chairs and just have the booths for sitting in. Food and drink are served from the counter and a flatbed trailer is parked in the street as a stage for the band. Works great." She grinned. "I already have my dress bought for the party. I'm savin' it. I hope to get Dal Allen to ask me to be his date."

"I'm sure you'll be able to," Ellie replied dryly.

Winter came full but mild. Life settled into a routine for Ellie, her world revolving around her girls, her job at the Last Chance, her house and her goats. Thanksgiving, Christmas, Sara's fourteenth birthday came and went. Rae finally got her horse, and the gift from Ellie's father was enough for all the needed tack as well.

The precious goats thrived; they hadn't lost a single one. Ellie and the girls counted and watched the pregnant does with glee, babying them, eager for them to deliver. Andrew and Gayla became frequent visitors to the McGrew house, bringing with them their easy laughter and bent for fun. The house brimmed with life and love.

But often Ellie found herself staring up at the house on the hill. She couldn't forget Wade Wolcott, no matter how much she tried. But then, she often thought, how could she, when she saw him almost every day? They didn't speak beyond a polite "hello," or "coffee's good today." But sometimes their eyes met. It was enough to allow the fire to kindle. A fire Ellie very much doubted would voluntarily burn itself out.

Chapter Eleven

Ellie awoke early and lay very still, listening to the quiet. Without the girls' regular Saturday morning noise the house seemed exceedingly empty. They'd gone the previous night to spend the weekend with their grandparents in the city. Though Ellie had been thankful for the prospect of a rare few days of peace and quiet and some time for herself, now she almost regretted it.

Quit being silly, she scolded herself, rising from her bed. The sky was clear and the sun on the rise, promising a balmy February day. The winter had been one of the mildest on record—an enjoyable blessing, bringing with it the certainty of an overabundance of insects for the coming summer months, one of the things of concern to Ellie now that she was in the stock business.

She laughed, admonishing herself not to borrow trouble. Her thoughts raced ahead to the goats and the farm as things stood at the present. In another week a crew would arrive to shear the goats, providing Ellie with her first profit from their fleece. As a general rule, a shearing crew wouldn't come to a farm with less than one thousand goats, but Andrew had arranged for the crew he used to come. One more thing she was indebted to Andrew for, though he never made her feel in his debt. It hadn't cost him anything but a few minutes of his golden tongue, he'd told her, laughing.

Ellie was beginning to suspect Andrew had a crush on her. The idea had dawned slowly, and still she rejected it as absurd. What would he see in her? she asked herself. He was a handsome young man who could have his pick of any number of young women. Yet, she tried to make certain she never did anything to encourage Andrew beyond friendship, just in case her uncomfortable hunch proved correct. She valued his friendship and wouldn't want to hurt him.

Hurriedly she showered and dressed, anxious to get out to the meadow and check on one goat in particular, a pregnant doe she'd come to call Jewel. Jewel had been acting strange lately, listless, skittish; Ellie couldn't exactly put a finger on it. The does weren't due to start delivering until the end of the month, but having carried three children herself, Ellie knew nature tended to disregard calendars.

Though she'd been aware Jewel could be in trouble, the picture that awaited her at the barn made her break out in an immediate cold sweat.

One of the heelers, Mutt, sat at the outer corner of the long barn, an unusual place to find him. Some sense telling Ellie she'd find a goat in trouble inside, she began to run. Entering, she stopped to look, giving her eyes a chance to adjust to the dimness. The barn was warm and damp, ripe with the musky odor of goats.

There were only a few of the animals inside, and they scattered away as she walked through. Several seconds later she spotted a goat lying at the far end upon a bit of straw near the corner. Jewel, she recognized as she came nearer. The doe lay on her side, her almost painfully rotund stomach humped into the air; her chest heaved, though she made no sound.

Ellie fell to her knees and ran a hand over Jewel's round side, crooning softly. Jewel's eyes were wide and pitifully filled with pain. She struggled to breathe. Mutt came in, sat down and looked at Ellie expectantly.

Help me, Lord, she thought. Her heart went out to Jewel in empathy. She, too, had struggled to bring a life into this world; Poppy had taken over thirty hours of hard labor to arrive. Birth was a hard, painful process, for the mother and, Ellie suspected, for the baby as well.

She examined the doe as best she knew how. Bloody mucus seeped from Jewel's birth canal, which had widened to a great extent. Ellie suspected by feel that Jewel could be carrying twins. Not a likely occurrence; only about ten percent of pregnant angoras would produce twin kids. Yet the chance existed. And although she was not a doctor, Ellie knew something was wrong with Jewel.

"I'll get some help, girl," Ellie promised the doe and stroked her head. "Just hang in there." She rose and ran, calling to Mutt over her shoulder. "Stay with her, fellow."

The instinct of one mother to help another gripped Ellie as she ran into the house and straight to the telephone. She had to do everything possible to save Jewel and her kid.

With a shaking finger, she found their veterinarian's number on the list above the telephone. She dialed and waited. One, two, three rings ... six, seven, eight—at last a voice answered.

"The doctor's over to the Hann farm, Mrs. McGrew," the voice told her. "I'll call over and tell him, but the Hanns have an emergency with their bull. Don't know how long it will take the doctor."

"Okay, please tell him ... thank you."

Ellie replaced the receiver and nibbled on her bottom lip. Again scanning the list of numbers, she dialed Andrew. Eight rings and she gave up, then called Gayla, thinking perhaps Andrew could be found there. But no one answered at Gayla's, either.

She squeezed her eyes against tears. She didn't know what to do. Brushing the tears aside, she ran through the house, gathering a blanket and soft rags from the linen closet and filling a plastic jug with water. Then she ran back to the barn.

Mutt lifted his head at Ellie's approach and watched her carefully, his ears cocked as if questioning. Dropping to her knees beside Jewel again, Ellie found herself breathing as hard as the doe. She spread the blanket over the doe, wet a rag with water and pressed it to the animal's mouth. Jewel licked the wet rag eagerly.

Wade, Ellie thought, glancing to the barn wall as if she could see right through it to his house. She rose to her feet, left the barn and began running up the hill, her lungs burning.

Duffy rose from where he lay in the morning sun and came, tail wagging, to greet her. Hardly sparing the dog a glance, she raced up the short steps and pounded on the side door. The time Wade had led her there in the misty rain flashed across her mind. Suddenly the door opened, and Wade filled the space. He looked down at her, surprise full upon his face. His hair was mussed, his shirt hanging open.

"I—" Ellie gasped for breath. "One of my does...is about to give birth. She's in trouble. Can you help?"

He stood there a moment, then turned into the room. "Come in...I have to get my boots on."

Ellie followed. Her eyes swept the room, seeing the paper and thin wooden dowels on the table, recognizing kite plans. Country music played softly from a small radio on the counter. The room was exceedingly warm.

"Little early for kidding," Wade commented from where he sat in the easy chair, pulling on his socks and boots.

Ellie nodded. "But mother nature does as she sees fit."

"She does that," Wade agreed. "Did you call Dr. Cross?"

"Yes. He's over at the Hanns, and I don't know when he can get here."

Wade rose, buttoned his shirt and went to a cabinet, pulling from it a small brown duffel bag. "Let's go," he said, reaching for his Stetson on a nearby rack.

Opening the door for her to go first, Wade followed. He noted the worry and strain in her face and in the set of her shoulders, felt the urgency of her concern. Yet he felt something more, too. A distinct gladness at the unexpected surprise of seeing her, of being with her.

One of the heelers met them outside the barn and growled at Duffy, who'd accompanied them. With a word from Ellie, the herd dog allowed Wade to enter but remained outside keeping Duffy at bay, heedless that the big red dog was about three times his size.

The doe was in great trouble, Wade saw at a glance.

"Twins?" Ellie asked.

"Looks like it could be..." Wade searched the doe's abdomen with his hands. "But she shouldn't be having too much trouble just because of that...I think...both kids are caught together, trying to deliver at the same time. I had a cow do that before. We've got to get one to come before the other." His mind focused on the problem at hand, forgetting his own emotions. A life—two or more lives—depended on him.

Wade gave thanks for a strong stomach as he and Ellie shifted the doe and pushed and prodded her abdomen, seeking to move the kid, or kids, inside to a different position. Ellie repeatedly stroked the doe's head and talked soothingly. Finally Wade was able to see what he thought were hooves. Using a pair of forceps from the bag, he pulled as gently as possible until he was able to use his hands. The doe struggled against the pain. Slowly, trying to assist nature, not take over the job, Wade eased a kid into the world. Barely a minute later a second angora miraculously followed.

Dr. Cross arrived as soon as the second kid had been born. "Just missed the crisis, did I?" he said, appearing in the doorway, his head silhouetted by the sunlight.

"Think we can use you, Doc," Wade told him. "This mother's still in trouble."

Leaving the mother to the doctor, Wade and Ellie cleaned the tiny kids. Ellie's eyes sparkled brighter than any diamond as she and Wade let the animals go and watched them struggle to stand on wobbly legs. They were very small and collapsed immediately, but seemed healthy enough, Wade thought. They'd survive with the right care. He was very aware of Ellie on her knees beside him.

"Your first new acquisitions, Ellie," he said, helping her to scrape fresh hay up in the corner for the kids.

She stopped and looked at him. "Thanks to you."

He shrugged and looked away, uncomfortable and pleased at the same time with the gratitude he saw in her eyes.

Dr. Cross pronounced the kids fit as fiddles and said he expected the doe to pull through. "Things just sort of got tangled inside," he said. "She hemorrhaged some, but I think nature will heal her up nicely. You two did fine." After handing Ellie some antibiotic along with terse instructions, the doctor hurried off to another emergency, grumbling about no rest for the righteous.

Wade stood beside Ellie in the sunshine just outside the barn and watched Dr. Cross hurry to his car in the drive. Duffy sat at Wade's feet, cowering at Mutt's threats. The sunshine lay warm upon Wade's head and shoulders and the sense of life he'd come to associate with being around Ellie filled him. He was reluctant to leave.

When the doctor's car pulled from sight, Ellie turned her eyes to look at him. "After I grain Rae's horse, I can offer you a cup of coffee and a piece or two of peach pie."

Slowly a smile started deep inside him. He was powerfully glad she'd made the offer.

"Sounds great," he drawled.

Bringing two plates, silverware and the pie to the table where Wade already sat, Ellie saw him cock his head, as if listening.

"Where are the girls?" he asked.

Until that moment, she'd forgotten they were alone—or had she?

"They're staying the weekend at my parents'," she answered as she slid a chair back and sat down. The coffee machine gurgled from on the counter. She sliced the pie, then glanced up to find Wade's eyes hard upon her. Warmth fluttered in her stomach.

They drank the warm coffee and ate the pie and talked about the goats they'd just saved, the upcoming shearing and recent goings on at the Last Chance. They talked easily, never at a loss for something to say, just as they had when they'd strung fence.

When Ellie rose to make a fresh pot of coffee, Wade reached out and grasped her wrist, holding her firm. She stopped in her tracks, didn't look at him. She'd known, had even hoped, he'd do something like this. That he'd make a first move. *Because she couldn't. Didn't think she could.*

He held her wrist until she looked at him. Then he tugged gently, pulling her close beside him, then down onto his lap, surrounding her with his arms. Her gaze remained on his, seeing the gold flecks in the warm brown iris of his eyes. His chest was hard against her arm, his legs firm beneath her bottom. A hint of manly cologne clung to him, a warm, enticing fragrance mingling with that of musky goat. Her heart beat rapidly; her breathing was shallow. It was a delicious sensation.

They kissed. Ellie wasn't certain if she lowered her head, or if Wade raised his lips to hers. She was aware only of kissing him, of thinking: at last. Blessed relief, blessed joy, blessed desire, as she slipped her arms atop his shoulders and curled her fingers into the thick richness of his hair. His very lifeblood pulsed beneath her fingertips, and it was as if her own blood suddenly rushed hot and pounding through her veins.

They broke apart, and Ellie pressed her cheek against his ear, clinging to him, reluctant to look at him, embarrassed to have him see the desperate wanting she knew was reflected in her eyes and across her face. His arms tightened around her; she could feel the beating of his heart against her own. He nuzzled down to her neck, his mustache tickling erotically.

Oh, my heaven, what was she doing?

It didn't seem wrong. It seemed so very *right*.

And she couldn't deny herself this . . . this beautiful, exquisite indulgence. For right now, in this moment, she wasn't lonely. She cared for Wade; he cared for her. The aching within her for a loving touch was eased, vanished.

She would take the joy, she decided clearly in that moment. Her girls were safely and securely away, would never have to know. There would be no tears, there would be no demands on Wade. Yes, she would take, and give, the joy of this time and be thankful and never ask for more.

His hands rubbed hard up and down her back, sending the desire spiraling within her. It was Ellie who moved her lips to find his. His kiss grew rough and demanding, his tongue parting her lips, flitting within her mouth, searching. Grasping her cheeks in his rough palms, he pulled back and looked into her eyes, a question upon his face.

Ellie smiled softly; he answered, his smile beginning first in his eyes. He helped her to stand. Her legs felt weak, and she clung to his hand. He rose and put an arm around her shoulders and walked with her to the bedroom.

She looked from the unmade bed to Wade, sudden hesitancy squeezing her heart. This was the bed she'd shared with Galen. But she wasn't thinking of Galen now. Was that wrong? And it had been so long since she'd lain with a man. She wasn't a young twenty-five anymore. Her body had carried and borne three children, and showed the effects. Maybe... Unreasonable, confused fears filled her.

The blue eyes she turned on Wade were clouded with hurt, with fear. It cut into him as a two-edged sword of amusement and concern. He thought he felt something of the same. What if he hurt her? What if he wasn't what she expected?

He reached out and pulled her to him. She trembled against him. Softly and repeatedly, drawn by the velvet of her skin, he kissed her temple and rubbed his cheek against her hair, hair that smelled of roses and sunshine. He kept thinking about stopping but never seemed able to. Very slowly her hands moved to rub up and down his back. He sensed the fear evaporate, the desire grow.

Somehow they made it to the bed. Crazy, but he didn't remember doing it. He took off his boots and socks, then sat up and watched her removing hers. While she was still about it, he reached out and released the clip holding her hair. Satisfaction swept him as, like rippling strands of spun gold, her hair fell across her shoulders. He'd been aching to do that for such a long, long time.

Ellie tossed him a smile over her shoulder, a naturally seductive smile as bold desire shone in her eyes. Suddenly Wade felt ten feet tall and all man—the biggest, the greatest man in the world. Tossing the hair clip across the room, he reached for her, pulling her down to the bed.

For long seconds he towered over her, allowing himself to look into her beautiful eyes. The heated love he found there caused a painful swelling within him. Taking his time, he ran his gaze over her hair, her forehead, her cheeks, her moist lips, then downward, tracing the silken skin of her neck down to the soft swell of her breasts. The creamy skin there beckoned, and he lowered his head to kiss and taste her warm flesh. She caught her breath, then sighed. Her body pulsed beneath his hands.

He looked again into her eyes. She was more woman than he'd held in a long time, perhaps ever. And for the second time in his life, he was in love.

Ellie gazed into Wade's eyes and her breathing stopped as she took in the pure look of love. Joy flooded her spirit. She felt loved, cherished, adored. And when he kissed her she felt claimed.

Hot passion flowed between them. Hurriedly they shed their clothes, each helping the other, touching, caressing without embarrassment. Just observing Wade's lean, hard body sent desire spiraling ever higher. Impatiently, she pressed against him, eager to feel his skin touching hers from her neck to her toes, joyous with the plain admiration showing in his face.

Then, with the feverishness of longings too long denied, they came together as man and woman. Wade took her to him smoothly. Ellie sensed his great tenderness and knew he was holding back, taking care not to hurt her. Love because of his care washed over her, again and again, as ocean waves upon a beach.

Passion engulfed her and her senses filled with him, with the overwhelming need to have him, to give to him, completely. Then came the wondrous, consummate, fire-hot release.

Afterward, he held her face between his palms and looked at her. She gazed back through the blur of unshed tears. His expression reflected the wonder she felt. Studying her face, he frowned.

"I didn't hurt you? I tried to be—"

She shook her head and smiled. "No," she whispered. "No, you didn't . . ." She pulled his head down, his mouth to hers.

Later she lay curled against him beneath the blankets. Tears filled her eyes and slipped down her cheeks. She turned her face and pulled the blanket beneath her cheek to prevent her tears from falling onto Wade's shoulder. She didn't want him to see, to misconstrue her emotion and feel trapped by a weepy woman. The tears came from emotional release, from relief, from thankfulness, from seeing and feeling the pinnacle of joy and love.

There was no comparing this time with the times she'd had with Galen. Wade wasn't Galen; the two were completely different, yet equal in their virility, in their passion, their tenderness, their strength.

And, miracle of miracles, Ellie once again lay in the arms of a man she loved. Once again the heart of a man she loved beat close to her own. She slept.

She awoke nearly an hour later, groggy, disoriented. In a rush it all came back to her, the why of Wade lying next to her, the reason her body felt totally and wonderfully relaxed, fulfilled. Wade still slept. It was the first time Ellie had seen the rugged lines of his face in repose; he looked exceedingly young, vulnerable. She indulged herself in staring at him for a long time, knowing her chances to do so were limited.

This weekend, if Wade wished, she would give to him, to herself. But that was all she had to give.

Taking care not to wake him, Ellie eased from the bed, grabbed up her robe and headed for the kitchen. Suddenly she was famished. In the hallway, just as she tied the sash of her robe, she froze.

She and Wade could quite possibly have made a baby.

It was as if a clanging alarm sounded within her brain. Walking slowly to the kitchen, Ellie went through the motions of preparing the coffee maker, her mind whirling with realities.

She was nearly thirty-five, she reminded herself; her most fertile years were behind her now. The thought brought some relief, but also regret.

Staring at the calendar on the wall, she counted the days of her body's cycle. It'd been so long since she'd done this, it was hard to remember the method. But counting days of her cycle had been the birth-control method she and Galen had employed. She'd used the method mostly for conceiving—not for preventing it. She knew there were days she would be more given to pregnancy, days she would not.

It appeared these days were safe days.

But what if something were wrong? What if she conceived?

Ellie knew she had to make a choice, knew that Wade's life as well as her own was at risk. She should say something to him, she thought then, reluctantly. How, what would she say? Was she presuming too much in thinking he wanted to stay with her as she did him? She tore her eyes from the calendar and turned away.

She was attending to frying the sausage when strong, male arms encircled her waist and warm lips pressed against her neck.

Ellie laughed and turned in his embrace to wrap her arms around him. Her look, her scent, her welcome of his attention sent a rush of pleasure through Wade. He'd wondered what she'd act like now, if she'd regret what had happened between them. He'd dreaded the thought.

But this...this reaction—it was wonderful! He kissed her lightly, then held her to him, rubbing his hands up and down her beautiful curves. He'd worried about hurting her. It'd been such a long time since she'd made love to a man, he'd known he had to be careful. But it had been good with her, so good. And knowing he'd given her pleasure made it all the more perfect.

He drew back and looked for long seconds into her face, as if to imprint her image and the moment in his mind. Her eyes told him she had no regrets, that she was happy. To know himself at least partly responsible for her happiness made him feel like a man holding the world in the palm of his hand.

She pushed from his embrace. "The sausage is about to burn..."

He turned to the coffee maker. A clean cup sat in front of it, waiting for him. He found it damned pleasurable to be spoiled in such a way.

"I thought you might be hungry," Ellie said. "I know it's closer to lunchtime, but I didn't have any breakfast this morning."

He grinned at her as he lowered himself into a chair. "I'm starved." His eyes slipped down her body, a reminder of the way he'd looked at her only a few short hours earlier. Ellie stored the pleasure of his look away in her heart.

They were drinking their after-meal coffee when a truck sounded in the drive outside. Ellie looked at Wade, confirming that he realized the same thing she did: no one could find them together like this. Quickly she rose to look out the living-room window. Andrew was approaching with his long, firm strides.

Suddenly Wade's hand clamped around her wrist, and he pulled her toward the hall.

"But I have—" Ellie began, wondering at Wade's actions.

"Shush..." Wade said, cutting off her protest.

Chuckling, he hurried her toward the bedroom. In amazement, Ellie stared at him and tried to keep her feet beneath her. Andrew's knocking sounded on the front door just as Wade fairly tossed her upon the bed, himself coming after, holding her down, kissing her neck. Ellie struggled against him and choked back her laughter. Then she wasn't laughing; she was returning his kiss, melting in his arms. She no longer heard the knocking, and when Wade broke away from her, the knocking had stopped.

With her arms around his neck, Ellie gazed up at him. Her blue eyes darkened with seriousness.

"We can have this weekend, Wade. I have no intention of continuing with you, hiding behind doors, making excuses to my daughters."

Her words were like a splash of reality in his face. He found them hard to believe, yet immediately hid the fact.

"You want that, Ellie?" He watched her eyes; a shadow crossed them.

"It's all I can offer." Her voice came soft and gentle. She searched his eyes for a moment, as if waiting for something. Then she said, "I don't want to mislead you."

He looked at her for a long minute. "Have you thought about pregnancy?" It'd all happened so fast, he hadn't thought of it before and cursed himself now for being so juvenile.

A soft smile of gratitude lit her lips and her face blushed becomingly. "I don't have anything to prevent it." She stroked his mustache. "But I think it's all right. These should be safe days for me."

Desire flickered, then flamed in her eyes and echoed within her own heart. Wade knew, risky business or no, they both intended to have each other. Then he kissed her because there was nothing else to be said. They made love again—slowly, languorously this time, learning what pleasured one another. Wade guessed, amused, that he still had quite a few miles left within him after all.

Much later they dressed and went down to check on the goats. Together they administered the medication to the nanny who now nursed her kids. Ellie drew a fresh bucket of water and filled another bucket with special feed. Again he helped her to care for the horse, and then, with her hand in his and the sun warm upon her back, she went up the hill with him.

He showed her his house. It had a long living room, a rock fireplace at one end and large, comfortable furniture that spoke of masculine living. There were three bedrooms.

Ellie walked around the one belonging to Wade, and she kissed him there. It seemed important somehow, one more precious thing to add to her memory of the weekend. Like a small boy eager for her attention, he showed her his kites, explaining the aerodynamics, which Ellie didn't think she totally understood.

Like children, they flew one of the kites. They laughed, poked each other, played chase and ended up rolling on the cool ground. When darkness closed in, Wade insisted on fixing them some of his own homemade soup. Afterward they sat in front of a blazing fire in the living room.

"I have to go home tonight," Ellie said. She stroked Wade's forehead, pillowed atop her legs.

"Stay here."

Ellie shook her head. "I'm sorry, you'll have to come down to my house. The girls will no doubt call me tonight." She chuckled. "This is the first time they've stayed away since we moved in. When they left, they were a bit worried about leaving old mom at home alone." She turned serious. "They'll expect me to be there."

Wade nodded that he understood.

Inwardly, Ellie sighed. It was one big example of her responsibilities—it was probably just as well for Wade to see it.

"You'll come with me?" she asked shyly.

In answer, he rose to his feet and extended a hand. "All I have to do is lock the door behind me."

Ellie rose to stand beside him, then threw herself against his chest, encircling his waist with her arms and rubbing her face against his bare skin where his shirt hung open.

After a second's hesitation his arms came around her. They held each other for what seemed a long time before walking hand in hand down to the little stone house.

They'd hardly been in the house fifteen minutes when the telephone rang.

"Mama?" It was Sara's voice. "Where have you been? We've been calling you and calling you today."

"I've been here, honey," Ellie lied, glancing at Wade. "You've probably just called when I was out at the barn. I had to be down there a lot today—we have two new members at the McGrew farm. Jewel gave birth to twins today.'' Wade had moved to hold her around the waist and teased her with kisses down the side of her neck. Ellie tried to keep her voice and breath even.

"Twins?'' Sara said eagerly, then Ellie heard her relay the news to her sisters. "Are they okay?''

"Yes...they're fine. Jewel had trouble, but...it turned out well. Dr. Cross said Jewel should be fine.''

Wade slipped his thumb beneath her bra to caress her breasts and blew softly in her ear. Her blood ran hot through her veins. She tried to keep her mind on the girls.

She talked briefly to Rae and Poppy, then hung up. Wade still held her. She turned to face him.

"The girls will be home tomorrow at five,'' she said, looking directly into his eyes. Her blood pounded with desire.

His answer was to lift her in his strong arms and carry her with long strides into the bedroom.

They made wonderfully passionate love, and Ellie fell asleep listening to Wade's heartbeat in the darkness. Once she awoke, instantly, fully. She stared into the darkness, listening to Wade's even breathing and delighting in the warmth of his body snuggled close to her own. And by listening very carefully, again she caught the sound and the feel of his heart beating steadily, close to her own. So sheltered, she again slipped into sleep.

When she awoke, she found herself alone. She sat up with a jerk, her heart squeezing with sorrow. And then she caught the smell of fresh coffee and sizzling bacon and heard the hint of a whistle.

She found Wade in the kitchen, looking quite domestic. It was a good sight. Ellie joined in the preparation of breakfast and tried not to think about later, when it would all come to an end.

That day was a repeat of the gorgeously sunny one before. With Wade on his horse and Ellie riding Rae's, they rode for hours, first on Ellie's acreage and then on Wade's. Leading her to a secluded place he obviously knew well,

Wade pulled Ellie from her horse, spread his coat and then her own upon the ground.

He undressed her, baring her skin to the warmth of the sun and the caresses of his hands as well as the breeze. Then, eager to feel him pressed against her, Ellie helped him to undress. The feeling was beyond any she'd ever experienced as they made love there in the open with the sun, the birds, the wind and perhaps a few critters looking on. It was as if they'd become one with each other and the earth. Ellie held it all to her heart, pressing it forever in her memory.

Late in the afternoon they stopped to check on Jewel and her kids. They saw to fresh hay, feed and water. But time was ticking away fast now.

Then, for some insane reason, Ellie thought, they sat on the hay in the barn beside the smelly goats. They talked of everyday things, each one seeming to listen for a car in the drive. Ellie was almost holding her breath as she sought to memorize Wade's face as he talked.

"Why this one weekend, Ellie?" he asked softly, startling her out of her reverie.

"How long do you think it would be before people found out?" she replied after a long moment. "And what do you think that would do to my girls?"

His expression thoughtful, he broke a blade of straw. "You want marriage."

"I haven't asked you, Wade," she said gently, not wanting him to feel guilt, not wanting to strain the beauty of the past days.

"I know. Why not?"

She found herself smiling at the craziness of their conversation. "Can you see yourself suddenly married and having not only a wife but three daughters as well? Your bathroom would be a jungle of laundered panties and nylons. You'd have to install another telephone line." She strove to sound light and joking, hiding the disappointment inside. He had no obligation to her; she wouldn't make him feel one.

"You don't think I'm father material," he said, his brow furrowing.

"Oh, Wade." She watched his expression darken with confusion. Gently she touched his cheek. "I have no regrets over this weekend. You owe me nothing. And I thank you so much for what you've given me. I'll carry this time in my heart forever."

As they looked at each other the sound of a car in the drive reached them. Wade rose to his feet. His eyes burned into hers. With a swift, rough motion, he pulled her against him. His kiss came hard and ended quickly. Then he strode from the barn.

For an instant Ellie stared after him, seeing only the open doorway, her head spinning. She felt as if her heart had just been ripped from within her, wanted to cry out, to stop his going. But she choked back the words. It wouldn't be fair to him.

"Mama! Mom!"

At the girls' call, Ellie forced herself to step from the barn. Her feet felt like lead; she blinked in the brighter light.

"Here!" The word came out a raspy whisper. She lifted her arm and tried again. "Here...here I am, girls!"

Chapter Twelve

No one ever could have guessed about their weekend, even when she and Wade met at the cafe. It was "Good morning." "Warm weather's holding." "How's the goat count at your place, Ellie?" "The girls are anxious for shearing."

It was all casual, as if the clock had been rewound on two wonderful days and time had started all over again. Nothing lingered to prove to Ellie she hadn't simply dreamed it. She wasn't pregnant. Thank heaven, she thought repeatedly as the fullness of what she would have had to face came upon her. There was no telltale male sock beneath her bed, no man's cologne in the bathroom. Nothing. Except beautiful memories and the heartache of something denied her.

Ellie tried not to dwell on it, tried only to give thanks for the wondrous experience and not long for more—as she'd promised. Yet, often in the night, she allowed herself the luxury of remembering that weekend in an effort to ease the loneliness. Of course, it didn't work.

Had she thought she could get wanting Wade out of her system by indulging in those two days?

No—actually, she hadn't thought about it at all. She'd simply reached out and enjoyed life as she found it. If she had it to do over, would she stop and think of the consequences? No. She had no regrets and never would.

One week later it was shearing time. Wade even stopped flying a kite to come down and watch. Excitement gripped Ellie as she watched her first profits being made. Andrew arranged for Ellie and the girls to give shearing a try. Only Rae seemed blessed with the knack. Ellie would so much have liked to talk with Wade about it, to share her joy and pride in the fleeces, which proved of good quality.

When she looked at him, she sensed he knew. And the energy vibrated between them higher and stronger than ever before. She worried that someone would pick up on what passed between them. Once, she found Sara looking at her curiously.

She didn't think she'd realized it at the time, but something deep inside her had hoped Wade would speak of marriage to her. And he certainly could have come to see her anytime since, to pursue a relationship of a more permanent vein.

But he hadn't. And she shouldn't have expected him to, she told herself. He wasn't the sort for a wife and a family. She'd known it then; she knew it now. And still, she refused regrets.

"Ellie!" Gayla called her name eagerly, and Ellie guessed whatever was coming would have something to do with the Last Chance Cafe Spring Blowout, only two weeks away. It was Gayla's main, almost only, topic of conversation.

Ellie looked up from the desk where she worked on a list of supplies to see Gayla bounce in the office door.

"Whew..." Gayla slipped from her dripping rain cape. "Oh, my hair—it'll just get wilder and wilder in this rain. 'Course the rain'll stop soon. Always does for the annual Blowout."

"Pretty certain of that, are you?" Ellie teased.

"Always has. It's rained before and after but never during." Looking terribly pleased with herself, she perched on the edge of the desk, giving her head a shake and sending her earrings rocking. "I'm awfully glad I hired you, Ellie. I haven't had to mess with this supply list in months."

"Glad enough to give me a raise?"

"Yes, I do believe I am!"

"My, what happened over at the bank? Did you rob it?" Ellie leaned back in the desk chair and observed Gayla with amusement.

"Dal Allen was there."

"Now I know why you went to the bank an hour earlier than usual today. So how goes the quest?"

"I'm officially Dal's date for the Blowout." Gayla gave a pleased, Cheshire cat smile.

"I told you I had no doubt it would happen."

"Well, I was mighty worried there for a while. Annie Cobb was paying him an awful lot of attention."

"Annie Cobb has nothing on you, Gayla."

"Tell that to Dal Allen."

Setting the supply list aside, Ellie reached for her purse, her mind turning to the errands she had to run before returning for the lunch shift.

"You got a date for the Blowout, Ellie?" Gayla asked suddenly.

Giving a dry smile as she slipped into her raincoat, Ellie said, "Sure—with three girls." Her smile turned genuine. "They're really looking forward to it."

Gayla's gaze turned searching. "You could ask Wade, nothing says he has to ask you."

"Gayla! I couldn't do such a thing. And why in the world would you think I'd want to?"

"I'm not blind, Ellie. I've seen the way you two look at each other." She stared pointedly at Ellie, then raised an eyebrow. "There's nothing between me and Wade, Ellie. Never has been." Her voice gentled. "I know I flirt with him a lot, but, well . . . it's just my way."

"Thanks, Gayla. You're a good friend. But there's nothing between Wade and me, either. He's been nice and helpful to me. That's all." Ellie found it surprising that the denial came so easily. But then she'd had a lot of practice denying so much to herself lately.

Gayla shrugged. "He's a handsome, available man."

"And I'm a woman with three growing daughters."

"Wade could help there."

Ellie spared her a look and no more.

"Hey! How about some service out here!" Hard pounding on the counter accompanied the booming male voice.

Startled, Ellie's gaze flew to Gayla.

Gayla waved her hand. "Calm down, that's just Andrew."

Together they walked out behind the counter. Andrew, perched upon a stool, sent them a broad grin. His gaze seemed to linger on Ellie, and though she smiled back, she was cautious to keep it a friendly smile. She had little doubt now about Andrew's feelings. He wanted their friendship to become more. Not only had he been coming with increasing frequency to the farm, but he'd also begun dropping in often at the cafe. She wasn't at all certain how to handle the situation and dreaded the possibility of hurting him.

"Hi there, ladies. Which one of you gets the privilege of getting me a soft drink?"

"Don't know if I'd go so far as to call it a privilege, Andy," Gayla said, turning to fill a glass with ice.

"Well, I'm off," Ellie said, moving past the counter. "I've got shopping to do before lunch."

"Hold on, Ellie." Andrew reached out and grabbed her wrist.

In surprise, Ellie stared at his hand an instant before raising her eyes to meet his.

"You got a date for the big Blowout?"

Ellie gave a soft grin. "Yes, my daughters." Inwardly she thought she'd be glad when all the furor over this party was over.

"Let me take you and the girls," Andrew said.

His green eyes held a charming, pleading edge. He looked so young and vulnerable.

Shaking her head, she gave him a soft smile. "I thank you for asking, Andrew, but I think it would be better for me to just bring the girls. I'll have to get them home at a decent time, you know." The disappointment sweeping his face touched her heart and caused her to add, "You'll save me a couple of dances, though, won't you?"

"Sure..." His grin came lopsided. "If this rain lets up."

"You know it always stops raining for the Blowout," Gayla said firmly. "Always has, always will."

Though Ellie didn't look in the young woman's direction, she sensed Gayla's speculative gaze and knew Gayla was thinking of Wade.

And Ellie herself thought of him as she bid goodbye to them both and turned to leave the cafe. She stopped for a minute beneath the shelter of the overhang. Rain pounded upon its aluminum top, ran in rivulets down the gutters and streamed down the street. By their own accord, Ellie's eyes moved to Wade's shop across the street. His truck sat parked out front.

Then, purposefully, Ellie pulled her hood up against the rain, ducked her head and hurried down the sidewalk to the bank. It came as a great shock to almost bump into Wade coming out of the bank. For long seconds they stood in the bank alcove, staring at each other.

"How are you, Ellie?" Wade asked, as if he didn't see her nearly every day at the cafe. But he gazed at her exceedingly intimately, and Ellie knew his question was more than casual.

"I'm fine, now... had a cold a few weeks back." Came down with it right after our weekend, she thought as she looked into his brown eyes. "That's why I had a few days off."

"Me, too," Wade said, "a cold. I'm fine now, too."

Ellie knew he was thinking what she was: they'd caught the cold and shared it with each other that private weekend. That and so much more. The warm sensation of a blush slipped over her cheeks. Then a tall man came up beside Wade and, realizing they blocked the entry, they moved aside.

"I have to get over to the..."

"I have to make this deposit..."

They spoke at the same time, then laughed at the same time. Ellie said goodbye and Wade politely tipped his Stetson.

She walked to the teller window without a backward glance. She didn't need one; she knew when Wade was gone.

She pulled an envelope of money from her purse and passed it to the teller. It wasn't much—just what she'd managed to save from her tips for the past three weeks.

Though she'd received good payment for her fleece, the price for mohair was down. After paying on the goats and the barn, there hadn't been as much left as Ellie had figured on. She was over six hundred dollars short of the payment due Wade, which loomed less than two months away.

She accepted the receipt from the teller and thanked her. Looking at the receipt, Ellie's heart squeezed. She'd known she'd been cutting it close, but she'd thought it would work out. It still could, came a whisper. Sure, she thought darkly, dollar bills like manna from heaven.

Wade wouldn't push for the payment. Ellie knew this. And she also knew she'd be able to make up the shortage come fall shearing, so it wasn't life-or-death serious.

Still, she didn't like it. She wanted to pay him as promised, as had been their deal. She needed to pay him; she didn't want to feel further obligated to him.

Deliberately she turned her thoughts from the problem. Worrying herself sick over it wasn't going to help. One day at a time, she told herself for the thousandth time.

"Wade, if you can't quit grumbling at everyone, go home," Gayla told him, anger sparking in her eyes.

Wade frowned and turned away to the window, staring out at the street, quiet for a Saturday. Behind him Dal Allen and another young man Gayla had sweet-talked into helping hauled tables and chairs out the front door and down the sidewalk to Brad Young's office to get them out of the way. Another two men worked at securing the flatbed trailer for the musicians outside in the street. Two teenage girls decorated with banners and balloons. In another three hours, caterers would arrive with trays of barbecued ribs, huge containers of beans and pans of corn bread. The day of the annual Blowout had finally arrived.

He knew perfectly well he was overly touchy. He just felt so wound up; the least little disturbance set him off.

"See, I told you it would stop raining," Gayla said, coming up to stand beside him. "Nothing to worry about."

Wade grunted. It had stopped raining early that morning, but gray clouds hung low and heavy. It looked as if it could pour any time.

"Wade, you gave me this job when no one thought I could do more than look pretty."

Surprised, he looked down at Gayla, wondering at her point. She averted her eyes, but sucked in a breath to say more.

"You helped me, had faith in me, and I feel I owe you."

"You don't owe me anything," Wade said, shaking his head. "If you did, it's a debt long paid."

"Well, I think of you as a good friend."

"Thanks."

"That's why I think I can say to you that you need to straighten this thing out with Ellie."

"What..." He stared down at her, wondering what in the hell she was getting at, and why she was getting at it.

"I know you care for her," Gayla said before he could get his breath. "It's time you did something about it. You're not getting any younger. It's time you found a good woman and settled down."

He rubbed the back of his neck and stared at the checked curtains, searching for something to say. "It's not that easy..." he began, then wondered why he simply hadn't denied Gayla's supposition.

"Why not? You're single. She's single."

"I don't know anything about raising girls. I don't know anything about being a husband." He scowled at her. "And I don't think I want to."

"You're one man I know who knows a heck of a lot about females, young and old. I think you could handle being a father and a husband just fine." She put her hand on her hip. "You're just making this whole thing more complicated than it is, and you're driving us all stark raving mad in the process."

"And you're forgetting I'm your boss again!"

"So fire me! Then I wouldn't have to put up with your bullheaded temper!"

Pivoting, Gayla stalked across the room and entered the kitchen, leaving him standing there staring after her. He blinked, then moved his gaze around the cafe and saw Dal Allen and the others staring wide-eyed at him. Emitting a low curse, he stalked to the counter, grabbed his hat, plunked it on his head and left.

His bad humor wasn't all his own fault, he fumed. Everyone was bugging him. And what business was it of Gayla's? She acted as if all he had to do was go up and ask Ellie to marry him, and she would fall at his feet. Ellie herself had said she could give him only that weekend. And she'd also said she didn't think he could be much of a father. She obviously didn't want anything more from him than the weekend they'd shared.

In the weeks since that weekend he'd studied her eyes, her face, looking for some sign she missed him, cared for them to have something more together. And while sometimes he thought he saw a warm welcome radiating from those sky-blue eyes, other times they were clear and cool, reflecting no emotion at all. Who could figure women, anyway?

But perhaps what bothered Wade the most was that he couldn't figure his own emotions. He felt empty inside, as if he'd lost a part of himself and would never regain it. And sometimes he looked down at the small stone house and longed to hear the noise, the laughter, even the arguing of young voices. He longed to have someone he could care for—and to care for him in return. And all these longings brought with them responsibilities Wade wasn't certain he wanted to take on or was even capable of handling.

The Last Chance Cafe Spring Blowout began at four o'clock that afternoon and was scheduled to continue until everyone had left that night. And if this year followed the pattern of the previous years, there'd be several fights, several engagements and several good pranks before it all ended.

Avid conversation and laughter filled the cafe and spilled out the open door right along with people. Toe-tapping bluegrass music filled the air. The rain held back; the temperature hovered at a comfortably warm level for early spring.

Wade circulated and greeted people; there were very few he didn't know. Gayla, too, greeted people, although neither she nor any of the regular waitresses worked during the Blowout. On this afternoon, the main street in front of the cafe was roped off and every business in Advance shut down. The caterers who provided the food and drink and handled the serving were hired from out of town, so as not to break the tradition of no Advance person working.

It was past five when Wade finally spied Ellie. She made her way through the people to the counter where soft drinks and beer were being served. Quickly excusing himself from talking with a group of businessmen, Wade made his way toward her. He was following his instincts, not having the least idea why—or what he'd say to her.

"See you made it," he said, stepping beside her at the counter.

Her blue eyes widened. In a glance he took in the dress falling softly over her full curves. A print of tiny blue flowers on white and buttoned to the neck with a lace collar, it was completely demure. Though it didn't seem so on her—at least to Wade.

"Hi, Wade." Poppy's voice drew his attention. Standing on the other side of Ellie, the small girl clung to Ellie's hand and smiled up at him.

Bending, Wade reached for Poppy and lifted her in his arms, saying, "Hi, Pumpkin. Feel like you're in a sea of legs?"

"Sure do," she answered, laughing.

He sat her atop the counter. "This seat is reserved for special guests. Tell this young man here what you'd like to drink." He turned back to Ellie. "What would Mama like?"

Her eyes reflected surprise, uncertainty and, dare he hope, pleasure?

"Cola, please."

She averted her eyes. Wade was suddenly reminded of how her face had looked in ecstasy when he'd made love to her that first morning.

Suddenly Andrew stood at Ellie's side. "Hello, Ellie." Andrew sent a smile all for her and added a greeting to Wade as an afterthought. Wade's shoulders tightened in irritation.

"Ellie, would you like to dance?" Wade asked.

"I imagine she would, Wade," Andrew said, before Ellie had a chance to speak. "And she promised me the first one. Second, too."

Even as he spoke, Andrew took the soft drink from Ellie's hand and passed it to Poppy. Then he pulled Ellie toward the door and outside. Wade stood beside Poppy and watched Ellie waltz past the window, securely held within Andrew's arms.

"I saw on a movie once where this man went and took this woman away from this other man and danced with her," Poppy said.

"What?" Wade said.

Poppy's blue eyes regarded him seriously. "This man...in the movie...he went over and knocked on the other man's shoulder, then danced with the woman."

Slowly Wade grinned. "You're right, Petunia. I owe you one."

"Poppy!" Her laughter rang in his ears as he made his way around people and out the cafe door.

Andrew smiled at her. Dressed in a pale yellow western shirt and brown sport coat, he was quite handsome. He moved her smoothly around the street, which served as a dance floor, expertly avoiding other dancers.

"I'm sorry, Andrew," Ellie said, "I don't dance very well. I haven't danced since...since before Rae was born, almost ten years ago. Galen took me dancing for my twenty-fifth birthday." If Andrew got the hint, he didn't show it. His eyes sparkled with enjoyment.

"You dance fine, Ellie, just fine."

Suddenly Wade stood there, resting a hand on Andrew's shoulder. "May I cut in, Andrew?"

Wade's voice was smooth and polite, but without waiting for a reply he took Ellie's hand from the younger man's shoulder. In seconds Ellie was whirling dizzily away from Andrew in Wade's arms.

Wade looked dashing, every inch the old-west gentleman in a white western shirt with a black string tie at his neck, slim-fitting slacks and gleaming black boots. Ellie felt overwhelmed by his effective claiming of her, by being in his arms, by Wade himself.

She looked up at him. A slow smile slipped across his lips beneath his thick mustache. His eyes held a memory. And Ellie, too, remembered. For a precious instant the commotion around them faded, leaving her and Wade the only two people in their very private world.

The tune ended and another began, and Andrew appeared at her elbow to claim her for another dance. At the end of that dance, Wade awaited his turn. After twenty minutes of changing partners, Ellie begged off.

"I must check on the girls."

"I'll help." Wade and Andrew spoke at the same time, then glared at each other. Ellie couldn't believe or quite comprehend what was happening.

Rae showed up, Poppy in tow, and complained about being followed. Allowing Rae to rejoin her friends, the four of them—Wade, Andrew, Ellie and Poppy—went to get dinner and something to drink. To Ellie they appeared very much an odd group.

"There's Sara," Andrew said a bit later, using his fork as a pointer.

They sat at one of the picnic tables arranged beneath an awning hung with lanterns, Wade and Andrew on one side of the table, Poppy and Ellie on the other.

Ellie followed his gaze and saw Sara with a group of other young people at a far table. A young man dressed in black with a black, wide-brimmed Stetson sat close to Sara's side.

His profile was turned toward Ellie; he seemed much older than the others.

"Wade, who is that sitting beside Sara?"

"Sloan Mundell," Both Andrew and Wade answered. Andrew glared at Wade, who simply smiled in return.

Ellie watched Sara and Sloan Mundell with the inner instinct a mother has when she spies someone who spells trouble for her daughter. Looking at Sara, Ellie tried to see her daughter as a young man might. A cool chill swept her spine. In spite of the fact that Ellie refused to let her wear makeup, Sara's features and bearing made her look far older than her fourteen years.

Sara and the young man rose and went to the dance floor. When the young man's hand strayed to Sara's derriere, Ellie rose, saying, "Stay here, Poppy."

Wade grasped her wrist, stopping her. "Let's dance over there," he said, rising and whirling her out onto the dance floor. Smoothly Wade two-stepped over to the young couple.

"Hello, Sara," Ellie said, leaning close. Sara's eyes widened. Ellie looked at the young man and offered a friendly smile. But her voice turned steely. "That young woman whose rear you have your hand on is my daughter, and she just turned fourteen." She pierced him with her gaze. "I suggest you remove that hand."

"Mama!" Sara gasped.

Sloan Mundell removed his hand and straightened to a proper position. Turning her head, Ellie allowed Wade to whirl her away. Blatantly watching, she saw Sloan Mundell lead Sara back to the group of friends. Then he moved away.

For the next couple of hours, Ellie danced with many other men besides Wade and Andrew, and the table where they sat became a hub of a number of the cafe's regular customers. Still, Wade and Andrew were never far from her elbow and Ellie felt like a pampered belle at the ball. And it worried her. But not more than it made her curious. Andrew's attention she thought she understood—but Wade . . . was he jealous? She couldn't believe it.

Ellie had just realized she hadn't seen Rae for over an hour when Rae appeared beside her. With alarm, Ellie saw that dirt streaked Rae's face and dress.

"What is it? What's happened?"

Rae fidgeted. "Mama...I didn't mean to..."

"Rae, are you all right?" Ellie grabbed Rae's arm.

"Yes, Mama...but your truck may not be." Looking at her daughter's remorseful face, Ellie had a distinctly sinking feeling.

She found her truck sitting in the low, grassy land beyond the small graveled lot where it'd been parked. The back wheels were buried nearly up to the axle in the muddy ground, and the front ones weren't much better off. The light of a nearby street lamp illuminated the truck with a faint silver glow.

They'd just been going to move it as a joke, Rae said, snuffling tears. It had been her and some schoolmates—boys, Ellie surmised, though Rae refused to name names. Rae had bragged the truck was a four-wheel-drive and that she could drive it. Ellie had the idea the joke had been on Rae, a payback for her bragging.

"My fault," Ellie murmured as she looked with a sinking heart at the truck. "I left the keys in it."

"Four-wheel-drives are nice," Wade commented, standing beside her. "But when you get them stuck, then you just have four wheels stuck instead of two. That land's a bog from all the rain we've been having."

When she looked up at him, Wade wished he hadn't said that last part.

"Aw..." Andrew said, "I'll get it out for you, Ellie. Pull it with my truck."

Andrew, the knight in shining armor, Wade thought dryly as Andrew backed his truck to the edge of the gravel. A small crowd had gathered, and there came the fluttering of applause as Andrew stepped out across the mucky ground to tie a tow rope to the rear bumper of Ellie's truck. Wade folded his arms across his chest and watched. After carefully walking back across the soggy ground, Andrew got in his truck, shifted into gear and slowly pulled away. The tow line tightened and the truck strained. The next instant, the rope had snapped loose from Ellie's truck bumper and lay like a dead snake on the ground.

A deep groan flowed over the small crowd.

Poppy pulled at Wade's hand. "I think you better help."

"You do?" Wade asked, keeping his face perfectly straight.

Poppy nodded seriously, and Wade glanced up to see a look of agreement across Ellie's face. With a large sigh, he shrugged out of his coat, handed it to Poppy for safekeeping and strode out into the mucky ground, following Andrew to Ellie's truck. The disgusting mud pulled his boots deeper with every step. His best boots.

"I can get it, Wade." Andrew fumbled once again, tying the rope to the bumper. "It was just weak—see, it snapped here at the end." He held up a frayed edge. "Need a new one."

"Here, let me show you a better way to tie it." Wade reached for the rope.

"I can do it fine," Andrew said shortly. "You're just out here to do some showing off for Ellie."

"Looks like you've been doing some showing off yourself, boy," Wade said.

"I happen to be serious about her. Can you say that, old man?"

"Why don't you grow up—and get me some slack on that rope."

Andrew pulled the rope, then shoved the wad of rope and his fist at Wade's chest. Desperately, Wade tried to get his balance, but, unsuccessful, he fell with a splat onto the soggy ground. He stared up at a laughing Andrew.

Hot anger shot through him. "Looks like you need a lesson in manners, boy," he growled through gritted teeth. Shooting out a long leg, he aimed a swift kick at Andrew's knee, sending him down, spread-eagled in the muddy marsh. The fight was on.

Hot damn! Wade felt a sudden, wonderful release of pent-up frustration. No matter that it wasn't all Andrew's fault. He was the one handy.

To Ellie's horror, Wade and Andrew were suddenly ex-
changing punches, pushing each other into the mud, then
rolling in it. People surged around her, cheering the fighting men on. And her truck remained stuck in the mud.

Lifting Poppy, who still clung to Wade's coat, into her
arms and commanding Rae to find Sara, Ellie moved to the
edge of the gravel, then took a step into the marshy ground.
Her feet began to sink, mud oozing into her fine leather
flats.

"Stop it! Wade! Andrew! Stop it this minute!" She
yelled. She looked toward some of the men present. "Get in
there and stop them!" But each shook his head, chuckling,
and stepped back.

Feeling helpless, she turned again to watch Wade and
Andrew. Wade's white shirt was now mostly brown, or
black; it was hard to tell in the dim light. Mud streaked his
face and clumped over his brown hair. And Andrew's shirt
and coat now appeared to be the same all over muddy color.
Ellie flinched when she heard the sound of fist connecting
with flesh. Then they grappled with each other again and
rolled on the wet ground, grinding whatever grass was left
into the muck.

Worrying that one or both of them would get hurt, she
knew with rising guilt that the fight had a great deal to do
with her. Well, she thought hotly, *she hadn't done anything! And her truck was still stuck!*

And if it was going to get unstuck, it looked as if she'd
have to do it herself. The boys were too busy playing. Making fools of themselves, more accurately, she thought, in-
dignant. Maybe Andrew could be excused, but Wade was
old enough to know better.

Ellie turned to hand Poppy to Sara, who'd come to stand
close behind her. "Stay here," she ordered the three girls.

She took off her shoes. Holding them in one hand and
lifting her skirt with the other, she stepped out into the
marshy mire. The muck sucked at her feet. Slowly, clench-
ing her bottom lip between her teeth and taking care not to
fling mud onto her new dress, she approached the truck by

way of a wide circle to avoid Wade and Andrew and their ruckus.

Just as she moved closer to the truck, Wade stumbled backward. Ellie managed to step out of the way, but one of Wade's flailing arms arched up and back as he struggled for balance and knocked against her shoulder. Not hard, but hard enough to set her off balance. So quick she couldn't believe what had happened, Ellie slipped, landing on the mucky ground with a resounding plop.

She sat there a moment, stunned. She looked down at her dress, her brand-new special-sale designer dress. Then hot anger erupted and took total control. Struggling to a standing position, she clutched her shoes in one hand and shook the muddy back of her dress from her legs.

With single-minded purpose, she stomped up behind Wade, and as he drew back his fist to aim a punch at Andrew, Ellie shoved him, hard, sending him forward into Andrew. Both men went tumbling into the mud.

Ellie turned, dragging her feet from the mud, and stomped to the driver's door of the truck. Pulling up into the seat, she tried to shake the slimy mud from her feet, legs and dress, then just gave up and sat down.

She slammed the door, pressed in the clutch and turned the key. She gunned the accelerator; the engine roared, and she glanced to see if the noise had gotten Wade's and Andrew's attention. It had. They stood apart, gaping at her. She leaned out the window.

"Get the hell out of my way, because I'm getting my truck out of here!"

Adrenaline coursed through her. Checking the gear shift, she started out in reverse. The truck surged backward, sending Wade and Andrew jumping out of the way, though the truck moved less than two inches before the wheels bogged down. Shifting, Ellie sent the truck forward. Each time the truck bogged, she sent it immediately in the opposite direction, until finally she'd worn ruts long enough to give her some traction.

"Okay, Ellie," she heard Wade call from behind. "You're going forward and out this time!"

A glance over her shoulder told her Wade and Andrew were behind the truck, ready to push.

Slowly Ellie pushed on the accelerator, at the same time letting out the clutch. The tires spun, the truck rocked with the effort of the men pushing. Then the tires grabbed and the truck shot forward, bumping over the ground to the street beyond.

Once up on the dry pavement, Ellie stopped the truck. She inhaled deeply. A small sound drew her attention to the bed of the truck. Wade sat there, his back against the tailgate. He was laughing, his teeth white against his mud-stained face. Bringing his hand to his forehead, he shot her a smart salute.

Immediately, though more slowly, Ellie drove the truck around to the gravel parking area. The crowd greeted her with applause and cheers. Pulling to a stop, she got out and strode to the back of the truck. Wade climbed stiffly over the tailgate. He held his chest as if he'd hurt his ribs.

"Wade! Are you all right?" She was angry, at Rae for the mischief, at Wade for fighting and scaring her half to death.

He stepped to the ground and stood slightly hunched over. Her anger melted to concern.

She touched his face. "Wade?"

He looked up and he was...laughing! The next instant his arm shot out and his muddy hand grabbed her firmly around the back of the neck. He planted a wet, muddy kiss full on her lips. Right there, boldly, not only in full view of at least fifty people, but in front of her daughters, too. She was too shocked to offer the least resistance.

She was conscious of the feel and taste of gritty earth, and of Wade's warmth. Then of a burst of applause and laughter from all around them.

"This may just be the best Blowout ever," he said when he pulled away, smiling broadly.

Chapter Thirteen

On the drive home, Ellie had the feeling the girls were staring at her as if she had horns sprouting from her head, or something equally wild. The scratchy mud soaking through her dress and coating her legs didn't help her discomfort any—or her mood.

"You got mud on your face from Wade kissing you," Poppy offered.

Ellie wiped at her mouth and wondered if she'd gotten all the mud off. She wondered what to tell the girls about the kiss. She could try to pass it off as just a friendly, spur-of-the-moment type of kiss, but they had eyes in their heads. And she'd always made it a point to be honest with them. They would sense it if she tried to lie.

"I'm sorry for what I did, Mama," Rae offered. "But you sure were something getting the truck out."

"You're grounded for the next ten years," Ellie said.

That effectively put an end to further conversation until they reached home.

Ellie went straight to the bathroom. She stared in the mirror. Mud stuck to her hair and streaked her neck where Wade's hand had been. And there were dark stains on either side of her mouth—where his lips had been.

Right there in front of everyone, he'd kissed her... fully... hotly. Blushing, Ellie turned from the mirror.

"Sara?" She called to her daughter passing in the hallway. "Will you unzip my dress?"

Quietly, Sara entered and did as she was bid. Ellie sensed her disapproval and knew the person most upset by Wade's kiss was Sara. Ellie met her eldest daughter's accusing eyes.

"I'm sorry for embarrassing you tonight," Ellie said.

Sara's expression didn't change.

"What are you most mad about—what I said to Sloan Mundell or Wade's kiss?"

"Both."

"Sloan Mundell is too old for you."

"He's eighteen. That's only four years."

"Honey, eighteen is much farther beyond fourteen than just counting years. I think he has a lot more experience than you."

"You don't even know him."

"True," Ellie acknowledged, inclining her head. "But I have to stand with my opinion of eighteen being too old for you."

"What about you and Wade?" Sara accused. "He's older than you."

Ellie surveyed her daughter, taking in the jut of her chin, the hand on her hip. "You know age isn't a factor between Wade and me," Ellie said calmly. "Please explain what it is you object to so strongly about Wade."

"Everything!" Sara gave a stamp of her foot. "He's not like Daddy. Daddy... didn't do the things he does. Daddy wouldn't have been out there fighting with Andrew, especially in the mud. Daddy was... reasonable... like a dad."

"Wade is different from your father," Ellie allowed. "It doesn't mean he's better or worse. He's just different."

Sara jutted her chin, but said no more. And Ellie had nothing else to say, either. How could she explain what was happening between Wade and herself when even she didn't know? Was it real? Was it leading somewhere? Where?

When the girls were tucked into bed, Ellie went to stand in the shadows of the porch. She'd heard Wade's truck go up the drive earlier. A light shone from his bedroom upstairs.

How she longed to lie with him, to feel his strong warm chest against her back and the shelter of his arms around her, to hear his heartbeat in the darkness. She gave no thought to whether it would be practical, or good in the long run for herself and the girls. She simply knew an aching emptiness and what would cure it.

Why had he kissed her this evening?

It had begun to rain again in the night. Ellie and the girls skipped church and, except for caring for the goats, stayed indoors. When Ellie heard a truck in the drive, she knew instinctively it was Wade. Peering through the curtains with Rae and Poppy confirmed it. The three of them watched as he alighted from the truck and, head bowed against the pelting rain, sprinted for the cover of the front porch.

"He's got flowers," Poppy announced in her reedy voice and smiled up at Ellie.

Ellie quaked inside. What was happening?

She opened the door before he had a chance to knock. He towered in the doorway, his height made even greater by his Stetson. His eyes looked hesitant and guarded. And a large bruise shone purple and gray beneath his left eye. Ellie's gaze strayed downward, taking in his almost formal attire: pale shirt, dark blue string tie, sport coat and gleaming boots.

After a moment's hesitation, he snatched his hat from his head, revealing neatly combed hair. "Hello, Ellie." He looked at her a long moment, and she felt touched, intimately, as was the way with his looks. "I came to apologize for last night." He held a bouquet of daisies and carnations toward her. "Can I talk to you?"

"Oh . . . come in, please."

"Hi, Wade," Poppy piped up.

"Hi, Pebble," Wade teased. He winked at Rae. "Hi, Rae. If I were you, I'd stick to that horse of yours."

"Oh, Wade." Rae blushed and rolled her eyes. "Mama said I'm grounded for the next ten years."

"Come into the kitchen, Wade," Ellie said, "and I'll put these in water. Then we can sit in the swing and talk, if you'd like." She found herself as shy as a teen on her first date. Her insides shook. When she entered the kitchen, remembered scenes from their weekend together shot helter-skelter through her mind. Wade remained standing far from her, twirling his Stetson in his hand.

She found a vase and arranged the flowers in it with shaking hands. She wondered where he'd gotten them on a Sunday—the nearest place would be a large grocery store thirty miles away. That would be sixty miles round trip.

"Where's Sara?" Wade asked.

"In her room, reading."

"And she wouldn't come out to see me, right?"

Ellie only nodded. When he gave a long sigh, she glanced over to see a thoughtfully sad expression on his face. Handing Wade a cup of coffee, she reached for a sweater and her own cup and they went to the porch.

Wade stiffly lowered himself into the swing and held an arm to his side. Catching Ellie watching, he gave a dry chuckle. "Not as young as I once was—proved that last night."

She sat beside him on the swing. His broad shoulder brushed hers; she sensed his nervousness, too. After a moment, he leaned forward and plunked his hat on the porch floor. He rubbed the back of his neck. Ellie's heart squeezed as she studied the bruise beneath his eye.

"I'm sorry about the fight last night with Andrew," he said, casting a quick grin. "Well, I'm not sorry about fighting with Andrew—I'm sorry about making it more difficult for you to get your truck out—" he paused "—and if my getting carried away and kissing you caused you embarrassment."

A smile slipped out. "It's all right...I'd have to be a fool not to have felt a bit flattered."

There was no way she could look at him without her heart melting. She was so glad he was okay; her anger had been motivated by fear for him and Andrew.

"There's nothing between Andrew and me, Wade," she said then. "He's a wonderful young man, but..."

Wade waved his hand, cutting her off. "I know that, Ellie. The fight wasn't anything serious. Andrew and I were just letting off a bit of steam." He cocked his head. "Andrew does care for you, Ellie."

She sighed. "I'll have to talk to him."

Wade nodded. They both fell silent. Ellie studied the porch flooring, wondering what to say, what she wanted to say. Glancing up, she found Wade's gaze steady upon her.

He looked long into her eyes. "I don't know much about love, Ellie." He paused, again rubbing at his neck. "After what happened to me with Beth, I sort of dried up. I took affection from women, enjoyed it, but never cared to pursue anything deeper." He looked over at her. "But I think I'm in love with you."

Her pulse pounded in her temples. "You don't know?"

"I know as much as I can right now... How about you?"

A small smile escaped. "I love you."

She knew it for certain, though she was surprised when the words came out. His eyes were very warm on hers; she thought she saw a gleam of joy.

"It's damn unnerving," he said, giving a small, nervous chuckle.

"Yes...it is."

Neither said anything for almost a full minute, Ellie searching her mind for words to express her feelings.

"Ellie, I'd like to see you," Wade said, speaking first. "Court you, to use an old-fashioned word." His expression turned anxious. "I'd like a chance with you."

"A chance for what?" she managed at last, wanting to know exactly where things stood.

"A chance to share a lifetime with you, if we both come to the conclusion we want to. I mean marriage."

Joy tried to burst through into Ellie's heart, but uncertainty crowded its way in, as well. She found it impossible to swallow.

"Is it all right, Ellie?"

For heaven's sake. Tears blurred her eyes. "Of course it is." She touched his hand. How much she'd wanted to touch him. "But Wade, our weekend together was a special time, not like everyday life. I have three daughters. And Sara...well, Sara remembers her father. She doesn't want to see you take his place."

"I don't guess I can, Ellie. I know how you felt about him." He frowned. "I'd like to make my own place in your life and the girls' lives."

"Oh, Wade..." She put a hand on his arm. "I know that, but Sara's a child. She doesn't understand—and she's jealous." She looked full into his eyes. "The girls and I are a package deal."

He gave a lopsided grin. "I know that full well. Let's just play it by ear, okay?"

He reached for her and she went willingly. It felt so good to be in his arms again. He held her tenderly until the desire grew unbearable between them. She didn't know who started what, but suddenly Wade's lips were hard, demanding upon her own, her own lips parting to receive him, her fingers curling into the rich thickness of his hair. She knew nothing beyond the sensation of his kiss, his embrace.

Until Poppy's voice rang out, "Mama's kissing Wade!"

Jerking apart, Ellie and Wade stared at the door, finding it wide open and Rae standing there, blatantly gawking at them, a knowing smile on her lips. Poppy's announcement again rang from the house, and Ellie knew she was telling Sara.

She raised an eyebrow to Wade. "Still interested?"

"You bet, woman!" He rose and yelled into the house. "Everyone get their raincoats. We're all going for hot-fudge sundaes and I'm buying!"

When Wade brought them home, he walked with Ellie to the porch but declined to stay. He didn't think he could stand being so near Ellie without touching her, and they had constant observers at the moment. It was damned unnerving, the way the girls kept staring at him.

"See you tomorrow morning," he said in her ear, allowing himself a quick taste of her satiny lips. He brushed her cheek with his finger, then turned quickly and ran through the rain to his truck.

His heart swelled to see her wait to wave goodbye. Turning the truck toward his own house, Wade allowed himself a good, resounding, old-west-style yell of triumph.

He'd made the right choice, he thought. Cautioning himself to keep his perspective, he reminded himself he was only openly dating Ellie. Didn't mean they were on the doorstep of the church.

But it was true that this was only the second time in his life he'd felt this way. And he'd chosen well this time.

Sara's image passed through his thoughts. She hadn't gone with them to get ice cream. Wade had been somewhat surprised, yet had approved, when Ellie hadn't insisted Sara come, leaving the girl alone at home. There wouldn't be any forcing a child's emotions into something. How well he knew that. His father had tried to jam a certain code of behavior down his own throat. It hadn't done anything but make him feel resentful. Although a child, Sara was a person; she had to be allowed her own feelings, her own way of being.

At home, Wade sat in the easy chair in his kitchen, the television going in front of him. He didn't see it. Instead, he heard Poppy's reedy voice, saw Rae's mischievous face and Ellie's warm eyes. There was a bond between them, a strong bond, a caring. They were a family.

Wade mused over it and wondered if he would be able to make a place in that family. And he wondered if any time soon, he and Ellie would have a chance to be alone. They'd find time, he vowed.

"Mama, are you and Wade going to get married?" Poppy asked after nightly prayers.

"No, darling," Ellie answered quickly, a bit flustered. She smiled. "At least not right this minute." Out of the corner of her eye, she saw Sara leave the room. "We like each other. We enjoy each other's company." Poppy climbed into bed, and Ellie tucked the covers around her and Rae. "We'll probably be seeing even more of Wade, but a person has to get to know another person before they think of marriage." She smiled. "And in this case *all* of us have to get to know each other."

"I already know I like him, Mama," Rae said.

"Me, too," Poppy echoed.

"And I know he likes you both, too. Good night, my loves."

Why couldn't they stay that age? Ellie thought as she turned out the light. Right now was so easy with them. But that would change as certainly as spring followed winter. They'd have plenty of puzzling growing pains, too.

She paused at Sara's door. "It's getting late. About ready for bed?"

Sara, her back turned toward Ellie, nodded. "Can I sleep with you tonight, Mom?"

"Of course. I'd like that. I'll be in myself in just a few minutes."

Sara's request tugged at Ellie's heart. Her eldest balanced between childhood and womanhood, and right now she was grasping for security.

Sara still lay awake when Ellie turned out the light and slipped into bed. Traditionally this had been their time for private talks. Ellie suspected that had been the reason behind Sara's request.

When Sara remained quiet, Ellie said, "Sara, Wade and I are only seeing each other. We like each other a lot. But we don't know, honey, about getting married."

"I don't want you to marry Wade. You make a big deal about us being a family. Don't my feelings count?"

"Yes...they do," Ellie said, and added after a long moment, "is it just Wade, or any man?"

Sara didn't answer right away. "I don't know," she said finally, her voice betraying her uncertainty.

Ellie could hear the clock ticking in the darkness.

"How can you forget Daddy?" The question came almost as a whisper.

Ellie searched her mind and heart and prayed for the words. "I'm not forgetting Daddy, Sara. Your father became a part of me in the years we were together. Things I learned with him and from him in those years are what make me who I am today. In that way, he will always be with me.

"But he's gone now, honey, and we all have to go on living and learning and experiencing all we can of this life." She felt around beneath the blankets for Sara's hand and gave it a squeeze. "Sara, I was wonderfully happy with your father. Don't you think he'd like me to find somebody who could bring me that happiness again?"

"I don't know," Sara said after a long second. Shaking her hand from Ellie's, she turned on her side, her back toward Ellie, and said no more.

Ellie lay there, staring up into the darkness, hoping she'd said the right words and that Sara would think about it. She worried over Sara's hurt and wanted so much to simply kiss it away. But those times were over. How could she help her daughter? Would she have to forfeit her own chance at happiness?

Wade. She thought of him and couldn't help smiling. Her whole being tingled with excitement. Could they do it? Could they merge their lives? Oh, thank heaven he wanted her. But what if he decided that she and the girls were just more than he wanted to handle? Her heart tightened and she brushed away the thought.

The payment she owed him popped into her mind. The day was less than two weeks away. She'd saved a bit more money, but still the payment was nearly five hundred dollars short. She knew perfectly well he'd brush the matter aside simply because of the way he felt about her. The idea stuck in her throat. Would it make her less in his eyes?

She considered asking her father for the money, knew he'd give it to her without question. But the idea wasn't any more acceptable than telling Wade she was short on the payment. It was her responsibility to pay. She had herself and no one else to blame for her predicament. She wanted to own up to it!

The only thing left to her was the sale of some of the goats. She hated the thought. It would mean cutting her herd in size, which meant a cut in the profits from the fleece in the fall, though she'd have enough left to make her payment to Wade then. But it was more than that: it was like selling off part of their family. The girls certainly wouldn't like it.

Her troubled thoughts turned to Andrew. What words could she say to straighten things out between them without hurting his manly pride? She didn't want to lose his friendship.

Her mind whirled with problems. Life in this moment was a muddle almost too big to even attempt to get through.

Listening to the steady, gentle rhythm of raindrops upon the roof, Ellie fell asleep at last.

The following morning was quite a test of Wade's strength, Ellie decided when she walked into the cafe. He looked at her with eager excitement. But she couldn't match his joy. She wanted, needed comfort.

"Ellie, what is it?" Wade said, his expression instantly concerned.

She kept on walking into the office, not wanting the few early customers to view her distress. She knew she was going to cry, even though she'd already had one good cry at home.

"Ellie?" Wade stepped in the office behind her.

Trying to hold on to her calm, Ellie put her purse away. Then she straightened to look at him and tell him. A lump caught in her throat and her bottom lip trembled.

"We lost a goat last night..." The words came out along with tears. She blinked and tried to look at Wade through the blur. The next instant she stepped into his open arms.

He held her to him, and she cried into his shirt. He stroked her hair and rocked her gently. Finally her sobs turned to sniffles. Wade handed her a tissue.

"How'd it happen?"

Ellie sniffed, then shrugged. "I'm not certain. She'd been sickly and all this rain...I went out and found her this morning."

"Did you call the vet?"

Ellie shook her head.

"You need to do it. He should do an autopsy," Wade said. "Where's the goat now? Did you bury it?"

"No, I didn't have time. I put it in an old truck in the barn. The girls didn't want to get rid of it without a funeral."

"A funeral?" Wade raised an eyebrow.

Ellie sent him a defiant look. "These goats are our family."

His expression gentled. "Yeah, I guess they are." He embraced her again. "You know, you will lose a goat from time to time, Ellie. Death is a part of life."

"I know," she mumbled into his shirt. Suddenly she realized where she was—held in the warm shelter of Wade's arms. For the first time in a long time, she didn't have to bear the hurt or burden all alone. Slipping her arms around his waist, she held him to her, luxuriating in the feeling.

"Think we could slip away this afternoon?" Wade said then. He kissed her temple and vibrations of desire quickly flamed within her.

"What about Poppy?" she asked, almost absently, her mind taken up with the feel of him.

"Doesn't she take naps or something?"

"Oh...no..." Ellie rubbed her face against his shirt, feeling the warmth of his body through the material. "I have something I need to do this afternoon, anyway."

"What?"

"I have to go see Andrew and straighten things out with him." She stared up at him, searching his eyes, seeing the frown sweep his face. "Want to come with me?" she asked, not wanting him to feel left out.

His frown remained for an instant, then a look of resignation took its place. "No," he said, sighing and shaking his head as he pulled her against him. "I guess you and Andrew better handle this alone. He wouldn't appreciate me tagging along on a personal conversation. Just remember—not too personal," he cautioned gruffly.

"Wade," she said, her voice muffled by his chest, "thanks for being here, for listening to me cry, for caring."

His fingers under her cheek, he lifted her face. Then very tenderly he kissed her. "Get to work before I fire you."

When they both turned, Gayla stood in the doorway, a peculiar smirk upon her face. Apparently she'd been standing there for some time.

"I know—" she raised her hand and laughed "—none of my business.... But I told you both so!"

Wade watched Ellie move around the cafe, waiting on tables. He tried not to be too obvious. He was aware of more than a few curious looks from people who'd seen him kiss her Saturday night. They were wondering.

And he was, too.

A part of him he recognized as being childish smarted from her less than enthusiastic greeting that morning. He'd had it all planned, how he'd hand her a cup of coffee, joke with her, enjoy her blue eyes looking at him with that hint of welcome he often saw. Instead she'd been thinking of goats. And now the afternoon would be spent with Andrew.

Suddenly there was a pot pouring coffee into his cup on the table. Looking up, Wade's gaze connected with Ellie's. Slowly her right eye closed in a wink. The welcoming look filled her eyes. Then she walked away, leaving Wade a beautiful view of her shapely behind.

Wade chuckled, at himself and with himself.

When Gayla offered to take Poppy with her into the city for some shopping that afternoon, Wade sent Ellie a questioning look. She answered with an almost imperceptible shake of her head. Frowning, he snugged his cap upon his head and strode away. Regret and uncertainty pulled at her, but she felt she had to speak with Andrew today, wouldn't have any peace until she did. He'd been awfully good to her; she owed him the consideration.

Even so, regret tugged at her. She dreaded Wade's anger or disappointment in her. And she almost couldn't face missing the opportunity to be in his arms. With a loud sigh, she thought how very tired she was getting of being torn in so many directions. Her girls, Wade, Andrew, her own desires.

She found Andrew tinkering with a tractor engine.

"Well, hi," he said with surprise, wiping his hands on a rag. A Band-Aid covered part of his right eyebrow and a small bruise colored his chin.

"Hello, Andrew." She looked at him. "Got time to talk?"

"Sure." That charming smile slipped across his face, along with curiosity and a certain guardedness he'd never held before. He inclined his head toward the patio. "Want to sit?"

Ellie nodded and walked beside him to the chairs. There was no hint of stiffness in his movements, and inwardly Ellie smiled, thinking of Wade.

It was a hard subject to ease into. She didn't know what else to do but speak what was on her mind.

"Andrew, I appreciate all you've done for me, and I cherish our friendship."

He looked at her a moment. "Sounds like placating talk to me."

"I don't mean it to. I mean to get some things straight. I value our friendship, but I don't mean to take advantage of it."

"You think I'm too young for you—that I'm a kid."

Ellie looked full into his green eyes. "You're a very handsome man, Andrew. I'd never make the mistake of thinking of you as a kid—I don't think I could. And it's very flattering to have you look twice at me. I suppose the difference in our ages has something to do with it, but it's just that we don't . . . click. We are good together as friends, but we'd never get along as anything else."

Andrew sighed. "I appreciate what you're saying, Ellie." He gave a half-smile, then a familiar wink. "Can't blame a guy for trying."

"No," Ellie agreed, giving a wide smile, "you can't. And thanks, Andrew."

"Thank you, Ellie."

Andrew walked with her back to the truck. She told him about the loss of her goat, and they mused over probable causes.

"Think the spring rains are about over," Andrew said, looking up at the gray sky. "You shouldn't have any more problem." He opened the truck door, she slipped inside and he closed it after her, leaning his hands on the open window.

"Does this mean I don't get to come for peach pie anymore?" Andrew asked, half teasing, half serious.

"Of course not," Ellie said, placing her hand on his. "You're welcome at our home any time."

"Maybe I'd better watch out for Wade." He touched the bruised place on his jaw.

Ellie blushed. "You're welcome at our home; our friends are always welcome." She raised an eyebrow. "I expect to see you there from time to time."

"You can count on it," he said with a smart nod. His voice turned serious. "If Wade don't treat you right, you give a holler."

Ellie suppressed a grin. Andrew meant it in a kind way.

"Thanks again, Andrew," she said with a parting wave.

For six out of the following ten days, Wade shared a late supper with Ellie and sat in the porch swing with her afterward. Sometimes the girls ate with them, other times they'd had their dinner earlier. Still, they were always around, needing help with homework, watching television, popping in and out to ask a question. Ellie found Wade a blessing for the questions pertaining to science and math, and soon Rae took to asking Wade for help, bypassing Ellie completely.

But there were two nights for themselves. He took her to dinner and to a movie. They sat forever in the restaurant, talking and just looking at each other. When he brought her home, she lingered in his truck, frustrated at being limited only to kisses, yet unable to keep her lips from his. It was gratifying, wonderful really, that Wade was equally frustrated.

Once, they'd gotten carried away and Ellie's blouse was completely unbuttoned when Poppy came running from the house, eager to have Wade come inside and watch a movie with them. Wade was certainly learning the realities of having children, Ellie thought, sinkingly. She would have gone up to his house with him, but there was no adequate way of hiding that from the girls. And she couldn't stand the thought of deceiving them.

No, she had to come in at a decent hour, and for safety's sake, the girls had to know where she was at all times.

On the weekend, Wade flew kites with Poppy, Rae and Ellie. He instructed Rae in riding and caring for her horse, he mended Poppy's bike tire, he repaired the toaster. He was just there, wonderfully there, bringing his humor and wit, his easiness with life.

But Sara refused to acknowledge Wade in any way. In fact, Sara was downright rude until Ellie insisted she show at least the minimum of politeness due a guest in their home. Sara would speak when spoken to, but Wade had really quit trying to talk to Sara at all. Saturday afternoon Ellie insisted, against Wade's advice, that Sara join them for a drive into town for soft drinks. It was a disaster, Sara's attitude dampening everyone's fun.

The situation caused bitter conflict between Sara and Ellie. Sara refused to agree with Ellie on anything; if Ellie had called the sky blue, Sara would have argued. Nothing pleased Sara, and it tore at Ellie to see her daughter so obviously unhappy. Especially when she knew that she could end all Sara's unhappiness simply by giving up her relationship with Wade.

Ellie hoped and prayed things would change, once more putting her faith in all-healing time.

When she was with Wade, Ellie felt such joy. He made her aware of her womanliness, and glad for it. Something as simple as walking across the meadow brought excitement, just holding his hand, discussing the goats, the land and the weather.

And always, in his eyes and within her own body and heart, was the desire.

On the morning of the day the land payment was due, Ellie looked hopefully at her savings-account book almost as if the numbers might have changed on their own. They hadn't, of course.

Closing the book with a firm snap, Ellie tossed it to the kitchen table. With resignation she went to the phone and dialed Andrew's number. Though not much past the crack of dawn, she knew he'd be up, had probably already seen to his stock.

His voice came across the line.

"Andrew, this is Ellie. Would you be willing to buy back some of your goats? And I'll also sell you a few of my kids."

She held her breath, hoping Andrew had the money to do what she requested. The adults would bring less than she'd paid; they were older now, one shearing behind them. But Andrew agreed to buy them and a few kids, as well, and these would bring a good price. It was a setback, but far from a major one; the McGrew clan still had more than when they'd started.

"Mom?" Sara, in flannel nightgown and rubbing her eyes, stepped into the kitchen just as Ellie hung up from speaking with Andrew. "You're selling some of the goats?"

Ellie nodded.

"Why?" Incredulity reflected in Sara's voice. She knew how much the herd meant to all of them—the work, the pride, the affection. Her face, now wide awake, filled with concern.

Ellie's first instinct was to gloss over the matter; she didn't want to burden her child with her concerns. Then a strong whisper urged her not to shut her daughter out. This was an opportunity to share with Sara, for them to draw close.

"Because I need the money to make the payment due Wade for the farm," Ellie said.

Sara frowned. "But the goats, Mom. Couldn't you just tell Wade you're short the money and will pay him...later? I mean...well, he likes you."

Ellie was gratified for the obvious attachment Sara had formed for the goats and now seemed to hold for their new home. She put her arm around her daughter and shook her head.

"I can't do that, darling. It's a matter of pride—of keeping my word. It's my responsibility to pay. Because he cares for me and I for him doesn't change that. If anything, it makes me want to keep my word even more."

After a moment, Sara nodded in reluctant understanding. "But please don't sell Jewel, or Avery...or Baby Belle. You won't have to, will you, Mama?"

"No, we won't," Ellie said gently. "Now go on. Get ready for school."

With the worry over making the payment lifted, another, smaller one tugged at Ellie. Something told her Wade wouldn't be happy when he learned how she'd raised the money. She considered briefly that he didn't have to find out, but the hope faded quickly. This was a small, rural area. Wade would hear.

But she just had to pay him. As she'd told Sara: it was a matter of pride.

Chapter Fourteen

Wade greeted Ellie with his slow grin and the brown eyes that twinkled with hidden knowledge—and not so hidden lust. For a brief moment when she looked at him, she forgot everything else.

Playful, laid-back as usual, he entered the office and sneaked a kiss on her neck. Ellie gave in to the urge to snuggle into his arms, to feel his warm strength. Then, just as she was about to mention the payment due, someone called Wade from the cafe dining room.

"We'll take this up later," he said with a teasing wink, then left.

When Ellie came out of the office she saw Wade sitting with two men, familiar faces if not names, deep into a discussion. The stream of regular morning customers began, and she went about the usual routine.

Andrew came by with a check for the amount they'd settled on. Slipping atop a stool at the counter, he passed the check over to Ellie and she pocketed it quickly, conscious of Wade's presence in the booth not far away.

"Ellie, if you're in a bind, we can make this just a loan," Andrew said, his gaze probing. "I know you're good for it."

She smiled, touched at his kindness. "Thanks, Andrew, but it's better this way. And I don't think selling these goats is going to break me. I have a good start on a herd now."

"Okay," Andrew said after a moment. "When do you want me to come get them?"

"This evening'll be fine—after the dinner shift. I'd better be there because Mutt and Jeff probably wouldn't let you near the goats."

Andrew stayed for breakfast, but both he and Wade had left by the end of Ellie's morning shift. Slipping on a sweater, she grabbed her purse, then walked over to the bank to cash Andrew's check and draw the money from her savings account.

Outside the bank, she paused and stared over at the Wolcott Machine Shop. Wade's truck sat parked outside. Though she'd just drawn nearly every cent she had out of her savings, Ellie experienced a growing sense of high satisfaction. It hadn't worked out exactly the way she'd planned, but it had worked out. She was going to make this payment, and she still had an investment in the goats. The fleece the remaining goats provided in the fall would more than meet the November payment due Wade on the land.

Just as she stepped out to cross the street, Gayla hailed her from the Last Chance. "Ellie! Ellie, can I talk to you for a minute?"

Catching a note in Gayla's voice, Ellie searched her friend's face. "What is it, Gayla?"

"Can you spare me a few minutes—have a cup of coffee?" Gayla asked, breathless from hurrying. "I need to ask you a favor. A big favor."

With a glance toward Wade's shop, Ellie followed Gayla back to the Last Chance. Gayla brought them both coffee and sat for several long seconds before speaking. Sensing something serious weighing on the younger woman, Ellie remained quiet, waiting for Gayla to explain in her own time and words.

"I need to borrow some money," Gayla said, at last raising her green eyes to Ellie.

"Okay..." Ellie said after a moment's surprise. She'd thought the problem would prove to be much greater. "How much?" She reached for her purse. "I made about twenty dollars this morning...let's see, I have..."

Gayla laid her hand over Ellie's. "I need about seven hundred, Ellie. Eight, if you can spare it."

Stunned, Ellie just sat there. *How could it be that she'd picked this particular time to ask her for that kind of money?*

"I'm sorry, Ellie, I shouldn't even have asked," Gayla said then, and Ellie knew dismay shone upon her face like a neon sign.

Gayla started to rise, but Ellie reached for her hand.

"Sit," she commanded, "and tell me about it."

After hesitating a moment, Gayla sat and leaned forward. "It's not really a loan I'm asking for—it's an investment." She shook her head, sending her earrings bobbing. "Wade considers it gambling, says I'm going to get into trouble someday. I guess I do have a bent for gambling, but it's no different from Wade investing in stocks or cattle or goats. Anyway, he wouldn't approve, so I couldn't go to him. And I can't ask Andrew. He hates Dal, says he's shiftless. Dal's got a heart so big, he doesn't even see Andrew's dislike..."

"Okay," Ellie said, waving for Gayla to stop prattling. "So Wade and Andrew wouldn't approve. What are you talking about, Gayla?"

Gayla took a deep breath. "Okay, this is it: Dal Allen has a horse—you know that's what he and his daddy do, board and breed horses?" When Ellie nodded, she continued. "Well, Dal has a horse he's positive is going to be a winner at the track this year." Gayla frowned. "You should know Dal has said this same thing just about ever since I've known him. His dad has for years. They were always going to breed the horse to take all the money. They never have."

Ellie seemed to recall hearing something about the Allens and their hopes of breeding a winning horse. It appeared to have become one of the town jokes. She took a deep breath, wishing Gayla would get to the point.

"Well, Dal's certain this year. He had a two-year-old filly he named Zoe's Secret, after his mother. He's clocked her and believes that she's running faster than anything at Oaklawn last year. I've seen her, Ellie. She is fast, and I do know a bit about the ponies, if I do say so myself."

"What do you need money for?" Ellie asked, puzzled. "Can't she just race and make it for you?"

Gayla shook her head. "Dal needs money to race her—to even get her to the track. He wants to take her over to New Mexico, to Ruidoso for her first race. That race will make her. When she wins she'll be worth ten times what she is now. But we need cash to get there: traveling expenses, entry fees and such. And the bank's breathing down Dal's neck. You know his daddy's been sick—kidney disease? Takes a lot of money for medicine and treatment. And Dal's afraid his daddy isn't going to make it, won't ever see them have a winning horse at last."

"And you're crazy about him?" Ellie added for her.

Gayla gave a sheepish smile. "I never thought it would happen, Ellie. Dal's asked me to marry him, but he wants to be able to provide for me—isn't that old-fashioned?" Her smile vanished. "I know Dal may not be much of a catch to some people, but Ellie, he treats me like a queen. And he's a heck of a horse trainer. Really. I want to help him, but I've just never been given to saving, and about all I've got is five hundred. Dal needs to make a bank payment and all those other things I told you."

Ellie sighed. There really was only one thing to do. Yet it was so hard. She had to force herself to reach for the envelope in her purse. She counted out bills. "Here—eight hundred," she said.

Gayla's eyes widened. "What are you doing with cash..." She took the money. Her eyes glistened with unshed tears, and Ellie's own eyes watered. "What I meant by an investment, is that now you own part of Zoe. If she... when she wins, you'll get all your money back and a heap more. Oh, thank you, Ellie!" She clutched Ellie's hand.

A lump rose in Ellie's throat. "Gayla, you're a good friend—if friends can't help each other, what do we have? You gave me a chance. Now I want to help you and Dal have one."

Gayla rose and pressed her cheek to Ellie's. Then a shadow crossed her face. "You don't need this money, Ellie? I mean..."

Ellie shook her head. "I was just out for a shopping spree," she lied, quite proud to know she sounded convincing. "I can wait until Zoe wins me some money."

"Oh, thanks!" A wide grin split Gayla's face. "I'm going to call Dal right away."

"When's this race?" Ellie called as Gayla sprinted away.

"Next weekend..."

Ellie sat there a few minutes after Gayla had left. She was perfectly aware that she might never see that money again. Dal hadn't raised a winning horse in all these years; there was no reason to think he had now. And no reason to think he hadn't, she told herself sternly.

In any case, it didn't matter. She'd meant what she said about Gayla being a friend. That and that alone was the reason for her decision. Gayla had helped her when she desperately needed it; she couldn't turn Gayla down now.

But as a result, Ellie was further behind in the money she needed to pay Wade than before she'd sold the goats. She took a deep breath, forcing her mind to face the fact. She couldn't sell any more goats, or she wouldn't have enough fleece in the fall to make her payment to Wade then. And he would wait; Gayla and Dal couldn't.

Reviewing the facts in her head, she rose and stepped out in the sunlight and looked to Wade's shop. She plain didn't want to tell him.

She found him in his office, tilted back in his desk chair, his red cap pushed to the back of his head. He gave a bare smile, his eyes hard upon her.

"I heard you sold some goats today." His voice was sharp.

She'd had this silly hope that he wouldn't hear for a few days. "Yes," she said, meeting his gaze.

"Ellie, you didn't have to do that!" He swept his hat from his head and tossed it to his desk, then raked his fingers through his thick hair. The planes of his face were hard and drawn. "You could have come to me instead of Andrew. *Should* have come to me instead of Andrew! I would have waited for the money. You could have made it up in the fall . . . I don't even care about the money!"

She stared at him, took a deep breath and said flatly, "Well, that's good, because you're going to have to wait."

"What happened?" he said after a moment, his expression measuring. "Didn't Andrew give you a good price?"

Ellie handed him the envelope. "Yes, Andrew gave me a good price. I . . . something came up."

Wade counted the money while she spoke, then looked at her. He had a right to know why she couldn't make the payment, she told herself. Even if she was afraid he'd think her a sentimental fool—and with his money, too.

"I lent the money to Gayla."

"You . . ." He blinked. "For Dal."

"Yes."

He stared at her a moment and Ellie was gratified to see his eyes slowly fill with warm amusement. He lifted a hand to stroke her cheek. "You're a hell of a woman."

For a fleeting instant her lips curved into a trembling smile, then for some crazy reason Wade didn't understand, her face fell and her shoulders slumped.

"I'm glad you think so," she said in a faint voice. She looked away, then back at him. "Oh, Wade, I'm so sorry. I guess I should have talked to you before I lent the money to Gayla. I wanted to pay you." Her frown deepened. "It's likely it'll take a couple of shearings to make all this up."

"I'm not worried about the damn money, Ellie. As far as I'm concerned we passed that debt a long time back."

Her eyes widened and took on an angry glint. "Oh? Do you mean I paid what I owe with my body?"

Wade's own anger flared. "What in the hell kind of thing is that to say?"

"If it wasn't for what's between us—if I were anyone else, you'd take the farm."

Wade watched her, baffled at the onslaught. "Well, what do you want me to do? Disregard how I feel for you? Take the farm?" he asked in a low tone.

Ellie rubbed her forehead, her anger fading instantly. "No, of course not. I just mean that no matter what our relationship is, I entered this deal in good faith. I want to pay you what I owe, just like we agreed in the beginning. I hate it that I've failed. I thought I could learn to be independent—most of the time I've been leaning on you, on Andrew, on Gayla. I never should have done any of this. Never should have bought the farm, moved out here..."

Suddenly Wade knew what he was dealing with—Ellie's pride.

"This is payment on the principal," he said, his voice brisk and businesslike. He shook the envelope. "And I think circumstances being what they are, we can waive the interest."

"I don't think we can," Ellie replied, her tone again turning sharp. "We agreed on twelve percent. It's what I owe."

"You let Andrew sell you those goats interest free," he pointed out, silently calling Ellie one stubborn woman.

"We both know that Andrew made a profit on those goats, interest or no."

"And I'm making a good profit on the land, close to double what I paid."

Ellie stared at him, stubbornness written all over her.

"Look," he said, grasping at a different tack. "You're behind on a payment. It's not the end of the world. And you only fail at something when you quit trying. I'll work with you on this, Ellie. Banks do it all the time. I don't want to lose my money. Taking the farm won't help me get my money. You have a good investment in those goats. Come next shearing time, you'll be able to make the payment and more—provided you hold on to those goats."

"If everything goes well," she said glumly.

He couldn't help smiling then and gave in to the growing ache to hold her. He was glad she didn't pull away when he enveloped her in his arms.

"If you hadn't come out here, crazy to buy that farm, I would never have met you," he said, his thoughts filling with how good she felt in his arms. "As for leaning...we all lean on each other, Ellie. That's the way it is for all people. And you've given as much as you've gotten. Before you went to work at the Last Chance, Gayla never dared take time off. You've blessed Andrew with enough home-cooked goodies for him to gain nearly ten pounds, and me—" Pulling back to look into her face, he smiled. "I've gained at least five pounds on your cooking. And I'm the luckiest man in the world right now."

Ellie leaned into his strength, grateful for his words.

"I love you, Ellie." Wade's deep voice came softly. His breath brushed her temple; his hands were warm and hard upon her back. "I want to do things for you. Don't make me feel guilty because of it."

"Oh, I don't mean to," she said, clutching at his shirt. "I love you, too, and I don't want you to think..."

She pulled back and searched his eyes, realizing then that they'd both spoken casually, openly, of loving one another. For the first time.

"I don't," Wade said firmly, looking long into her eyes. "It's your pride. I understand that. And Ellie, I could never think less of you. You are more woman than I've ever known. You've got more guts, more strength than many a man."

Ellie, suddenly conscious of the windows all around them, tried to push from his arms. "Wade," she protested when he tightened his grip. "People can see!"

"Who cares?" Wade chuckled and fell down into his chair, firmly pulling Ellie into his lap. A strong hand at the back of her neck, he forced her lips to meet his.

At first, self-conscious of being in full view of chance passersby, Ellie resisted. But the sweet feel of his lips and the warmth and hardness of his chest against her quickly melted any resistance. Hardly realizing what she was doing, she slipped her arms around his neck and parted her lips. Hot flashes of desire sparked in her veins as his tongue flickered across her lips and into her mouth. He smelled of flannel, old leather and manly cologne.

"I've missed that," Wade said, finally pulling away just when Ellie was certain she'd lost her breath—and didn't care. He buried his face at the side of her neck.

Ellie inhaled deeply and tried to focus her thoughts, to remember why she'd come here in the first place, but all she could do was feel. His lips searing her skin, the hard muscles of his shoulders, the heated swell where her hip pressed against his groin. Her heart pounded, sending pulses of hot longing from the recesses of her feminine body.

"Wade...don't...oh, it's not fair." She couldn't seem to clear her mind. "Do you know what you do to me? Does it happen to you, too?" It was too extraordinary to express in words.

He gave a low chuckle and continued nuzzling her neck, his hand moving surreptitiously to cup her left breast. "Yes—on both counts. And we're going to have to make a decision soon...or something."

"The girls will be taking a weekend at Grandma's," Ellie murmured.

Wade pulled back to look at her. She touched his cheek, her gaze absorbing the hard planes of his face. Handsome. So dear.

He raised an eyebrow. "You thinking of carrying on behind their backs, Ellie?" he scolded playfully.

"I...yes. I love you."

"What about marriage?"

"I don't know..." What could she say? It was dangerous to speak her true feelings—it would leave her bare, unsheltered, open for hurt. "What do you think?" she countered, turning things around.

He nodded, his brows furrowed slightly, his eyes watching her closely. "Will you marry me, Ellie?"

Her breath caught. She hadn't expected...not so soon. She searched his eyes and found love there. Her heart swelled and she knew she loved Wade, wanted beyond anything else to be his.

"We have problems." Ellie gazed into his shimmering brown eyes. Her heart tugged as she saw them darken with hurt. But there were things that needed to be said. "Sara. She needs time, Wade. If we can have only stolen weekends, can you accept it?"

Pain flashed across his face. "I don't know for how long, Ellie. I've never been very good at lying."

Pain squeezed her own heart. She was grateful for his honesty, and he was right, of course. What she'd asked had been unfair.

"I love you, Wade," she said very clearly. "I want very much to marry you. Can you give Sara just a little more time?"

He nodded, though Ellie saw it was with reluctance.

Before she left, it was she who kissed him, completely ignoring the fact they could be observed.

Ellie thought of Sara. There was no simple choice; Sara was her daughter. Besides, what kind of life would she and Wade—any of them—have if Sara was unhappy? Ellie would be pulled in two trying to be the buffer between Sara and Wade. Strife would reign, dividing and killing love.

And what of Wade? Would he truly be happy suddenly finding himself in a home filled with females after he'd spent the better part of his life living alone? He'd never had the responsibilities of a family to hem him in. He did what he wanted, when he wanted. He breezed through life on the vagaries of the wind, Ellie thought, like a soaring eagle—or one of his kites. Not allowing anything to weigh him down.

Marriage, even committed love to another person, didn't allow for that. Marriage to her would certainly be a shock to him. And she didn't want to change Wade. She loved him as he was, wanted him to be happy.

What if he found it unbearable? What if he left? She'd lost Galen; she didn't think she could stand another loss in her life.

What ifs were an endless, useless cycle. There was nothing to do but wait and see how things turned out. Take it a step at a time, Ellie, she reminded herself.

* * *

Wade wasn't a man to brood, but he spent the afternoon doing just that. He had a big ache inside him, and part of it was an irritating knot at the conjunction of his thighs, which didn't help his temper any.

Though he didn't like it, he knew Ellie was right about Sara. For one thing, Sara was her flesh and blood; he respected the way Ellie looked after her daughters as fiercely as a wild cat protecting her cubs. He also knew full well that if Sara refused to accept him, their life, Ellie's especially, would be pure hell.

But, damn it! Didn't he and Ellie have a right to live their own lives?

It's not that simple, came the whisper into his mind. He didn't like it; he'd always found life simple enough, if a person let it be.

While trying to balance the company books, he found himself musing over Sara. But what could he do? The kid had set herself against him.

He pictured her, her heart-shaped face with a few freckles still in evidence, her eyes so like Ellie's. Her attitude angered him, but he found that a soft spot lingered in his heart as well. Sara was confused and hurting. He'd been the same way at her age, maybe for different reasons, but hurting all the same. And she was Ellie's child. His love for the mother made it impossible to dislike the child.

He hadn't told Ellie, but he'd seen Sara twice in the company of Sloan Mundell. Once with some other kids and once alone, at the gas station. Sara had been sitting in Mundell's truck while he got gas. When she'd seen Wade, she'd ducked to hide. He hadn't said anything, hadn't let on about seeing her.

He wondered if he should tell Ellie. But it would only add fuel to already heated emotions. Sara would feel defensive, and Ellie might not care for him butting in.

How had he gotten himself into all this? he wondered in exasperation, when he'd added a column of figures for the third time and for the third time came up with a different total.

Leaning back in the chair, he allowed his thoughts to wander. Immediately they conjured up the image of Ellie. As if she were there before him, he saw first her shining hair, spun like strands of silk, then her blue eyes, then her creamy skin. As if looking at her with his eyes, his inner gaze moved downward, remembering just how creamy and soft her heavy breasts not only looked but felt.

"Damn!" He swore aloud, finding no peace in the picture.

The telephone rang and he answered, fairly growling, "Hello!"

It was Ellie. How glad and irritated he was at the same time. No doubt about him being in love, he thought sarcastically. Catching his mood, her voice turned shy as she asked if he wanted to come to dinner.

"Thanks, but not tonight," he said, forcing his voice to a gentler tone. "I'm going with Virg over to a car auction in the city." It was a good excuse. He just didn't think he could stand seeing her this night and knowing he couldn't have her.

"Okay," she said, her voice sounding quite small. He heard Poppy and Rae in the background. "I will, Poppy," came Ellie's voice across the line. "Wade? My parents are coming for dinner tomorrow night. Would you like to join us?"

"Sure."

He heard again the girls' eager young voices in the background as he hung up. He knew he wanted not only Ellie but to be a part of the life she had.

Wade was heading home that night when, just outside of town, his headlights flashed across a figure walking at the edge of the road. Instinct picked up something familiar about the figure, and, slowing, Wade checked his watch. It was past eleven. And the figure he'd seen was too small to be anything but a kid.

The truck's reverse lights caught the small figure in a silvery-red glow. A girl in a short denim skirt.

Sara? Wade thought wildly, unbelieving. He had to be mistaken. But the hair appeared similar to Sara's short-cropped style, the size was about right.

Cautiously, the figure moved further away from the road as Wade approached. Obviously she'd had some trouble, he thought. Girls didn't just walk along lonely country roads in the dark.

He pulled back far enough to catch whoever it was in the glow of his headlights. And dumfounded, he saw it was Sara. In an instant his mind played the scenario that must have happened. Sloan Mundell. She'd had to run away from Sloan Mundell.

After freezing with surprise and uncertainty, Wade shifted gears and eased the truck up beside her. He rolled down the window, noticing her small frame tighten, as if readying for flight. She began to jog forward.

"Sara! It's me—Wade," he called.

She stopped and turned, her eyes squinting in the bright headlights. Wade pulled beside her and stopped. He switched on the overhead cab light so she could see him clearly. The light spilled out to illuminate her pale, drawn face, her saucer-round eyes.

"Get in," he said. "I'll give you a lift."

She didn't move; uncertainty crossed her face. "I don't want to go home," she said.

Another surprise, but Wade took it and let it slide. "Where to, then?"

"Maryann Vogel's." She watched him carefully.

"Okay." He nodded. "Up here about two miles? To the left?"

She nodded as she opened the door and stepped up into the truck. She slammed the door behind her and sat very rigid, her face straight ahead.

Wade let out the clutch, starting off. "Are you all right?" he asked very quietly. Out of the corner of his eye, he checked her appearance for signs of violence.

She nodded. "Yes."

Minutes ticked away. "Where does your mom think you are?" Wade asked.

"Maryann's slumber party."

The answer eased Wade's mind, and he relaxed. He didn't want Ellie to be sitting home, going out of her mind with worry.

He let the silence lie. Just as he turned from the highway, Sara spoke.

"Aren't you gonna lecture me or something?"

Wade took a breath. "I can guess what happened. And I also guess you're feeling foolish enough right now, without me saying anything." He continued on down the dirt road. "Which house?"

Sara nodded. "There—the third one."

Wade rolled to a stop in front of the large sloping lawn.

Sara made no move to get out of the truck. The dash lights showed her eyes large and dark. "Sloan, he...we were parking down Naylors Road. I didn't think...he tried to..." She left off talking, a sob catching in her throat.

"You okay, Sara? He didn't hurt you?" Wade said anxiously, placing a hand on her shoulder.

She shook her head. Wade turned on the overhead light to have a better look. Placing a hand to her chin, he turned her face to look at him. "Tell me the truth."

She blinked, and he saw her fight the shame. "He didn't hurt me. He just got mad and said I could walk home. I even think he came after me to give me a ride, but I hid from him. I was afraid."

Wade nodded, satisfied she was telling the truth.

"It was my own fault."

"It was that," Wade agreed, then he smiled softly. "But I have yet to meet the world's perfect person."

"You gonna tell Mama?"

Wade shook his head. "You're all right. I think telling your mom is something you'll have to decide about."

She didn't look as if she believed him. Then she was out of the truck and running up the door of the house. Wade turned out the cab light and waited to see her enter the house before driving home.

He was a man who rarely changed his mind, once he decided something, and such was the case with his decision not to tell Ellie what he knew. The last he allowed himself to think of it was later, in the early hours of the morning, as he stared down at the small stone house, wishing he could hold Ellie in his arms. He very much hoped Sara would tell Ellie. The two of them didn't need to be so far apart they couldn't talk about such a thing.

The thought gone, he was never tempted to speak of the incident, considering it as if it hadn't happened, though he wasn't completely unaware of Sara's curious looks and edginess when he visited Ellie the next afternoon and sat with her on the porch. Twice, Sara came to the door, saying nothing really but looking at him as if she couldn't figure him out. Wade, on his part, acted no differently.

Sara helped Ellie set the table for the elaborate dinner. Ever since she'd come home, Sara had seemed extremely quiet and withdrawn. Her face was paler than normal. Ellie had checked her for a fever and stopped stirring the cheese sauce now to check her again.

"You feeling all right, honey?"

Sara gave a wan smile. "Fine, Mama."

Ellie was not reassured. Something was wrong with her eldest. Mother's instinct again.

But then her parents arrived and, soon after, Wade. He amazed and pleased her. He looked every inch the gentleman land baron in a tweed, western-style crease. He further amazed her by bending to plant a kiss upon her lips in a familiar greeting. His eyes twinkled, and Ellie suspected this was his way of making his intentions known to her parents.

She wasn't unaware of the glances exchanged between her parents. Her mother frowned. But the frown and reserved manner gradually melted during the course of the evening. Wade cajoled, blatantly flirted with, and outright charmed them. And Ellie knew it was all done deliberately.

They'd set the table with the best linen cloth. The fine china and silver gleamed. Gallantly, Wade produced a bottle of excellent wine. "Didn't think I knew about anything other than beer, did you?" he whispered teasingly in her ear.

He swept the chair out for Ellie's mother and even extended the courtesy to Rae and Poppy, while Ellie's father did the same for Ellie and Sara.

Wade commented to her mother that now he knew where Ellie got her good looks. He even winked. And Ellie's mother actually blushed. Wade drew her father out about his business and talked sports. Then he managed, in a very unassuming way, to impart the knowledge that he owned eleven hundred acres, the Last Chance Cafe and the Wolcott Machine Shop.

As if in a conspiracy, Rae and Poppy did their part. Repeatedly they bragged about all the things Wade had done for them—bike repair, riding lessons, kite flying and, of course, Poppy's almost daily ice-cream cone. Even Sara seemed to help matters. At least she didn't frown and huff and puff.

Ellie found it all close to hilarious. More than once she had to choke back a chuckle. Wade was the equal of Cary Grant in charm and grace, and he enjoyed every minute of it.

Then her parents were gone, the dishes cleared, the girls at the sink washing them and Ellie and Wade sitting at the table. Suddenly Wade reached for the wine still sitting in the ice bucket.

"There's some left," he said, holding the bottle to the light. "Come on." He reached for Ellie's hand and grabbed two glasses with his free hand. "Girls, I'm taking your mom to the barn for a few quiet minutes."

Caught off guard, Ellie pulled back. "Wade..." She glanced at her daughters, seeing the grins across Rae's and Poppy's faces, the blank stare from Sara.

And then Wade was pulling her toward the door. She caught the flash of his smile, the warm light in his eyes. And she wanted to go. She wanted beyond anything that could hold her in that house to be alone with him.

Chapter Fifteen

Ellie left the girls in the kitchen and went with Wade. Holding her hand, pulling her along—both of them laughing for no reason at all—Wade led the way to the old barn. They stopped just inside and climbed up to sit on hay bales. The outside pole lamp provided a silvery light. Rae's horse snorted at the intrusion into his barn. A fresh spring breeze brought the scents of growing things, and Ellie shivered in the coolness.

"Oh...here, my lady," Wade said, removing his coat and settling it in a courtly manner over her shoulders. His hand brushed her neck, and they looked long into each other's eyes, sharing the happiness—happiness sprung from nothing, as it often did with people in love.

With a flourish, Wade filled the two glasses with the last of the wine. They clinked the glasses together in a toast.

"To me," Wade said.

"Not conceited, are you?" Ellie commented, then sipped her wine.

Wade shook his head. "Not at all. You have to admit, I was magnificent tonight."

"I do admit it." She averted her eyes, conscious of his heavy gaze slipping down her body. "How did you know what to expect from my parents? I don't remember ever saying anything."

"Ah, but you have. Small comments here and there. And Rae and Poppy are a wealth of information. They warned me, in a matter of speaking."

"They warned you? Poppy?"

"She didn't realize it."

His eyes rested on hers, and she saw desire there. Her breathing became shallow; her heartbeat sped in anticipation, though she tried to talk sense to herself.

"You're pretty high on yourself tonight," she said. He seemed almost drunk with self-satisfaction.

"Isn't the wine," he said, taking another deep drink. "Haven't had enough." His gaze turned decidedly sensual. "Maybe it's the company I keep." His arm slipped around her shoulders. He finished his wine.

Ellie turned her face and took another sip from her glass. She wanted him, there, at that moment. But her mind strayed, as always, to her daughters only yards away in the house. She needed to get back. *What if they came looking for her?*

The next instant Wade had taken the glass from her hand and set it aside. Then he was kissing her and pressing her back against the hay. He tasted of wine and garlic and sweet warmth. The romance of the moment swirled around her, and she accepted it, grasped it. Inhaling the scent of him, she forgot everything but the way it felt to be in his arms with his lips pressed to hers.

When his hand slipped inside her blouse and stroked tenderly across her ribs, Ellie shuddered at his delicious touch and kissed him harder. Tender, demanding, drugging, he led her into their own private world. All she could think of were the hot sensations rushing over her and the need for more.

"Mama?"

Ellie froze as if ice water had just been thrown over her. Wade did the same, his hand still around her, his cheek pressed against hers. Slowly he moved, and Ellie looked beyond his shoulder to see Sara standing in the wide entry, staring at them. The light streamed from behind her, so Ellie couldn't see her expression.

"I . . . was . . . wondering about letting Poppy stay up to watch the movie with us," Sara said. Her hands hung at her sides.

"Oh?" Ellie managed, hot anger bursting inside her. "I'll be up to the house in a minute, Sara. You go now."

Instantly Sara turned and fled.

Ellie realized she was shaking; Wade's arm trembled against her. She pushed away from him and straightened her blouse where he'd unbuttoned it.

"I'm sorry, Wade . . . but it's like that a lot with kids."

"She knew what she was doing." Wade replied in a short tone.

Ellie looked over to see him raking a hand through his thick hair. "What do you mean by that?"

"Just what I said."

"Okay—but she's just a child."

"I know that, Ellie." He looked hard at her. "Come up to my house with me. Tell the kids we're going up there, give them the phone number to call if they need to."

"I can't do that."

"Why not? Those girls know all about what goes on between a man and a woman, Ellie. Even Poppy. And what in the hell is wrong with having a date with me?"

"Nothing . . . only, not now, like that. Yes, the girls know about the facts of life—all the complete details. I'm the one who taught them. We've never hidden sex in our home. But I'm their example." When Wade let out a disgusted sigh, she said, "Would you want your daughter doing what you've asked me?"

"If I knew the man's intentions were the same as mine," Wade answered after a long minute. "If I knew he loved her the way I do you. I'm not playing around, Ellie. I'm willing to pledge all that stuff about for better or worse for the rest of our lives, 'cause I think living the rest of my life with you will be pretty damn good. And you're only the second woman in my life that I've said as much to.''

Ellie just looked at him, feeling tears well in her eyes. She knew it was hard for him to say those words. She touched her fingertips to his cheek. "I want to marry you, too. And I know spending the rest of my life with you would be good...and eventful." She chuckled and brushed at her eyes.

"Ellie, I'm damned tired of not being able to hold you when I want, kiss you when I want. Let's get married. Sara will come around."

"Wade...I don't think you know what it'll be like. Something like Sara's interruption tonight will probably happen nearly ever night, not only when we're kissing, but when we're talking, when we're working on something around the house..." She lifted her arm and let it drop.

"You don't think I can handle it?"

What could she say, how could she express her doubts without hurting him?

"Ellie, give me credit for knowing *something*. I may not be the same as your precious Galen, but I think I'm man enough to be a husband to you and a father to those girls." His voice rose with anger. "I'm not only going to take from you, Ellie, I have something to give, too."

Ellie felt slapped. She'd never imagined the hint of jealousy of Galen she heard in Wade's voice. Immediately she sought to cool that jealousy.

"I didn't say you weren't man enough," she said levelly. "You're a hell of a man." She searched her mind for the words. "I'm just saying that you've been a bachelor for thirty-eight years. And seeing me and the girls like you have and living it day to day are two different things. What are you going to do if you don't like it? Leave?"

"You afraid of that, Ellie?" His voice came cold.

"Maybe." She averted her eyes. It was uncomfortable facing such feelings within herself.

"You don't think any more than that of me?"

"Oh, it has nothing to do with my esteem for you. It's cold facts. And there's Sara to think of." Ellie felt torn in two by the people she loved most on this earth.

"Yep, there's Sara." Thick sarcasm traced the words. "You know, Ellie, you say you want to live your own life, but you're letting a little fourteen-year-old run it for you. Every time we've been out together, you kept thinking about getting home to her for fear of upsetting her. Well, maybe Sara needs a little less kid-glove handling. The world's not going to be so careful with her, Ellie. She might as well learn that now."

The cold rebuke in his voice sent anger flashing through her. "Oh, are you suddenly the child-rearing expert—you, who've never lived with a child?"

"I've been a kid. I haven't forgotten. And I'll tell you something else, I'm damn tired of you putting her over me. I have feelings, too. I want to hold you. I want to make love to you." For this last he stepped to the barn entrance and shouted. "There, now there can be no doubt. I want to laugh with you and share problems with you. Now, we don't have to have a piece of paper to let us do all those things. And I'm not going to sneak around about it just because we don't." He paused and placed a hand to his hip, looking at her. "That's it, Ellie."

"That's it? You want this all your way or not at all?" She said. Her anger rising to meet his, her instincts were to hit back at his hurtful words.

"If you see it that way."

"Well, then . . ." She searched for words.

"Well, then, you just sit here with those girls and let little Sara run your life."

"You know what your problem is?" she said acidly. "You're all hot and bothered and don't know what to do with it."

"Oh, no . . . I know exactly what to do with it. And I'll just go find me someone who will appreciate my attentions." He snatched up his coat and threw it over his shoulder. Then he walked to the far opening in the barn.

"You just do that!" Ellie called after his retreating back. "If that's all you want, you're welcome to it—because, honey, I can get that any time myself!"

Closing her mouth firmly, she bit back the ugly swear words that wanted to spew forth. She'd already gone too far. Pivoting, she ran for the house, the anger and hurt churning around within her. Damn him! Damn him! She opened the door and three shocked faces with three pairs of blue eyes stared at her. And damn them, too! she thought, running on through the kitchen to her bedroom.

Closing the door behind her, she even locked it. Then, throwing herself to her bed, she buried her face in the pillow and cried. Her body fairly ached with frustrated longing and rejection.

Soon, over her sobs, she heard muffled whispers outside her door and there came a tentative knock. Ellie lay there. She couldn't answer, not yet. She had to have a few more minutes to get some sort of control over her emotions.

Ten minutes later, she came out, like a good mother should, she thought, feeling drained and dry. With mechanical motions, she saw to finishing up in the kitchen, lifted the linen tablecloth and put it in the dirty-clothes basket, made sure the girls brushed their teeth and hung up the bathroom towels.

"Mama?" Poppy asked shyly. "Did you and Wade have a fight?"

"Poppy!" Rae gave her sister a nudge.

"Yes, Poppy," Ellie answered, pulling a nightgown over Poppy's tiny head.

"Did you fight with him because you care for him so much?"

Ellie gave a tired smile. "I guess so. Come on now—get a brush and I'll brush your hair."

The girls declined the late movie, and Ellie tucked them in bed.

She paused in Sara's room. "Sara, I'm very angry about you coming out to the barn tonight. You did it on purpose, and not to ask a question. It was very rude."

Sara's eyes filled with tears. "I know. I'm sorry, Mama."

Her daughter's contrite expression melted the remaining anger within Ellie. She bent to kiss her daughter's cheek. "It's all right. Go to sleep now."

Alone in her bedroom, she listened to the quiet. Trying not to think or feel, she changed into a nightgown, washed her face and brushed her teeth, then checked on the girls. They slept. Sara's hands were balled into tight fists. Tender love swelling Ellie's bruised heart, she gently opened Sara's hands and stroked them into relaxing.

When she stepped into her bedroom, her eyes fell on the wide expanse of bed. A sharp pain stabbed into her heart. *I didn't mean it,* she thought, as if crying out aloud to Wade.

She sat on the edge of the bed and hugged a pillow to her. *How had they come to say all those awful things?* She'd just been so frustrated with wanting him, feeling pulled in a dozen directions. And then she'd flared up at his attitude. It was as if a spigot of unreasonable and unexplainable anger had suddenly been turned on within her.

She hadn't meant much of what she said—at least the way it had come out. So she'd been putting Sara first. What was she to do? Sara was fourteen, Wade an adult. And it seemed to him that she allowed Sara to run her life, but all she was doing was trying to be patient. The girls had lost their father; they only had her. She'd brought them into the world, and not by accident. She'd planned those babies; she owed it to them to provide the best life she could.

Recalling the argument, her mind whirled with confusion. She couldn't remember the exact words, but she did remember Wade saying plainly that he wanted her. Regret welled up and settled heavily on her shoulders. She hadn't told him that—and she should have. She did want him. She wanted him very much.

When she recalled his stated intentions upon leaving, she dropped her head into the pillow and cried again. Right now he probably lay in some other woman's arms.

Well, so be it! she thought angrily. If he could go to someone else so quickly, she didn't need him. *Not at all!*

The next day, although she felt foolish, Ellie hoped to see Wade at church. Disappointment struck deep when he wasn't there. When they returned home and saw his truck up the hill, she considered going up to talk to him. But, no, she couldn't do that. He'd said last night that he would find comfort elsewhere. The thought made anger rise afresh. She would not go to talk to Mr. Wade Wolcott. He obviously didn't want to be bothered with her.

At the sound of a knock, Wade hurried down the stairs to open the door. High expectancy rose in him as he prepared what to say to Ellie, to greet her and kiss away the hurt between them. But it wasn't her at the door. Instead, Sara stood there.

"You forgot your hat last night," she said, extending the Stetson toward him.

"Oh...thanks." He took the hat.

Sara didn't turn to leave. "May I come in for a minute?"

"Sure," Wade said after a moment's surprise. He moved aside to allow her to enter. "Want to sit?" He inclined his head toward the couch.

Sara shook her head. She stood, clasping her hands. "I never did thank you for helping me the other night."

Wade shrugged. "It's okay."

Sara took a breath. "That fight you and Mom had last night. It was because of me, huh?"

"Don't give yourself so much credit."

"Well, do you want to marry my mom?" Her blue eyes were wide with strain.

"Sara, what's between me and your mother will stay between us. It's our business." Wade considered his words. "I guess you have a right to know I love her. But you should know better than anyone that she will never do anything she feels is not the best for you girls. You do know that?"

Slowly Sara nodded. "I wanted to apologize for coming out to the barn last night."

He looked at her for a long minute. It had taken a great deal for her to come here like this, and he respected her for it.

"Apology accepted."

"Well, goodbye..." She turned to leave.

"Goodbye, Sara."

He watched her from the doorway as she walked back down the drive and slipped through the fencing, continuing to the small stone house. Wade's gaze moved to the windows of the house and then to the porch, seeing Ellie even before he realized it. Just as the night before he'd spent hours looking out the window, deliberating with himself about going back to straighten things out. Yet, he hadn't cooled down enough to do so.

He'd said things last night that, while true to a certain extent, had been motivated by frustration and anger. When he couldn't have what he wanted, he'd lashed out.

And that anger still lingered. He briefly considered going down to see Ellie now. He longed to see her. But nothing good would come of it in his current frame of mind. Hell, she probably didn't want to see him. Besides, he'd told her where he stood. If she wanted him, she knew where to find him.

The week dragged by. Ellie was astonished when Wade wasn't at the Last Chance when she came in Monday morning. And he didn't show up the rest of the day, nor the next. She learned from Gayla that he'd driven down to Dallas and wasn't expected to return until Thursday. Though terribly disappointed, Ellie figured it was probably for the best. She wasn't at all certain how she'd behave around him. It would be mortifying beyond belief to break down in tears in front of all the customers.

When Gayla asked what was going on, Ellie just shrugged and refused to talk about it. Luckily Gayla, preoccupied with Dal and Zoe and the upcoming race, didn't pursue the matter.

Ellie didn't see Wade until Friday morning when she came into work. She didn't cry. She simply looked at him, wondering what she should do or say. She almost ran into his arms, but there was no welcome in his eyes. She turned away, and minutes later he left and did not return.

She was probably going to have to quit her job, she thought sinkingly. She certainly didn't want to be the cause

of Wade not even frequenting his own cafe. But what would
she do? Where would she work? And she didn't want to
leave all her friends.

And she didn't want to leave Wade. She wanted more
than anything for it to be right between them again. She
longed to snuggle into his strong embrace, to feel his lips on
hers. She considered going to him, but, too fearful of being
rebuked, she just couldn't bring herself to do it. He'd said
he'd find comfort elsewhere. The thought that he might no
longer want her cut through her heart like a dagger.

She didn't think it possible, but Saturday was worse than
the previous days. Every chore seemed to take all her
strength to complete. The girls came and went, visiting
friends, their friends visiting the house. The chatter got on
her nerves, and she was appalled to find herself actually
yelling at the slightest infraction.

And always she looked for Wade's truck or to see him
standing on the hill flying a kite. When she did see him, she
would turn away, longing overwhelming her.

In an effort to deal with her heartache, Ellie retired to her
bedroom, seeing some bit of solitude and peace in the midst
of a house of active children. She was propped against pil-
lows in bed late Sunday afternoon, reading a novel, when
Sara peeked her head in the door.

"Mama, can I talk to you?"

"Of course," Ellie said, patting the bed beside her. Her
mother's radar instantly sensed something troubling her
daughter.

"I have to tell you something," Sara said, settling herself on the bed. She didn't meet Ellie's gaze. "Something I
did."

"Okay," Ellie said quietly.

"I went out with Sloan Mundell."

"You what?"

"Now, Mom, please listen." Sara's voice and eyes
pleaded.

Swallowing indignation and roiling anger, Ellie quieted.
"I'm listening."

"It was the night of Maryann's slumber party," Sara continued. "We girls all met in town and some boys joined us. I went off with Sloan." Ellie held her peace with iron discipline. Sara watched her closely. "He tried to make me...well, you know, and I refused. He got mad and said he wouldn't take me home. So I got out and started walking to Maryann's. Sloan came after me, to give me a ride, I think, but I hid from him."

It all fairly took Ellie's breath away.

Sara focused on the bedspread and played with a loose thread. "Wade came along and gave me a ride to Maryann's."

"He did *what*?" Ellie couldn't believe it. Why hadn't he told her?

"He gave me a ride. And he said he wouldn't tell you— that it was my responsibility to tell you."

Ellie sat there, digesting the information for a long second. Then she opened her arms and Sara pressed against her. "Oh, my darling, I'm just so glad you weren't hurt."

"Me, too," Sara murmured.

They stayed a full minute in the quiet embrace. Then Sara pulled back and looked at Ellie.

"Mama, have you and Wade split up because of me?"

Ellie didn't quite know how to answer. She searched for the truth, but wasn't even certain what that was anymore. "We've argued over you, yes. But it's all so much more complicated." She sat there. "We just argued over a lot of things."

"Do you love him, Mama?"

"Yes," Ellie said slowly. "Yes, I do."

"As much as you loved Daddy?"

"As much as I loved your daddy when I married him. You'll find when you finally meet a man to love and marry him, that love grows to more than you can ever imagine, but it takes years."

"Do you want to marry him?"

"Yes, I'd like that, but I have to think of what would be best for all of us, make us all happy."

Sara looked thoughtful. "I've been thinking about what you told me that night about Daddy and living and stuff." She cocked an eyebrow and for one instant reminded Ellie so much of herself. "Don't you think if you're happy, all the rest of us will be, too, and if you're sad, it makes the rest of us sad?"

After a moment, Ellie nodded slightly. "Yes . . . it can be that way."

"Mama, don't you think maybe you should go see Wade? You always tell us to talk out our problems with people."

At Sara's words, Ellie chuckled softly. "I do, don't I?" She had a feeling she was receiving a dose of her own often-given medicine. And that perhaps it was exactly what she needed.

Sara gave her a parting squeeze, then left the room.

After several minutes Ellie moved to fling back the sheet. "Perhaps I should go see him," she murmured aloud. "To apologize for things I've said, if nothing else."

Her hands shook. She paused to look in the mirror. Should she really go and talk to him? *Could she?* She went into the kitchen for a cup of coffee and glanced up the hill at the same time, checking to see if Wade's truck was there. The late afternoon sunlight shone upon its dark blue surface.

What if he didn't want her anymore? How horrible it would be to see pity in his eyes. Lord, he won't know what to say. Her body tightened with aversion. She didn't want to embarrass him. Or to feel any more foolish than she already did.

But then came another voice into her mind: he could want her. Like her, he could be waiting . . . and she'd never know unless she went up there to talk to him.

Quickly, before she could lose her courage, she went back to her bedroom to change clothes and make herself as pretty as possible. She didn't know if Wade still wanted her, but she did know she intended to find out.

"I'm going up to Wade's, if you need me," she told the girls. She smiled at Rae and Poppy's grins. And oddly enough, a soft smile touched Sara's lips as well. Ellie sent her a look of thanks, and Sara answered with her own look of acknowledgment.

"His number is right beside the telephone, if you need me," she said over her shoulder as she went out the back door.

Chapter Sixteen

The telephone rang and Wade answered it. To his immense surprise, Sara's voice came across the line.

"Mama's coming up to see you, and if you're half as smart about women as people say you are, you'd better know enough to meet her halfway."

A click sounded and the line went dead. Wade stood there for a second, foolishly staring at the receiver. Slowly he replaced it, his mind trying to sort out the words he'd just heard. He strode to the door and looked out the window. Ellie indeed was headed across the pasture toward his house. He started immediately out the door, then realized he wore only his socks. Racing back, he tugged on a boot and hopped to the door as he tugged on the other. Then he was out the door and heading down the hill to meet her.

Uncertainty tinged with hope flickered across her face. A tentative smile touched her lips. He walked faster, holding her gaze with his. When they were only a few feet from each other, Ellie stopped, an anxious question sweeping her face.

Wade kept going toward her, and she smiled. Then she was in his arms.

How good she felt! Her gentle, feminine shoulders beneath his hands, the smooth line of her back. Joy burst within him like an exploding star.

Ellie clung to him, rubbing her cheek against the softness of his shirt. His heartbeat pounded in her ear; he smelled of after-shave lotion, cotton and male warmth. She pressed the moment into the secret places of her heart, always to remember the incredible feeling of being wanted, being fully loved.

At last she drew back and looked at him through a blur of tears. Amazing, but his eyes watered, too.

"I'm sorry," she said.

"Me, too."

Neither said I love you, but the air vibrated with the unspoken knowledge.

Ellie took his hand and stepped toward his house. "I told the girls they could call me if they needed me."

"You did?" A slow smile spread beneath his mustache; pleasure lit his face.

"Uh-huh." She smiled, too.

In his kitchen, newspapers covered the floor by his chair, jeans and shirts sprawled across the couch, soup bubbled on the stove, the makings of it still strewn across the counter, and the television echoed with racing cars.

"I wasn't expecting company," Wade said sheepishly.

Ellie just looked at him, thinking how close she'd come to never being able to look at him so intimately.

He rubbed the back of his neck. "Look, about what I said the other night . . ."

He stopped speaking when Ellie pressed her body seductively against him and curled her hands around his neck. "We both said things in anger, things we didn't exactly mean." Giving a bare smile, she raised an eyebrow. Just before she spoke, she told herself not to ask. But she did anyway. "Was going elsewhere for comfort one of those things?"

A look of surprise swept his face, followed quickly by one of amusement. "Do I detect a note of jealousy?"

She pushed from his chest, feeling foolish and childish. she never should have asked, didn't need to know, should have trusted. He grabbed her around the waist and pulled her back, looking long into her eyes.

"That statement of mine was as empty as I hope yours was. There's no other woman for me, Ellie."

She hugged him to her and whispered, "We don't need to talk."

The next instant he amazed her by sweeping her into his arms. "No we don't, woman," he said, a low chuckle tracing his words.

They made love in his big bed. With his every touch, his every caress, Ellie felt his unequivocal love, and she abandoned herself to the passion. She strove to give back to him all that he gave her, measure for measure. Wonderful love. Their bodies, minds and hearts merging with one beautiful accord.

And when the tears came afterward, she didn't try to hide them. They were the evidence of the magic she'd felt, the magic she'd shared with him.

"Did I do that?" he whispered lovingly, moving his lips to kiss away the tears, then downward ever so slowly to tease and caress her breasts. He stopped and held her fiercely to him. "I love you, Ellie. Lord, I do."

Clinging to him, she felt his intense passion, his heart pounding against hers, his sweat mingling with hers. "And I love you, so very much."

She trembled as he ran a callused palm softly, even reverently, over her breasts and downward over her stomach and hip.

His brown eyes bore into hers. "You going to marry me tomorrow, Ellie?"

She nodded. A lump in her throat closed off any words. His eyes narrowed as he studied her face. "Sara?" he questioned.

She smiled and touched his hard, precious cheek. "Sara's working on it...she told me about the night you helped her.

I'm so grateful . . . for then and afterward. It was better she told me herself. Better for her, better for me.'' She looked at him in wonder, thinking how rare a man he was.

"I was a kid once," he growled, as if dismissing it all. He continued to search her face. "You still afraid I might up and leave you sometime?''

"Some . . .'' she managed huskily. "I wonder . . . if it will work out, if you'll be happy taking on the responsibility you are."

Understanding lit his eyes just before he pressed his cheek against hers. "I guess we all do a lot of that kind of wondering. It's okay, honey. Time will handle it.''

Ellie melted into his embrace, thanking God for the strength and goodness of him. And that he loved her.

They lay there, loathe to move, enjoying caressing each other's bare skin, gazing into each other's eyes. Then Wade rolled to his back and pulled her into the crook of his arm. Her gaze strayed around the room, taking in the pale blue walls, the framed pictures of kites, the old fashioned dresser with the top so cluttered it couldn't be seen. It was a nice room, a homey room.

"Think you can be happy in this house?''

Wade's voice startled her, and she realized he'd been watching her, had guessed her thoughts.

"Of course," she said, touching his mustache, wondering if she could ask him to give up something more than he already had. Her balancing act was beginning in earnest: what was best for Wade, best for her daughters. But it was worth it, she thought.

"Think you could fit me in down at your place for a while?'' he asked, his voice soft. He nuzzled her ear.

"Oh, Wade . . . you wouldn't mind too much? I know it's small, but the girls have enough changes to contend with . . .'' Her breath came faster as he played his hand across her ribs. "And we love that little house.''

He chuckled then. "I'd live in a cracker box with all of you. We'll manage.''

She drew back and looked into his eyes. "Thank you . . . thank you for understanding.''

"Oh, lady, you keep me happy like this and I may just build you a new house—room for three girls and maybe a couple of boys."

"Just like that?"

"Just like that." His gaze turned heavy with desire and he leaned down to claim her lips, effectively claiming her body, as well. Then suddenly, he broke away and growled, "Let's go tell them."

Ellie laughed aloud. "I don't think they need to be told much."

She sat with Sara in the kitchen. The hour grew late, but the children wouldn't be going to school the following day, nor Ellie to work. Wade sprawled his lanky frame the length of the couch in the living room, Poppy on his lap, Rae propped against his thigh, watching the end of a television show.

Ellie looked at her eldest daughter, whose head bent over paper on the table. Sara had virtually taken charge of the wedding, making lists of things to do. Ellie knew it couldn't have been easy for her daughter and that throwing herself into all the preparations was Sara's way of making amends—and also of coping with her lingering fears and resentments.

"I love you," Ellie said suddenly, placing her hand over Sara's.

Sara looked up. "I love you, too."

Ellie rose and drew Sara up beside her. "Thank you for all you're doing. Now come on, it's way past time for us all to get to bed."

With her arm around Sara's shoulder, they stepped into the living room. For long seconds she and Sara observed the occupants of the couch. Sara looked up at Ellie and grinned.

"Hey, guys," Ellie said, "time for bed."

There were the usual grumblings as Rae and Poppy moved to follow Sara. While the girls made ready for bed, Ellie snuggled next to Wade on the couch. She smiled a contented smile. Wade answered with one of his own. His thumb moved to stroke the sensitive skin beneath her ear.

Happiness bubbled up in Ellie and seemed to flow over to all parts of her body.

Had any woman ever been as blessed? she wondered as she considered Wade, her daughters. Her family.

The girls came back, Poppy and Rae giving Wade good-night kisses. When Ellie rose to escort them off to bed, Poppy stopped. With a furrowed brow, she looked from Ellie to Wade. The next instant she ran forward and threw herself into Wade's lap.

"Are you here forever, Wade?" she asked anxiously. She touched his cheek; her lower lip trembled.

Wade cleared his throat and looked at the little girls staring at him. He felt like a bug beneath a magnifying glass. He met Poppy's gaze last of all. Her large eyes beneath her frowning eyebrows made his heart seem to melt. Holding her in his arms, he stood and stepped toward Sara and Rae. They hadn't really been consulted on much of this, he thought very clearly. They'd simply been told what was to happen. He hadn't made his feelings plain.

"Yes, Poppy, I'm here forever," he said, looking first at her, then at Sara and Rae. "I love your mom." His gaze moved to Ellie, and his heart swelled to see the love shining there. "She's consented to have me, to be my wife, and I'm going to be at her side from now on. I'll be around forever." It was a promise to Ellie, to the girls and to himself.

"And you'll be our daddy, now?" Poppy asked.

Wade looked from her to Rae and then to Sara. "If you'll all have me," he said, his gaze meeting Sara's. He hoped he hadn't imagined the flicker of warmth in the young girl's eyes.

Poppy hugged him around the neck. "Will you carry me to bed, like the daddies do on television?"

Wade chuckled. "Of course, Pumpkin. I'm not too up on this daddy business, though. I guess you'll have to teach me."

Like a small platoon they all trooped into Rae and Poppy's room. Poppy still clung to his neck, Rae remained at his side and Sara hovered near the door.

"I love you, Daddy," Poppy whispered just before Wade lowered her to the bed.

Immediately a lump grew in his throat, making it hard to swallow. "I love you, too, Poppy," he whispered in return.

"Good night, Wade," Rae said, her voice and manner unusually quiet, but her smile genuine. "Dad," she added. Wade ruffled her hair, uncertain what else to do. Then she raised her arms for a hug. He complied, feeling awkward, but pleased.

"Good night, Wade," Sara said softly, standing back in the doorway.

"Good night, Sara," he answered with equal seriousness and respect.

He watched Ellie tuck the covers around the small girls, then turned and went to the kitchen and poured the last of the coffee into a cup. He listened to the sounds of Ellie stirring in the back part of the house.

He felt crowded; high, unfamiliar emotions tore at him. He needed some space to think about these feelings.

Poppy and Rae had touched him deeply with their immediate acceptance and love. Imagine, him, Wade Wolcott, a rough, everyday guy, he thought, falling into a bed of roses like he had. It seemed a blessing he didn't deserve in the least. And a heady responsibility.

The responsibility seemed to grow in his mind. Maybe he, like Ellie, hadn't counted the cost, he thought.

He'd intended to stay in Ellie's bed that night—couldn't imagine being separated from her. But now, he didn't know if he should be lying in that bed with her. He squirmed inwardly, recalling the three pairs of blue eyes regarding him so intently. He had three daughters to consider now. And he and Ellie weren't legally married—never mind that he considered himself already her husband, she his wife. Or that they'd already been a man and wife.

He thought about going home, but that seemed pretty silly, considering what he and Ellie had been doing up at his house that very afternoon. He felt damned unnatural and irrational. He didn't like it, but he couldn't seem to wriggle away from it. He wasn't used to being in a house with so many people, for one thing. So many *females*.

He lifted the cup to his mouth only to discover it empty. A sound drew his gaze to the kitchen entry. Ellie stood there. He caught his breath at the sight of her.

Her hair fell to her shoulders and framed her face like a shiny halo. She wore a pale pink gown, edged with lace at the low, scooping neckline and at the cuffs of the long sleeves. It flowed over her figure softly, like the gown of an angel. A very desirable angel. Her face looked hesitant, uncertain, much like the time when he'd first seen her.

Wade set his cup aside and opened his arms. She came quickly and he pressed her to him, inhaling her enticing scent and seeming to absorb her gentle serenity.

She pulled back and looked up at him and smiled.

"I'm going home for tonight, Ellie," he said.

Her eyes widened. "But...I thought..." she left off, her eyes questioning.

He wasn't certain if he could put it into words. "I just think it will be the best thing all around. I need some time, just for tonight. And I have three daughters to consider now—I understand now what you meant all this time about having to think of them."

He felt a coolness slip over her, as if she were withdrawing from him, though she remained within the circle of his arms. She searched his eyes. "You and I together tonight won't hurt the girls, Wade. What they need is to see us, day by day, standing beside each other in love."

He gave a deep sigh then shook his head. "I just don't feel right about it, Ellie." He tried for a smile. "Maybe I'm not as liberal as I thought—I don't know. I do know I need some time." He knew his answer was inadequate but couldn't seem to do better. "Just trust me, even if I'm not able to make much sense. Okay?"

Conflict played across her face. Then she smiled and nodded and turned her head to lean against his chest. Holding her, feeling her warmth and feminine curves pushed against his body, he thought maybe he should reconsider this whole idea.

"Mama?" Sara's voice sounded just before she appeared in the entry. She stopped, a stricken look on her face. "I'm sorry..." she stammered. "I didn't..."

"It's okay, Sara," Wade said quickly. He kept one arm firmly around Ellie as she turned to see her daughter. With the other arm, he motioned the young girl into the room. "I don't want you to ever think you can't speak to us at any time. We're a family, aren't we?"

Ellie saw joy and understanding pass between these two people she so loved. Remaining within the security of Wade's embrace, she extended an arm and grasped Sara's hand in her own.

"Now, ladies, I'm going. I'm getting married tomorrow. I've got to get my rest." He kissed Ellie fleetingly and paused to touch Sara's shoulder. Then, quickly, he walked out into the night.

Ellie watched the door close behind him, then turned to smile at Sara.

"He's...different," Sara offered, a wide smile on her face. "I thought he was going to stay."

Ellie chuckled. "Try not to burst his bubble about fourteen-year-old girls, Sara." She looked again at the door. "He's special," she said, slipping an arm around her daughter's shoulder. "A very good and special man." She paused her hand over the light switch. "Oh, what did you need, sweetheart?"

Sara looked perplexed. "I think I forgot... oh, I remember. We need to add cleaning out the refrigerator to the list." Hurriedly she scribbled on the paper lying on the table.

Finished, she came back to slip her arm around Ellie's waist. Ellie turned out the light and together they walked through the darkened house.

They stood in the quiet, sun-bright church before the minister and pledged their love, their lives, to each other. Behind them Ellie's parents, her daughters and Andrew looked on. When Wade took her hand to slip on the ring, a ring he'd magically procured in the hours just before the wedding, pictures of the morning flashed through Ellie's mind.

Waking that sunny mid-morning—later than she'd intended because someone had turned off her alarm—she'd opened her eyes to a bright bouquet of daisies and irises lying on the pillow beside her. On a small card, scrawled in Wade's handwriting, was: I love you. She'd pressed the flowers to her, inhaling their sweet scent. A scent she could almost catch again as she looked up into his smiling brown eyes and listened to him pledge his life to hers.

The morning had been so strange, yet so normal. Children who couldn't find underwear, socks, shoes—and one child missing: Rae, who'd gone to town with Wade to place a special Closed sign in the window of the Last Chance, announcing Wade and Ellie's wedding.

Ellie'd had to hurriedly press her dress, the white one with the blue sprigged flowers; it was Wade's favorite. Then there'd been the little goat who'd managed somehow to get his horns stuck in the fencing. Wade had helped deal with the panicky animal before hurrying home to get dressed and packed. Rae and Poppy had rushed through their own preparations, intent on going up to Wade's house to "help" him. Of course Wade couldn't deny them. Ellie refrained from scolding; this was no day to scold.

She had no ring for him, but with her hands securely clasped in his, she pledged her life to him. He kissed her, and they were man and wife.

They turned and everyone was hugging everyone else. Andrew grabbed her, saying to Wade, "Kiss for the bride, ol' man." Andrew's lips pressed overly long, and Wade tugged her away, though he and Andrew chuckled at each other.

A shout sounded from the door of the church, and Ellie looked up to see Gayla hurrying forward, eager excitement on her face. Dal Allen followed close behind.

Gayla hugged Ellie, then Wade. "Oh, my heavens, to think I missed this! Congratulations!" She brushed tears from her eyes. "And we can give you a wedding present."

She beamed up at Dal, who shifted his feet. A wide grin split his face.

"What . . . how did Zoe do?" Ellie asked, suddenly remembering. Her heart raced as she searched Gayla's face.

"She won!" Gayla cried. "We can pay you back, Ellie, and now you have an investment in that horse."

"Both of you do," Dal added.

"Both of us?" Ellie looked up at Wade. He gave a sheepish grin.

"Wade fixed my horse trailer for free at the shop," Dal provided. "The charge for that gave him an investment in Zoe."

"Well, just let our money ride with that horse," Wade commanded suddenly, pushing Ellie through the knot of people. "We'll see everyone in a week." Then, laughing, he pulled her down the aisle, while the others followed.

She hurried happily by his side, but halted at the door and turned. Shaking away his hand, she rushed to her daughters. The three of them embraced at once, and Ellie held them tightly to her. "I love you," she whispered fiercely.

"We know, Mama," Sara said, her voice breaking. "Now go on!"

Ellie paused just long enough to send a smile of thanks to her parents, then, propelled by cries of best wishes, she joined Wade.

He waited by the truck with an expression of patient love on his face. He held the door and she slid onto the seat. The girls and Andrew had written Just Married with shaving cream across the rear window. Tin cans and an old shoe hung from the rear bumper and clanked against the ground as Wade pulled away from the church.

Ellie sat beside him, unable to say anything for fear of crying, her mind awhirl with both happiness and sadness. She'd never left the girls before and had the terribly irrational urge to run back and bring them along. But this subsided quickly enough as she looked at Wade's manly profile and thoughts of another sort took their place. After fifteen minutes she managed to ask where they were headed.

"The Texas Gulf, my lady, if that meets with your approval." He raised a questioning eyebrow.

"Oh...yes." She chuckled, thinking she would have gone to the moon with him.

About ten minutes later she said, "Zoe won." It was a stunning thought. "Could she have made enough for me to make up the payment I owe you?" The next instant her heart leaped in her throat as Wade steered the truck off the road and came to a halt. "What is it?" Her gaze flew to his face.

He turned to her. "You made enough to pay me for next year, too, from what Dal told me about Zoe before he left. But that money's yours. Keep it in that horse and it looks like you'll have something good going for years to come— for the girls. Our girls." He grinned wickedly. "And maybe our boys."

Then he kissed her, deeply.

"Wade?" Ellie said, breathless with wanting. "We don't have to drive all the way to the gulf tonight, do we?" She allowed her longing to show in her eyes and in her touch as she reached up to loosen his tie.

A smile began first in his eyes, then spread across his lips. "I made reservations for us in Dallas," he said, his words slow and drawn. "I calculate we'll be there in just under three hours. Well before sunset, sweetheart."

* * * * *

FOUR UNIQUE SERIES
FOR EVERY WOMAN YOU ARE...

Silhouette Romance

Love, at its most tender, provocative,
emotional...in stories that will make you laugh and
cry while bringing you the magic of falling in love.

6 titles per month

Silhouette Special Edition

Sophisticated, substantial and packed with
emotion, these powerful novels of life and love will
capture your imagination and steal your heart.

6 titles per month

Silhouette Desire

Open the door to romance and passion. Humorous,
emotional, compelling—yet always a believable
and sensuous story—Silhouette Desire never
fails to deliver on the promise of love.

6 titles per month

Silhouette Intimate Moments

Enter a world of excitement, of romance
heightened by suspense, adventure and the
passions every woman dreams of. Let us
sweep you away.

4 titles per month

Silhouette Romance ™

Legendary Lovers Trilogy

BY DEBBIE MACOMBER....

ONCE UPON A TIME, in a land not so far away, there lived a girl, Debbie Macomber, who grew up dreaming of castles, white knights and princes on fiery steeds. Her family was an ordinary one with a mother and father and one wicked brother, who sold copies of her diary to all the boys in her junior high class.

One day, when Debbie was only nineteen, a handsome electrician drove by in a shiny black convertible. Now Debbie knew a prince when she saw one, and before long they lived in a two-bedroom cottage surrounded by a white picket fence.

As often happens when a damsel fair meets her prince charming, children followed, and soon the two-bedroom cottage became a four-bedroom castle. The kingdom flourished and prospered, and between soccer games and car pools, ballet classes and clarinet lessons, Debbie thought about love and enchantment and the magic of romance.

One day Debbie said, "What this country needs is a good fairy tale." She remembered how well her diary had sold and she dreamed again of castles, white knights and princes on fiery steeds. And so the stories of Cinderella, Beauty and the Beast, and Snow White were reborn....

Look for Debbie Macomber's *Legendary Lovers* trilogy from Silhouette Romance: *Cindy and the Prince* (January, 1988); *Some Kind of Wonderful* (March, 1988); *Almost Paradise* (May, 1988). Don't miss them!

SRT-1

For the millions who can't read
Give the Gift of Literacy

One out of five adults in North America
cannot read or write well enough
to fill out a job application
or understand the directions on a bottle of medicine.

**You can change all this by joining the fight
against illiteracy.**

For more information write to:
Contact, Box 81826, Lincoln, Neb. 68501
In the United States, call toll free: 1-800-228-8813

**The only degree you need
is a degree of caring**

LIT-A-1R

Silhouette Special Edition

COMING NEXT MONTH

#427 LOCAL HERO—Nora Roberts
Divorcée Hester Wallace was wary of men, but her overly friendly neighbor wasn't taking the hint. Though cartoonist Mitch Dempsey enthralled her young son, convincing Hester to believe in heroes again was another story entirely.

#428 SAY IT WITH FLOWERS—Andrea Edwards
Nurse Cristin O'Leary's clowning kept sick children happy, but her response to hospital hunk Dr. Sam Rossi was no joke. Would the handsome heart specialist have a remedy for a lovesick nurse?

#429 ARMY DAUGHTER—Maggi Charles
Architect Kerry Gundersen was no longer a lowly sergeant, but to him, interior designer Jennifer Smith would always be the general's daughter. As she decorated his mansion, resentment simmered . . . and desire flared out of control.

#430 CROSS MY HEART—Phyllis Halldorson
Senator Sterling couldn't let a family scandal jeopardize his reelection; he'd have to investigate his rascally brother's latest heartthrob. To his chagrin, he felt his *own* heart throbbing at his very first glimpse of her. . . .

#431 NEPTUNE SUMMER—Jeanne Stephens
Single parent Andrea Darnell knew Joe Underwood could breathe new life into Neptune, Nebraska, but she hadn't expected mouth-to-mouth resuscitation! Besides, did Joe really want *her*, or just her ready-made family?

#432 GREEK TO ME—Jennifer West
Kate Reynolds's divorce had shattered her heart, and no island romance could mend it. Still, dashing Greek Andreas Pateras was a powerful charmer, and he'd summoned the gods to help topple Kate's resistance!

AVAILABLE NOW:

In response to last year's outstanding success, Silhouette Brings You:

Silhouette Christmas Stories 1987

Specially chosen for you in a delightful volume celebrating the holiday season, four original romantic stories written by four of your favorite Silhouette authors.

Dixie Browning—*Henry the Ninth*
Ginna Gray—*Season of Miracles*
Linda Howard—*Bluebird Winter*
Diana Palmer—*The Humbug Man*

Each of these bestselling authors will enchant you with their unforgettable stories, exuding the magic of Christmas and the wonder of falling in love.

A heartwarming Christmas gift during the holiday season...indulge yourself and give this book to a special friend!

Available now